SON OF A TRiCKSTER

SON OF A TRiCKSTER

EDEN ROBINSON

ALFRED A. KNOPF CANADA

PUBLISHED BY ALFRED A. KNOPF CANADA

Copyright © 2017 Eden Robinson

www.penguinrandomhouse.ca

Library and Archives Canada Cataloguing in Publication

Robinson, Eden, author
Son of a trickster / Eden Robinson.

Issued in print and electronic formats.

ISBN 978-0-345-81078-6
eBook ISBN 978-0-345-81080-9

I. Title.
PS8585.O35143S65 2017   C813'.54   C2016-903143-8

Book design by Jennifer Lum
Cover image © Tanor / Shutterstock.com
Interior images: (feathers) © Tanor, (ravens) © SPYDER, both Shutterstock.com

Printed and bound in the United States of America

6 8 9 7

Penguin
Random House
KNOPF CANADA

For Sam & Leenah & Damon
'Cause you rule

Some of Coyote's stories have got Coyote tails and some of Coyote's stories are covered with scraggy Coyote fur but all of Coyote's stories are bent.

—Thomas King, *A Coyote Columbus Story*

CONTENTS

NANAS I HAVE LOVED

His tiny, tightly permed maternal grandmother, Anita Moody, had never liked him. As far back as Jared could remember, she'd watched him suspiciously with her clear black eyes. She never let him come closer than an arm's length from her, making him sit on the ratty blue couch while she sat in the kitchen of her small house near the Bella Bella Band Store. Once, when she was chatting with someone, she stopped when she noticed him, tensing as if she expected him to go haywire.

"Wee'git," she'd say if his parents left them alone. "If you hurt her, I will kill you and bury you where no one can resurrect you. Get, you dirty dog's arse."

"I'm Jared," he'd said.

"Trickster," she'd said. "You still smell like lightning."

She was a cuddly grandma with his cousins, sitting them at the kitchen table and giving them popcorn balls, homemade fudge and caramel apples. She knitted mittens with their names embroidered on the back. The last birthday present she'd given him was a jar of blood with little animal teeth rolling around the bottom.

"Fucking cuntosaurus," his mom had said, snatching it from him. "She doesn't believe me, does she? No faith. None."

"Jared, buddy, this isn't about you," his dad had said.

"She doesn't like me," Jared said.

"She doesn't mean it," his dad said.

His mother spat. "Sonny boy, it's got nothing to do with you and everything to do with what a fuck-up she thinks I am."

"She'd never hurt you," his dad said.

"Because I will fuck her up one side and down the other if she lays a single finger on you," his mom said. "I will fuck her up good."

When Jared was almost five, his mother decided they should move, so his dad found work at Eurocan, a pulp-and-paper mill in a town called Kitimat. His mom showed it to him on the map, tracing his finger over the ferry route they were going to take up the Inside Passage. They packed up their townhouse in one weekend, forfeiting their damage deposit. As they were loading the last boxes late in the evening, his grandmother came and stood in front of the moving truck. Jared ducked behind his mother.

"Don't," his dad said, grabbing her arm. "Maggie. Think."

His mom jerked her arm away. His dad lifted Jared and propped him on his hip. His mom got into the driver's side. She revved the engine. His grandmother stared at his mother, waiting.

"Maggie," his dad said.

"Momma," Jared said.

His mom turned the engine off. She got out and went to stand nose to nose with her mother. His dad slid behind the wheel.

"I've lost all patience with you, old woman. Don't push me."

"Be careful," his grandmother said. "You know what he did to me. That isn't your son. It's the damn Trickster. He's wearing a human face, but he's not human."

"You're one to talk."

"Marguerite, listen to me. He's dangerous."

"Lay your old-school crap on my boy one more time and I will fuck you up your dry, lifeless ass."

"I tried," his grandmother said, backing down, moving to the side of the road to stand in the grass. "You have no ears."

"Fuck off and stay fucked, cunt."

His dad placed Jared's hands on the steering wheel.

"Toot, toot," his dad said. "Let's blow this Popsicle stand, Jelly Bean."

His mom got in the passenger side and slammed her door shut.

"I think you missed a couple of swears, Hon," his dad said.

She gave him the stink eye. They started off for the ferry terminal. His grandma was a shrinking figure in the side mirror.

His dad stopped at a stop sign, looking both ways even though no one was around. "You should learn some French so you can swear at her some more."

"Are you taking her side?"

"Lord Almighty, no. Don't run me over, Mags. Ahhhh."

She'd slugged his shoulder. Jared rocked with his dad, whose laugh started in his belly, bouncing him against the steering wheel.

"I'm just saying Jelly Bean here is going to know the best curse words in kindergarten."

"Damn . . . tooting right, he will," his mom said.

Jared hadn't been on a ferry since he was a baby and he was so excited when he saw it, he bounced up and down, clapping. Driving inside was like being swallowed by a giant whale, like in the stories his babysitter Barbie read to him from the Bible. His dad grabbed a backpack and slung it over his shoulder before tucking Jared under his arm like a football. They crammed into the elevator with other sleepy passengers. His dad sat Jared on his shoulders. His mom rested her head against his dad's arm.

"It's okay, Hon," his dad said.

They found some seats, but Jared whined to go onto the deck and his dad agreed to take him while his mom set up their sleeping bags on the floor. The wind was cold and the ferry gave a toot before pulling away from the terminal. Jared covered his ears until he was sure it was the only toot. The lights sparkled on the black water. The mountains were giant black lumps against the starry sky.

The ferry rounded a point and Jared's dad lifted him up so he could say goodbye to Bella Bella. The buildings and streets looked different from the ferry. He waved.

"Goodbye to all that," his dad said.

Nana Sophia, his father's mother, lived in Prince Rupert with her fourth husband, Jim-Bob, whose real name was Reginald. No one had ever explained the nickname to him. They laughed in a way that told him it was a grown-up joke.

They drove off the ferry at the Rupert terminal and his mom wanted to visit her friends, but his dad wanted to stop in to see his mother first. Nana Sophia's house was on a steep hill and her front yard was a cliff. A wooden ramp with rickety railings led from the sidewalk to her front door, and Jared ran back and forth while they waited for Nana Sophia to answer the door. The ramp jiggled and rattled. They waited and waited and his parents argued about who had been supposed to tell her when they were coming in. They went out to a restaurant and Jared ate fish nuggets dipped in ketchup.

Then they went to see his mom's friends, who lived in a long series of grey townhouses. Her friends were having coffee in the kitchen and his mom joined them and screamed a lot with the other women. They compared children, and Jared was brought forward and stood back to back with a girl, and then made to hold babies and told to smile while flashes went off.

Once the grown-ups were blabbing, the kids brought him outside and told him they were playing tag and he was it. Jared didn't think it was fair because he didn't know their apartment complex, but he also didn't want to sit around the kitchen hearing the women swapping birth stories, dishing on who was fooling around or what they thought the sockeye run would be like this year.

He tagged a little girl named Becky, who was his age, and was slow and couldn't catch anyone. She moped, kicking the ground and whining about them all being too fast, until someone else volunteered to be "it." After a while no one bothered to tag her so they could keep the game going. She cried and stomped around, telling everyone that they were going to be in big trouble if they didn't play with her. She left and they kept playing. Becky's mom came out and gave them hell for excluding Becky. After that, the game broke up and Jared was left alone with Becky, who still wanted to play tag.

"You're it," she said.

"I'm tired," Jared said. "I'm going in."

"You can't go in," she said. "You're it."

"It's stupid to play with only two people," Jared said.

"You have to play," Becky said.

"I don't."

"Do."

"Don't."

"You don't play fair," Becky said. "I'm telling."

"That's why no one wants to play with you," he said. "You're a big, whiny tattletale."

"You're mean. I'm telling. And then you're going to get in big trouble, mister."

"Go fuck yourself and the high horse you rode in on," Jared said.

Becky took off running and Jared tried to remember which apartment his parents were visiting. Then he remembered their moving truck and looked for that. He was sitting in the driver's seat, pretending to drive, when his parents came out and glared at him. Jared locked the driver's-side door.

"Cute," his dad said. "Real cute, Jared."

"Did you f-bomb Becky?" his mom said.

His dad took out a fob and pushed a button that unlocked the door. He swung the door open and they waited for him to answer.

"No," Jared said.

His mom cocked her eyebrow.

"Maybe," Jared said.

"My daddy would have washed your mouth out with soap," his dad said. "But I'm not him. And we haven't exactly been shining examples, have we?"

His mom turned to glare up at his dad. "Really, Phil?"

"No dessert for a week, Jared," his dad said.

"Baby," his mom said. "You aren't getting any dessert either."

His father laughed. "No sugar for daddy."

"Ew," Jared said. "I know what you guys are talking about."

"You do, huh?" his dad said.

"Kissing and stuff."

"March your hiney inside," his mom said. "And you say sorry to Becky."

"She started it."

"And we're ending it," his dad said. "Make nice, Jelly Bean."

Becky snapped her eyes at him and wouldn't look his way while he mumbled sorry. Becky's mom looked like she was going to rip into him, but Jared's mom stepped forward and put her hand on Jared's shoulder. Becky's mom faked a smile. Jared's mom faked a smile.

"It's been a slice," his dad said. "We should say howdy to Mom before we hit the road, Hon."

The lights were all on at Nana Sophia's house. His dad bounced up the ramp and Nana Sophia flung open the door and he bear-hugged her, spinning her around the porch. His mom sighed. She held Jared's hand as they walked slowly towards the house. Nana Sophia's dark hair curled on her head as fluffy as cotton candy. She wore a tightly belted dress that puffed out around her knees. She had dark, shiny lipstick and a perfect birthmark on her left cheek.

"Maggie, aren't you hot as hell," Nana Sophia said. "Phil here pooched my tummy so bad I had to get a tummy-tuck. But you look like you haven't gained an ounce."

"Hi, Sophia," his mom said.

"And who do we have here? It's my handsome grandson! It's been so long I almost didn't recognize you, my cutie patootie," Nana Sophia said.

Jared pressed himself against his mother's leg, squeezing her hand hard.

"Hey, Cutie," Nana Sophia said. "Come give your nana a hug."

His dad picked him up and plopped him in Nana Sophia's arms. She kissed his forehead and nuzzled her cheek against his. She smelled like flowers and old wood.

"I missed you," Nana Sophia said.

"We missed you too," his dad said.

"Why don't you leave my grandson here with me so we can catch up," Nana Sophia said. "Go to the casino. Go dancing. Go be young and in love."

"He's shy," his mom said.

"Are you shy, Cutie?" she said, kissing him. "Come have some cookies."

"Uh, no desserts for Jared this week, Mom. He's been dropping the f-bomb with the other kids."

"My silly Jared," Nana Sophia said. "Don't you know that only hot chicks are allowed to swear like sailors? We get away with murder until our looks go. Then we're thrown on the trash heap of life and forgotten."

"Mother," his dad said.

"Fine. No cookies for my cutie."

"Where's Jim-Bob?" his mom said.

"Whoring," Nana Sophia said.

"Jesus, Mother."

"He's a walking dick these days," Nana Sophia said. "Thank you, Viagra. I hope his heart pops like the cancerous zit it is."

"Jared's right here," his dad said.

"Fine. No cookies and no unpleasant truths. Dry toast and stern lectures for everyone. Should I throw in a couple of hair shirts for good measure?"

"Why don't you dump his sorry ass?" his mom said.

"I want the house," Nana Sophia said. "I'm hoping he humps himself to death so I don't have to waste money on private investigators and lawyers."

"Classy," his dad said.

"Your dad was classy," Nana Sophia said. "Jim-Bob was fun until he became the star of *Geezers Gone Wild*."

His mom snorted then laughed her head off.

"You're a pip," Nana Sophia said to his mom. "I like you. But I looooove my cutie. I do. I want to cuddle you and hug you all night. What do you say? I have *Monsters, Inc.* or *Toy Story*."

"*Monsters*, please," Jared said.

"Oh, pretty manners, Jelly Bean," his mom said. "Let's get your jammies on."

His mom helped him change into his jammies in the bathroom. The counter was covered in perfume bottles that his mother touched and lifted to her nose.

"Are you okay alone with Nana Sophia?"

Jared nodded, even though he suspected Nana Sophia might wait until they were alone to say mean things. But he also hoped that once his parents were gone, she'd give him cookies.

"You're mine," his mom said. "Remember that."

He brushed his teeth and his mom gave his face and pits a good scrub with the washcloth. He told her he wanted to pee by himself and his mom hugged him even though his back teeth were floating as his dad would say.

Nana Sophia had her big-screen TV all set up. She'd made cocoa, which she claimed wasn't dessert because it had calcium in the milk plus she'd left off the whipped cream. Jared thanked her and put the cocoa on the coffee table. The cup was baby-sized and Jared could finish it in a single gulp, but he was going to wait until his dad was gone. When Nana Sophia was amused, her eyes sparkled.

"Don't keep him up too late, Mother," his dad said.

"Remember love is not all about your orgasms, son," Nana Sophia said.

His mom giggled.

"Take everything she says with a bucket of salt," his dad said. He ruffled Jared's hair.

"See you in the morning, Jelly Bean," his mom said, kissing his forehead.

"Night," Jared said.

"No desserts, good buddy," his dad said.

"Love your guts," his mom said.

"Shit or get off the pot," Nana Sophia said. "We're trying to watch a movie here."

His parents left. They heard the moving truck rumble to life and then pull away and fade. Nana Sophia turned her head to check the door. She looked down at him.

"Have you seen *Spider-Man* yet? There's a nine-thirty show. I don't think it's in 3-D, but they have popcorn, which isn't dessert. It's roughage."

Jared paused in the middle of reaching for the cocoa. "I'm not allowed to play outside after nine."

"Your parents are going to get plastered and spend the rest of the night holed up in a hotel room. You could be out robbing gas stations and they wouldn't care."

Nana Sophia had a sewing mannequin that they wrapped in a nightgown with pink fluff and arranged on the couch. She went into her bedroom and got a Styrofoam head with a wig pinned to it and placed it on top of the mannequin. She then stuck a pillow under a blanket so it looked like Jared was snuggling up to her, and loaded the DVD player with five different Disney movies so they'd play non-stop until they came back.

"Your dad is awfully suspicious of his own mother," she explained as they were loading the DVDs. "He'll probably drive by sometime tonight to make sure we're behaving."

Jared chugged his cocoa.

Nana told him to put on his shoes but not to bother changing into clothes. Jared felt an electric thrill going outside in a rain jacket and jammies. His nana had a powder-blue Vespa in her garage with a matching helmet that she gave to Jared.

"What about you?" he said.

"Two dedicated professionals sweated blood to get my do this perfect," she said, wrapping her hair in a plastic scarf. She hefted a fur cape around her shoulders and shrugged it into place. "I will not dishonour their fine craftsmanship with helmet-head."

Jared sat in front of his nana with his goggles and helmet slipping as they buzzed up and down the hills of Prince Rupert. Her dress fluttered around them like sugared-up butterflies. Her black sunglasses reflected the street lights. His nana let him honk the horn all the way to the parking garage, laughing when cars honked back. She left the helmet and goggles hanging off the handlebars like she'd never heard of robbers and they skipped past the line of people waiting to buy tickets. Nana slipped the ticket-taker something that made the girl's eyes boggle and she happily waved them through. Nana paid one of the guys in the lineup to get them popcorn and root beers.

"Tell them to go heavy on the butter," she told him. "None of those cheap squirts, either. We're talking *Last Tango in Paris* butter. Got it?"

"Heh, heh, heh," the guy said, his face turning electric red while his buddies cackled.

The theatre was half empty. Nana chose seats in the middle of the row close to the back. She plunked down a hard plastic booster seat and then laid her fur cape over it. Jared didn't want to sit on it in case he spilled, but Nana said he could fart so hard he pooped and she wouldn't give a fig. The fur was cold at first, but warmed up. Nana wrapped an arm around his shoulders and kissed his cheek. He rested his head on her until the guys came with the popcorn and root beers. They said to holler if she needed anything and Nana smiled at them in a way that made them shy. Nana let him hold the bucket of popcorn and it took up his whole lap with popcorn piled up to his chin. He was tempted to bend over and eat it with his mouth, and he was sure it would make Nana laugh, but he ate it the good way, with careful, non-spilling handfuls.

"They should have called you Phil Junior," Nana Sophia said.

"Granny Nita thinks I'm Wee'git," Jared said.

"She would. That Trickster's been a huge dink to your mom's family for generations," Nana Sophia said.

"Really?" Jared said.

"Can I tell you a secret? Will you promise to never, ever tell anyone? Hope to die? Stick a needle in your eye?"

Jared nodded. "I promise."

"I had a test done when you were born. You are part 'Namgis, part Heiltsuk, and all trouble."

"What kind of test?"

"A DNA test. A lab geek looked at the tiny, tiny bits that make you and the tiny, tiny bits that make your dad and your mom."

"Did you think I was Wee'git?"

Nana Sophia pursed her lips. "Did you know you're named after your grandfather Benny? Oh, I loved your pop-pop so much. It was like my heart got buried with him. Then you came along. I was afraid you were too good to be true. Your momma is so pretty and so many boys wanted to be with her."

Jared felt the popcorn stick in his throat. "But she loves Daddy."

"She does," she said. Nana Sophia kissed him. "And I love you and I would never hurt you. But if you weren't Philip's and your momma tried to pass you off as his, I'd have slit her throat and left her in a ditch to die like a dog."

Jared used his best printing to write a letter to Granny Nita, stealing an envelope and a stamp from the bill drawer:

Hi Granny. I am well. How are you? Nana Sophia did a siense test. My daddy is Philip. She said you can ask her for the test. I am not a Trickster. Okay?

After a few weeks, he found an envelope in their mail with her careful, curly printing. He hid it underneath his mattress, scared to see what she had written. He was aware of the letter even as he tried to ignore it. Late one night, he couldn't stand not knowing anymore.

Dear Jared,

Sophia is Halayt. She would know if you were a Trickster without a science test. If Wee'git visits you, be careful. He does mean things because he thinks he's funny. When I'm angry I say bad things. I'm sorry. I hope you understand someday, but I can't say more right now. Our story is too dark for your young ears. Until then, stay safe.

You and your mother are in my prayers every night, Anita Moody.

2

SIMULTANEOUSITY

Think of magic as a tree. The root of supernatural ability is simply the realization that all time exists simultaneously. Humans experience time as a progression of sequential events in much the same way we see the horizon as flat: our reality is shaped by our limitations.

If you blasted off in a rocket and achieved a low, stable orbit, you would see the planet's horizon curving into a sphere. But how, you may be wondering, can you blast yourself out of time? We don't know how to build those machines yet.

Close your eyes. Concentrate on your breath. Remember that you were not always earthbound. Every living creature, every drop of water and every sombre mountain is the by-blow of some bloated, dying star. Deep down, we remember wriggling through the universe as beams of light.

THE FOOD OF WORMS

Jared hadn't realized he loved his dog until they decided to put her down. His mom and the vet agreed on a time, like her euthanasia was just a regular appointment. While he went to school, Baby would stay at the vet's, sedated. In a way, he wanted them to do it right now, so it wouldn't be hanging over them all day, but he was kind of glad there were rules to follow. Jared scratched Baby's head. She was the result of a pit bull mixed with a boxer, a heavy, deep-chested dog with scraggly ears from a fight with her brother. Her fur was mottled orange, black and grey, a squiggly pattern like a toddler had coloured her with fading markers. Her face looked like it had been flattened by a shovel. She farted constantly from a diet of cheap dog food and a tendency to eat whatever landed on the floor. She had once shat marbles. Baby wheezed like a hardened smoker and then coughed. Jared's throat tightened. The room blurred as his eyes watered. He swallowed loudly. Baby roused from the exam table and licked his arm. Jared leaned his head against hers.

"I'll give you folks a moment," the vet said.

After he left, Jared's mom sat, shoving her hands deep in the pockets of her leather jacket. The fluorescent lights hummed. His mom's left leg jiggled impatiently. Jared wiped his nose on his sleeve. The harder he tried not to cry, the more he cried. The painted concrete walls echoed his sniffling back at him.

"I'm going for a smoke," his mom said.

Baby thumped her tail when his mom came over to squeeze Jared's shoulder. His mom's eyes darted around the room, but she avoided meeting his. Normally, she'd be telling him sixteen was way too old to be acting like a big fucking wuss, but they could hear the vet and the receptionist talking in the front room, so she stayed quiet. She patted her jeans as she walked out. Probably forgot her lighter in the truck.

The world is hard, his mom liked to say. *You have to be harder.*

Baby licked his cheek.

"Gonna miss you," Jared whispered in her ear.

Baby lifted a leg and farted. Jared laughed, and then it turned into crying that faded into more sniffling. His heart was a bruise because Baby's heart was full of worms. The X-rays showed them curled in its chambers like glowing balls of wool. Time stretched and folded so it went both too fast and too slow. After his mom finished smoking, she'd come back and drive him to school. He hugged Baby hard and she grumbled. He wasn't going to be alone after she died, but the world was going to be a lonelier place without her.

A few years earlier, Jared's mom had been dating a rebound guy nicknamed Death Threat, who'd left Kitimat suddenly, pushed out by a biker gang that moved to town at the start of the oil and gas boom. The gang had announced their intentions with a series of violent home invasions of the local drug-dealing community. Death had left a trail of debts that one guy in particular expected his mom to pay.

The guy'd dropped by the North Star when it was her shift and then left freaky-ass messages on their machine. One morning, he'd pinned a note to their front door with a buck knife.

His mom yanked the knife out of their door and examined the note, rolling her eyes. She crumpled the paper and casually tossed it off the porch. "Some fucktard sure laid a monster hex on us. Bastards don't know who they're dealing with. Karma's a witch."

"Later," Jared said.

He walked away from her down to the bus stop and huddled into himself, stamping his feet against the cold. His mom stood on the porch, watching him. He'd caught her tracking him a lot lately. She lifted the buck knife in a salute before she went inside. The curtains twitched. He sighed, then cranked his iPod touch until his headphones vibrated. That was the year the cats in their neighbourhood started disappearing because a family of wolverines had moved onto the nearby golf course and started snacking on them. Sad, crayon-printed signs offering rewards for finding Mr. Fluffy or Kat Mandu fluttered and faded on telephone poles. His mom had claimed she was watching him because she was worried when the wolverines ran out of cats they'd move up to kids, but the animals seemed to have migrated south for the winter. He knew she was really worried about the buck-knife freak but didn't want to admit it.

She'd had a tight circle of friends before she and his dad got divorced, but they'd all moved away when Eurocan shut down. His parents used to have something going on every weekend— barbecues or hockey parties or campground parties—and the kids would watch movies in the basement or in someone's SUV and the parents would get increasingly loud and sloshed upstairs or in the backyard or around the campfire. Now they were struggling to make the mortgage, and their fridge was filled with scraps from her job at the North Star. They had a four-bedroom house, but when they were alone it felt like a one-room shack. She'd talk to him through the door when he was on the can. The red glow of her cigarette was his night light as she sat beside his bed in the darkness. He smelled her Craven Ms in his dreams. A trail of her texts followed him through his day. Death Threat had been a temporary break from her one-hundred-percent attention.

Jared heard dogs barking loud enough that they penetrated his headphones and he looked up and across the street in time to see a tall, swaggering man pause and stare back at him. The man wore a leather jacket too light for the weather and had two pit bulls straining at their chains. His face was burnt brown and his head was shaved and unshapely, bumpy and folded. His nose had a crooked, off-kilter look, like it had been broken then reset in the dark. His mom had described Richie just in case he showed up when she wasn't around, but Jared had never seen him before that moment.

Richie dropped the chains. The orange, black and grey pit bull leapt up and its legs skittered in excitement as it took off down the street, biting at the snowbanks. The other dog, the larger one with dark fur and a yellowed eye, leapt over the ditch and took two bounds to cross the road.

Jared experienced the subjective nature of time. "Party Rock Anthem" played on his iTouch, a cheerful and jittery song dedicated to the party lifestyle. You should run, he thought, noticing the pit bull had surprising flecks of gold in its dark fur. You should run now. But he knew it was too late. Jared dropped his backpack off his shoulder and flung it. The momentum made his headphones slip and dangle around his neck. Richie wore a big shit-eating grin as he followed his dog across the road to get a close-up view of the action. The pit bull was locked on the backpack when Jared's mother hit it with her truck.

The dog bounced off the grille and smacked the pavement, yelping. Jared's algebra assignments broke free of the backpack and swirled down the street. His mom turned to look behind her, backed up a few feet and then calmly shifted gears again and squashed the pit bull under the front passenger tire. The unmistakable crunch of bones ended the yelping. As her tires spun, blood sprayed the snow and steamed in clots. His mom rolled down the driver's window.

"Kindly leave my boy alone," she said.

Richie stared at her like she'd surprised him with a lovely present.

His mom backed up, holding Richie's gaze. She revved the engine. "This is grown-up business, wouldn't you say? Something that should be kept between a man and a woman."

"Yeah," Richie agreed.

They smiled at each other. Passing cars slowed to gawk. A police siren grew steadily louder.

"Sorry 'bout your dog," she said.

"I got another," he said.

A police car parked behind his mother's truck and shut off the sirens but left the red and blue lights twirling. His mom put her hand to her mouth and her eyes welled with tears. Richie apologized and apologized and they lied like they'd been practising for years: *Damn mutt's been acting up since he got that infection. Oh, God, I feel so horrible! No, I'm the one who's sorry. I was so scared! Yeah, I know they need muzzles, but my boys needed a piss in the worst way.*

The cop tilted his head skeptically. Jared shook with fading adrenalin. His bus pulled up and let people off. He automatically tried to get on, but the cop put a hand on his shoulder, saying, "You might want to change your pants."

He looked down. Blood and chunks had turned the front of his jeans red. And of course his homework was blowing down the street and he didn't want to arrive late, get stared at for his dog-splattered jeans and not have his homework done. His mom wrapped him in her arms while the cop asked Richie to describe his other pit bull. She squeezed him until his ribs creaked.

"Richie could be the answer to a lot of our problems," she whispered in his ear. "If you keep your cool and don't take this personally."

He choked on his answer, trying to pull out of her grip.

"I'd kill and die for you, Jelly Bean," she said. "Don't ever forget that."

While the other students were running basketball drills, Jared ran around the track in the rain, feeling his chest burn. His track coach was also his PE teacher and let him skip classes to train.

"This is your year," his coach had said. "If you want it bad enough."

Jared didn't miss any practices, but he wasn't the most dedicated team player. He did like running, though. The rain stung. His windbreaker was sopping wet. Snowflakes streaked white in the grey downpour. Looming in the background, higher than the other mountains, the sharp peak of Mount Elizabeth was draped in a bridal-white blanket of new snow. The snowline had been creeping down the mountains in the valley all week and Jared's friends were psyched about the fresh powder. He stopped to check the time. Friday afternoon and school was almost out. The days you want to last go the quickest, he thought. He could go inside if he wanted, but his eyes were swollen and kids had been staring. He didn't want to explain his mood or the reason for it.

Richie's other pit bull had turned out to be as dumb as the day was long. Intruders had been greeted with tail wags and sticks to throw. Once Richie'd moved in with Jared and his mom, Baby Killer's feeding and poop disposal had fallen to Jared. He'd done those chores quickly and without eye contact.

Baby Killer, however, had managed to crawl into Jared's bed one night and he woke snuggling the pit bull. When Jared'd tried to carefully move away, Baby'd nuzzled in and lazily licked his face. Baby had cried for him every time he left for school and had waited anxiously at the end of her chain for him to come back. If Jared sat down, Baby tried to get in his lap. After a month, his mom had renamed her Baby Ka'o, a pet name for a demanding, needy child. Richie had been plain disgusted that his expensive weapon of intimidation was now Jared's lapdog.

Jared's legs started to wobble, so he slowed to a walk. He'd never heard of heartworm. Baby had become a little lazy, but Jared thought she was getting old, that's all, until she horked up blood. By the time they brought her to the vet, her heart, lungs and kidneys were too far gone to start any treatment.

He bent over, panting, and then went and stretched on the concrete dividers near the doors. Dylan Wilkinson came and stood beside him, hunching into a blue ski jacket with the hood flipped up. Dylan was Native too, but from the nearby reserve, Kitamaat Village. He was also a jock who hung with the sporty crowd, not a random town Native like Jared.

"I heard you're selling," Dylan said.

"My mom's boyfriend sells."

Dylan blew in his hands. "I heard it was you."

"Wrong guy," Jared said. "Sorry. Want Richie's number?"

"Your cookies are 'da bomb,' I was told."

"Cool. Yeah, I fundraise for the track team," Jared said. "Our next bake sale is on Halloween."

"Special cookies," Dylan said.

"We make chocolate chip cookies with real butter," Jared said slowly. "And the track team would appreciate your support."

Dylan frowned. "Are you shitting me?"

"I shit you not."

"I'm not a narc."

"Okay."

"I'm good for it."

"Look, dude, people talk out their asses all the time, right? Hasn't anyone ever made shit up about you?"

Dylan glared at him. He moved in close and their breath steamed together. Jared blinked rain out of his eyes and coughed, maintaining eye contact. Normally, he'd say something sarcastic to get rid of Dylan faster, but he'd just started dating Ebony Stewart. Jared remembered her from grade school. She knew how to hold a grudge.

"Whatever," Dylan said. He turned and went back inside.

The end-of-day buzzer blared and kids poured out all the exits. Jared knew he should go and get his stuff before his mom came and brought him back to the vet's office. He didn't want to say goodbye to Baby. He tilted his head up, letting the rain hit it until his face was numb. He was afraid he was going to blubber like a dumb-ass again.

———

After they put Baby down, his mom stopped at the liquor store and got them a six-pack. Baby was covered with a tarp in the bed of the truck. When they got home, they sat in the basement drinking quietly.

"You should move back upstairs," his mom said, looking around. "It's fucking depressing as hell down here."

"Yeah," he agreed.

He'd suggested his move into the basement with Baby because he wanted some privacy. She was renting out two rooms to cover the mortgage and he told her, if he moved downstairs, she could also rent his room to cover hydro. Paying the electricity was an excuse, but it was valid. Even with the rental market as tight as it was, the most they could charge for a room in their house was five hundred dollars a month and the tenants were not keen on chipping in for utilities on top of that. Richie had resentfully put up a wall separating Jared's side of the basement from the laundry machines. They'd dragged his mattress down, along with a toaster oven, a hot plate, and random pots and utensils. Until he got a dresser, he had his clothes separated into blue totes.

His mom popped open another beer and handed it to him. She leaned back and put her beer can on her chest, closing her eyes. Jared could hear one of the tenants on the other side of the wall stuffing the washer and pushing the buttons. The water hissed through the pipes. The laundry room had the stairs that came down from the kitchen. Jared's side had the utility tub, the toilet without a seat and a door that led outside with its own lock. Maybe, when he got more money, he'd spring for his own Internet service. Their wi-fi router was so overloaded, the Internet ran like molasses. Downloading a song could take all night.

His paper route money had bought a dented Canucks mini-fridge at a garage sale. He'd also bought the orange couch they were sitting on that smelled like Baby Killer because she'd used it as a dog bed.

"We should paint," his mother said.

No amount of paint was going to make the basement less depressing. It was damp, dingy and cold. Baby Killer had added a mix of wet fur and stale dog farts. The utility sink dripped. The laundry machine on the other side of the wall chugged.

"Just spend the night upstairs," she said.

Yeah, Richie would be thrilled if he was booted to the couch so his mom could cuddle her giant-ass crybaby. And the tenants would never let him hear the end of it.

"I'm good, Mom. I'm okay."

"I never saw you as a dog person."

"Me neither."

"Baby was such a dumb-ass."

"Yeah, she really was."

They finished the six-pack. His mom went upstairs and got a bottle of vodka and they did shots. Later, Richie drove them up a logging road. Leaves fell on the windshield, curled, gold paper boats sailing to the ground. The truck wiggled through mud troughs soggy from the solid week of rain. The air had a bite that promised serious snow. Their breath frosted above their heads in thin clouds. Jared dug a grave and put a blanket down and they laid Baby on top of it. He was pretty sure he was crying, but his mom said later he was singing "Like a G6."

"Real Irish wake, haha," Richie said on the drive back.

4

ALL SHOOK UP

One week after they put Baby down, Jared lay in bed and considered not getting up. He'd thrown out Baby's food, her food dishes and all her toys except her squeaky squirrel, which he kept hidden under his bed. The spot on the couch where she used to sleep was empty. But hanging out alone in the basement wasn't any better than school, and he had an essay he had to turn in. He talked himself into putting his jeans on and brushing his teeth. He put a face cloth under the tap and tried to use it to take down some of the swelling around his eyes. Crybaby was not a look he wanted to cultivate.

Jared was out of cereal, so he went upstairs and poured himself a bowl of Lucky Charms from his mom's cupboard. Two of the tenants were watching news in the living room. Kenny was old, mid-thirties, and clean-cut with no tattoos. The other guy, Dave, was barely out of high school and had so much ink he could walk around naked and you'd never notice. Jared nodded to them and was about to plunk himself in the recliner when his mom showed up.

"Think fast," his mom said.

She tackled him and his cereal went flying.

"Stop it!" Jared said. "God! Get off!"

"Fight back," his mom said. "Come on, fight back!"

Jared turtled. There was nothing weirder than wrestling your mom in front of strangers. The guys exchanged amused glances. She eased up on her headlock.

"Do you want a new dog?" she said.

"No," Jared said.

"Do you want to move back upstairs?"

"No."

"The way you've been moping around the basement, you'll start growing mushrooms."

"Can I get up now?"

"Gimme sugar."

"Mom."

"Nope. If you're not going to fight your way out, you pay the piper."

He pecked her hand. She grabbed his cheeks, smooching his face like he was a toddler. Richie scowled in the doorway.

"That's my cereal," Richie said. "All over the fucking floor."

"Shut it," his mom said.

"I don't eat your cereal," Richie said to him.

"You're not eating anything if you don't shut it," she said.

"Ew," Jared said. "Mom, total overshare."

She smirked. The guys laughed. Richie gave him a death stare. If they were alone, Jared had no doubt he'd have a face full of fists.

Some days after school, the neighbours paid him twenty bucks for some yardwork. They were an old couple. He was glad there was a lot of space between the Jakses' house and theirs because he knew their house got noisy. Mrs. Jaks, her long salt-and-pepper hair in a bun, would feed him mountains of food when he was done, which was the real pay. She was Nadleh Whut'en from Fort Fraser and her husband was Czech from Brno. Jared couldn't point out either of those places on a map. Northern British Columbia was a mystery to him, much less Europe. He'd lived down south in Bella Bella with his mom's family when he was a kid, and then they moved up here for his dad's job, but he'd never been to his dad's home in Alert Bay. It was on a small island a ferry ride away from Vancouver Island. Nana Sophia had wanted to adopt Jared into her clan so she could give him his dad's potlatch name, but his mom had told Nana she could shove her clan up her ass.

Today, Mrs. Jaks wore a turtleneck under a plaid work shirt. The weather forecast said they were due for the first big dump of snow tonight, and she was anxious to get the yard put away before it was too late. Jared raked the leaves and mowed their lawn. The grass was stiff with frost and the leaves were mucky brown and dissolving. He helped Mrs. Jaks wrap her rose bushes in burlap, and then covered them with plywood tents. They collected a single green pumpkin and a tangle of fat zucchinis. They dug up the last of the potatoes and the carrots. Mr. Jaks woke up, came outside in his pyjamas and demanded the car keys.

"We sold the car," Mrs. Jaks said.

"We didn't," Mr. Jaks said. "You're lying."

"Oh, Petr," she said. "Dinner's almost ready. Come eat. We'll find the car later."

"I'm going to be late for work."

"You're retired, Petr. Remember?"

They sat in the breakfast nook. She gave Jared a bowl of moose stew with liver dumplings. He liked her potato soup better, but he was starved and the stew was hot. Her husband stared out the window, his mouth moving.

"What is the time?" Mr. Jaks said.

"Suppertime," she said.

"Oh."

Mrs. Jaks gave Jared a cup of tea loaded with milk and sugar. She argued with Mr. Jaks some more about the time, and then he finally ate his stew.

"*Kdo je to?*" Mr. Jaks said, suddenly noticing Jared.

"He's Maggie's son, Jared," Mrs. Jaks said. "He's a good boy."

"*Já ti nevěřím.*"

"Leave him, Petr. More stew?"

"Yes, please," Jared said.

After stew, they ate moose sausages and boiled potatoes with a side of sauerkraut. Mrs. Jaks said her brother had brought fresh moose down from Fort St. John, and their German friend in Cable Car had ground the meat in return for a share. She'd boiled the bones for the soup broth, and promised Jared moose-nose stew. Jared wasn't sure if she was kidding. They had blueberry dumplings in maple syrup for dessert. After, he helped her with the dishes. She gave her husband tea laced with liqueur. Halfway through *Wheel of Fortune*, he started snoring.

"I wish you knew him before he got sick," she said. "We went through hard times, me and him, but he always made me laugh."

He was comfortable and tempted to park, but soon Mrs. Jaks was nodding off, so he said good night and locked the door behind him.

On Friday, Jared took the bus downtown after school to meet some buds, Kelsey and Blake. Kelsey lived down the hill and Blake lived in an apartment building near the golf course. They'd been gaming together since they all got the same Game Boys and Mario Kart 6 one Christmas. They were currently getting their asses handed to them by some random online players in Halo 3. They hadn't played Halo in years. Plus they'd hotboxed in the old tree fort out back, so they had the reflexes of noobs. They'd hosed themselves down with Febreze and then Axe body spray to cover the smell of Blake's skunkweed. Blake had an overly literal mind, so when Kelsey said he was high as a kite, Blake scanned the ceiling like he was looking for the kite. Kelsey killed himself laughing.

"Ah, shut it," Blake said, dropping an incendiary grenade on Kelsey's avatar, effectively ending their game as all their avatars burned.

Kelsey rolled around the floor, deep in a stoner giggle fit. Blake's shit was okay, but the aftertaste was as subtle as mouthwash. Cotton mouth Jared could deal with; weak weed pumped up with mystery crap gave him a headache. But it was bad form to criticize a free high.

"I got the munchies," Jared said.

"Mom banned snacks in my room," Kelsey said.

"Okay, I'm off on a junk food run," Jared said. "See you later."

"Later," Kelsey said, already searching for another tournament while Blake sulked on his beanbag chair.

Jared tiptoed down the hallway to the mud room, where he found his sneakers with Bounce dryer sheets tucked in the toes. Kelsey's mom again. He suspected she didn't like Natives, because she disappeared into her bedroom whenever he was around, but Kelsey said she was a massive neat freak who hated talking to people in general

and Kelsey's friends in particular. The house did have a joyless clean-
liness where the furniture never moved and every surface shone like
an empty surgical suite. They hardly saw Kelsey's dad, who travelled
a lot for work.

Jared zipped his jacket against the bitter wind and flipped up his
hood. A raven glided overhead. The sun poked through the high,
wispy clouds. Light snow blew along the sidewalk, dusting the bushes.
The mall would be open for another hour and he didn't want to go
home right away. The basement was pretty empty. Kelsey was okay
and he liked hanging out with him, but you couldn't mention school
shit without weirdness. His friend had flunked out of most of his
subjects, so they didn't have classes together this year. Kelsey wasn't
stupid; he just lost track of time when he was gaming. The pot probably wasn't helping. Blake too was teetering on being expelled. He'd
been caught setting a Dumpster fire in a construction site and was on
probation. He'd always been a bit of a pyro, getting off on fireworks
and bonfires. But last year Blake's dad had been caught embezzling
from work. They'd lost the Bimmer and the house. When his dad got
too haywire, Blake slept over at Jared's.

Blake and Kelsey had been ragging him about being a suck-up
nerd. And it was true that Jared had gotten some average grades,
but only because Nana had set up an "academic extortion fund."
She gave Jared a hundred dollars for every A he got on his report
card and fifty dollars for every B. Cs got him ten dollars. Passes got
him nothing, and Fs got him text messages and e-mails of animated
pictures of steaming poop. She'd told him to keep the bank account
secret, so he did. His mom didn't like Nana. As far as his mom was
concerned, his dad and everyone related to his dad should be cut out
of their lives.

The mall was quiet. Jared walked past the keno tables and one old lady watching the keno board. He grabbed some chips and a couple of chocolate bars and some Mountain Dew. He was considering going to the penny candy store when he bumped into David.

"Jared," David said. "What a surprise."

His mom's ex-boyfriend wore a soft blue sweater over a crisp white shirt and ironed dark jeans. Jared looked up at David, at his bland expression and his casual stance, the first white guy his mom had ever dated. Jared tried to go around him and David stepped in his way. His heart started thumping and his stomach clenched.

"Small towns," David said. "Gotta love bumping into people you don't want to see. How's your mom, by the way?"

"We have a restraining order, shithead. You have to stay away from us."

David chuckled and shook his head. "Call the police. I dare you. I can smell the marijuana on you, you idiot. I'm sure a pothead like you is going to be taken very seriously."

"I wouldn't call the cops," Jared said. "I'd call Mom."

"My condolences. Heartworm is so easy to prevent. If you were less ignorant, your dog would still be alive."

"Stalk much?" Jared said.

"Need a ride home?"

"It's your funeral," Jared said, pulling his cellphone out of his back pocket.

"Still hiding behind Mommy," David said. "Some things never change."

Jared fake-dialed as David walked away. He put the phone to his ear until David left the mall, giving him a cheerful wave through the glass. Fuck. Fuck, fuck, fuck, Jared thought. He went to the bathroom and locked the door. He sat on the can until the mall started closing. He went to the bus stop and paused at the door, scanning the parking lot through the window. He didn't see David around, but he stayed inside until his bus came. David didn't follow the bus, so Jared got off at the stop near his house. He sat in the bus shelter, vibrating.

A raven landed on the sidewalk in front of him, black and ominous. It cocked its head, studying him. Jared liked crows because they were small and goofy, but ravens with their deep croaks and their large size unnerved him.

"FYI," the raven said, "advertisers lie to get you to buy their product. If you coat yourself in Axe body spray, girls aren't going to pull your clothes off. They're going to hold their noses and back away."

Holy crap, Jared thought. I am still way more stoned than I thought.

The raven hopped closer. "So do everyone a favour and stop bathing in it. Okay?"

"'Kay," Jared said.

"Don't worry about David," the raven said. "Your mom and Richie paid him a visit. They put the fear of God in him, so he's moving soon. He's pissed, but he knows if he touches you again, your mom will skin him alive. In the most literal way possible."

"Good to know," Jared said.

"Seriously, I'm getting a headache from your Axe fumes."

"You're pretty judge-y for a pot hallucination."

"Ah, well, that explains things," the raven said. "Don't tell anyone I talked to you, okay? I have enemies and I don't want you to be any more of a target than you already are."

"You got it," Jared said, wondering how he could be a target for anybody but his mom's crazy ex.

The raven flapped off and Jared sniffed himself, then coughed. Maybe his own headache was cologne-induced. And the pot must have had a good dose of LSD. Jared hated acid. He never had good trips with it, and today was no exception. What a weird, fucked-up day.

When his mom had told him she was bringing her new boyfriend home, she had warned Jared to be on his best behaviour.

"Hey, Slugger," David had said, handing him a catcher's mitt.

"Hi, Dave," Jared had said.

"It's David." His mouth had kept smiling, but his eyes had stopped.

David had knelt down to show him how he could balance a baseball on the tips of his fingers. Jared had flinched.

"David's taking us out for dinner," his mom had said. "Isn't that nice?"

"Anywhere you want," David had said, tossing the ball in the air and catching it behind his back.

His mom had dressed in her Sunday-best blouse, hair neatly wrapped in a ponytail. Her toothy smile, her eager laugh, bending, aching to please.

Jared hadn't liked David. David had pretended to like him. They'd all pretended they were happy until the bitter, bitter end.

Jared spent Saturday afternoon at Kelsey's. His mom was on an epic cleaning binge, so they hung out in the backyard. Kelsey took a giant roll of plastic wrap from her Costco collection and Blake mummified Jared and Kelsey. They played Sumo Worm, trying to butt each other out of a circle drawn in the snow, while Blake refereed. After they were bored with that, they threw themselves down the hill out back that dipped into a ravine. The first guy who had his plastic wrap dissolve lost. Jared bumped off a couple of trees as he sped down, laughing his ass off as Kelsey tumbled past him. He was declared the loser, and had to spin a plastic cocoon around Blake, who kangaroo-hopped over to Kelsey and jumped up to kick him.

Afterwards, Jared took the bus back to their neighbourhood and helped Mrs. Jaks shovel the snow out of her driveway while Mr. Jaks searched the house for snow tires for the car they'd sold. They had venison pie for supper. She asked him if he could watch Mr. Jaks on Wednesday while she went to a doctor's appointment. She promised to make his favourite, spaghetti with moose meatballs.

When Jared got home, the tenants invited him up for a beer. Kenny had got on at Bechtel, the company that was contracted to modernize the Rio Tinto aluminum smelter. The pay was good and, better yet, he could move into the company's work camp and save even more money, so Kenny was taking the guys out to the strip club to celebrate. He popped a Corona and handed it to Jared. They stood around the kitchen and Kenny couldn't stop smiling. He'd left his family in Hamilton, Ontario, in hopes of getting a job so he could catch up with his mortgage.

"Shit," Kenny said, "it'll be good to get out of the fucking hole, hey?"

"Ah, don't talk about your wife like that," Dave said.

The tenants hooted like kids. Richie came into the kitchen, took Jared's beer and said, "Thanks, Useless."

The guys went quiet.

"Gotta go," Kenny said. "Strippers ain't gettin' any love if I ain't there."

"Have fun," Jared said.

"You should crawl back downstairs," Richie said.

Suddenly the pots hanging in the rack above the butcher's block jiggled and banged. The ground shuddered, and for a long minute the house rolled like a large ferry on big swells. An earthquake. Jared had been in small quakes that had lasted a couple of seconds. This one shook the pictures on the walls crooked and then settled into a gurgle then stopped.

"Damn," Kenny said as they all looked at each other.

"Okay," Jared said. "Who farted?"

The guys laughed. Richie checked his cellphone, hit it and then tried the land line, clicking the receiver a few times. He slammed it into the cradle.

"Where's your mom?" he said.

"Not worrying about you," Jared said.

"Shut it, Useless."

"We're pretty fucking close to the ocean," Dave said. "Shouldn't we, I dunno, evacuate or something?"

"We're already on higher ground," Jared said. "But the bar's down the hill by the river. You might have to rescue the strippers."

The guys wahooed.

"You need your ass kicked into tomorrow," Richie said. "You goddamn fucking goof."

His mom knocked on the outside basement door. She unlocked it, came down the stairs and sat beside him. He kept playing Grand

Theft Auto as she wrapped an arm around his waist. She rested her chin on his shoulder. Her breath tickled his ear. He shut the game off.

"How was the end of the world?" she said.

"Awesome."

She pulled him down and kissed the top of his head. "That's my brave brat."

"Mom."

She shifted into a headlock. "The polite thing to do after an earthquake is to fucking text me back when I text you."

"I thought Richie was texting you enough."

"Jealous?"

He laughed. "All right, all right. Get off me."

She let him up. He offered her the other Xbox controller. She shook her head.

"Someone asked Richie if he could put in a good word with you. They wanted cookies."

Jared turned the game back on. His mom reached around and unplugged the TV. The screen flickered and went black. "What's up?"

Jared shrugged. "I do a batch of cookies now and then."

She stared at him, eyes narrowing. "And you decided you didn't want to cut me in because . . . ?"

"Mom, it's me and a couple of friends. I didn't think you and Richie wanted to deal with lunch money–level shit."

"But someone's got a big mouth," she said. "And you're going to get jumped and beat to hell. Sweetie, this can go wrong all kinds of craptastic ways."

"I'm careful."

"Not careful enough. If you're going to keep doing your little bake sales, we should get you out on the range."

"Mom."

"Jesus fucking Christ, don't *Mom* me, genius. You can't fight worth shit and you weigh eighty pounds soaking wet. Don't fucking argue with me, 'cause I'm not in the mood."

"Richie was pissed, huh?"

"You really are too smart for your own good."

"Sorry."

She sighed. "Cock-sucking Richie tonight is the only thing between you and Emerg."

"Ew," Jared said. "I really, really, really didn't need to know that."

"You're welcome. And you're packing. End of story."

After she left, Jared leaned over, grabbed a beer from the fridge and took a long, deep swig to get the image of his mom and Richie out of his head. He wished she'd find someone less psychotic. With all the hard-hat work, the town was a total sausagefest. She could have her pick of guys and she picked that dill-hole.

He felt his throat get a lump. About now, Baby Killer used to put her head in his lap and look up at him. She would pad right behind him around the room, so if he stopped, she'd bump her head against the back of his knees. She was a bed hog. She liked to bury her nose in his armpit and snort. She whined in his ear to wake him up at the crack of dawn so she could whizz in the backyard.

George Strait burst out of the speakers above his head, singing "Here for a Good Time." The guys must be home from rescuing the strippers. Jared changed into flannel pyjama bottoms and a sweatshirt. He pulled on noise-cancelling headphones and a pair of wool socks then sat watching the wood bugs trundle across the painted concrete floor. He finished his beer and opened another. Thumps made it through the headphones. Jared held one side up and listened for a fight, but it sounded like a bad attempt at dancing. He shut off the lamp. The bars on the basement windows were dusted white. The street light turned the falling snow orange.

A spot of yellow light blazed on the wall. No, Jared realized, it was light from the laundry side of the basement coming through a small, perfectly round hole. As he watched, another brightly lit hole appeared an arm's length away from the first and then the first hole went dark. He felt his way through the darkness to the wall. By the time he peeked through the first hole, the laundry room was empty.

Early Sunday morning, Jared patched the holes on his side of the wall and then the laundry room side. He didn't want to know how long they'd been there and he didn't want to know who'd made them. He knew exactly what his mom would do if she found out. She had enough aggravated assault charges that any jury wouldn't blink twice before assuming her chainsaw-killing spree was premeditated.

His mom called him upstairs for pancakes and bacon with the tenants. They all sat around the kitchen table, laughing and swapping stories about their Saturday night adventures, and Jared wished he didn't know one of them had been spying on him. People were like that, though. Basically good until they thought they could get away with shit without being caught.

5

THE ADVICE & WISDOM
OF NANA SOPHIA

Nana Sophia had posted a picture of herself in the sunken Jacuzzi on the balcony of her cruise ship, some cathedral towering gritty grey and sparkling glass in the background. She wore nothing but froth and a smile, lifting a glass of champagne to her dark red lips. After he Facebook-poked her and she poked him back, a chime signalled that she wanted to chat. Jared turned on the chat feature he normally kept off.

Dullest honeymoon ever, she wrote in the chat window. *How go the boonies?*

I must have eaten babies alive in my last life, Jared wrote.

Come spend Christmas with Nana.

I can't get a passport without Mom and Dad's signatures.

There is no problem so insurmountable a little charm and buttloads of money can't solve it.

Miss you, Nana.

Loyalty is admirable unless it's misplaced. Then it's stupid.

Jared snorted. Staying with Nana would mean a shitstorm of drama. His mom would see it as a betrayal. *Thanks, but I don't want to miss the Christmas grudge matches.*

If your mom and her Neanderthal get too carried away with the holi-day booze-fest, can you stay with the pride of my loins?

Dad's fresh off Oxy. Shirley's on a tear. Her daughter's knocked up and staying with them with her chihuahuas.

Well, I think Norman Rockwell painted that picture already. No one's original anymore.

Jared googled Norman Rockwell, then hooted and gave Nana a *LMFAO!*

You're going to have to charm Richie or he will continue to be a thorn in your ass.

Ew.

Mind out of the gutter, darling. CHARM, not copulate with. Do you remember when Death Threat first moved in? We discussed ways of show-ing him the respect he craved? It's only a hunch, but Richie probably doesn't get a lot of that either.

I dunno.

We're moving back to Canada in the spring. If you haven't figured out a way to get the Neanderthal off your back by then, you can stay with us. My Neanderthal's got a house on Salt Spring. You'd love the island. The tourists are annoying, but we'll have fresh oysters.

Thanks, Nana.

Sweet dreams, Cutie.

6

POWDER HOUSE RULES

With the exception of team fundraisers, he didn't socialize with Teresa Anselmo de Carvalho outside of track because she never smoked weed or drank booze. Ter had once studied until she fainted. Her grandfather was a founding member of the Luso Canadian Club of Kitimat and her grandmother was a Luso lady famous for her custard tarts. Jared's mom had shown up to one of his track meets with a bullhorn, belting out Queen's "We Are the Champions" until officials warned her to stop singing or she'd get tossed from the school grounds. She'd kept singing and no one had tossed her, but she never showed up again.

Ter put herself in charge of the bake sale and organized a dough-making party at her house the night before. Jared brought the unsalted butter and took charge of creaming it and adding the brown sugar. They spooned the dough into Tupperware containers. In the morning, Ter's mother drove around and picked up toaster ovens, which they lined up on tables in the hallways. They served the first round free to the teachers, bringing hot, gooey cookies into class to remind everyone that the bake sale was starting. Then they spent the lunch hour baking tiny toaster-oven batches of chocolate chip cookies and selling them. Because it was Halloween, Ter had wanted everyone to wear angel costumes, but even the squarest of the track squad had rebelled and worn their usual jeans and T-shirts. Only Ter had a feathery halo and glitter-sprinkled wings.

Jared was manning one of the toaster ovens in a hairnet and oven mitts. It was lame, he knew it was lame, but when kids outside his trusted circle asked him for cookies, he could play dumb and tell them to come to the next bake sale. It was a good cover. And, possibly, a source of future character witnesses.

"Do you have any *other* cookies?" Alex Gunborg said, stopping in front of Jared's table. He was a tall, skinny, blond-to-the-point-of-albino Goth who'd invested in contacts that made his eyes look like they had cataracts. His trench coat sleeves didn't quite come down over his wrists. Even though a lot of kids were dressed in costumes, this was Alex's typical look.

"Just chocolate chip," Jared said.

"But they're hot," Ter said.

Alex gave her a sneer. He stared intently at Jared. "I'm looking for *greener* cookies."

"We have a vegan option where we use fair trade virgin coconut oil," Ter said. "It's the last toaster oven."

Jared kept a straight face. "It's eggless, too."

"I'm looking for something *stronger*," Alex said.

Holy clueless telegrapher, Batman. "Where's your school spirit, Alex? Be a team player. Buy a cookie." And get lost.

"Jared," Ter said.

"Sorry."

After Alex left, she said quietly, "We don't use guilt to sell cookies. Cookies sell themselves."

"Amen," Jared said.

———

He took the rest of the afternoon off to watch Mr. Jaks while Mrs. Jaks went to her doctor. She thought she might have a lingering case of the mumps or an infected gland in her throat and was annoyed that her doctor was insisting she go to his office to get that news. Mrs. Jaks wanted them to watch TV and left tranquilizers on the nightstand in case Mr. Jaks got agitated. Jared turned the heater on in the garage instead and put Mr. Jaks in an old jacket. They opened up the weed whacker and replaced the thread. Mr. Jaks gave instructions in Czech. Jared nodded and frowned. They tuned up the lawn mower. Jared sharpened the blades. Mr. Jaks threw the flashlight across the room, which Jared took as a warning that the old man was tired. They went inside and scrubbed up.

They were sitting in the kitchen drinking tea when Mrs. Jaks came back with a cooked chicken. She put it on the table and disappeared into her bedroom while Mr. Jaks repeated her name. Jared knew it was bad news. She hated rotisserie chicken and thought serving it was against the holy sacrament of supper.

"No one has pride anymore," she always said. "Half-assing through life when a little effort makes a good meal you can be proud of."

Every Wednesday after school, Jared delivered the *Northern Sentinel*. He'd start two streets over from his own. Near the end of his route, Mrs. Brantford would wait for him in her lift chair in the front window and wave as he came up her walkway. Her son grew medicinal marijuana and regularly gave her a plastic grocery bag of odds and ends for her glaucoma. Death Threat had sold her a vaporizer a few days before he left town and had tasked Jared with delivering it and collecting the money. His mom hadn't liked it, but Death Threat had said Mrs. Brantford wouldn't rat out a fourteen-year-old, and if Jared was caught, his juvie record would be expunged when he became an adult. Jared had been very, very careful with Mrs. Brantford, but she turned out to be game for new pot experiences. She'd asked him how to work the contraption and they'd spent an afternoon getting completely blitzed in her sitting room and eating their way through her collection of Cadbury chocolates.

"Were you home for the earthquake?" she said today, as he stomped his feet on her porch.

"Wild, huh?"

"I was putting in my Xalatan drops and must have wasted half a bottle," she said. "So annoying."

"Do you need your walkway shovelled?"

"Aren't you thoughtful. No, dear, I have someone coming over later. Would you like a cup of cocoa to warm you up?"

"Sure," Jared said.

He kicked off his boots and followed her into the kitchen. Mrs. Brantford could probably smoke a bong in the City Centre Mall and no one would blink, but she liked a little mystery in her life. So they had a code: if she invited him in for a beverage, she had something to sell him. He handed her the money in a newspaper and her eyes lit up like a kid at Christmas.

She passed Jared a tiny cup of cocoa. "This just hasn't been my week."

"No luck on the slots, huh?"

She was always talking about her seniors' group, which regularly bussed to Terrace for shopping followed by an early supper at the casino. While the other ladies were Bingo-inclined, Mrs. Brantford had a thing for the one-armed bandits.

"It's been all donations and no love." She opened her breadbox and took out a zip-lock bag stuffed in a bread bag. Jared tucked it in his delivery pouch.

"Sorry, Mrs. B."

"Win some, lose some."

Jared put his teacup in the sink. "Thanks for the cocoa."

"Say hello to your mother for me."

After he finished his route, Jared took the bus to the Nechako Centre. In the summer he biked, but now the sidewalks were too icy. At the Pizzarama, he ordered a small pepperoni that he ate at a stool, scrolling through his phone. The cook knew his mom from her party days and, when he didn't have any money, sometimes gave him the single slices that she would normally have thrown out.

He'd gone to Nechako Elementary and knew the kids in the neighbourhood. He sometimes visited friends, sometimes hung out at the skate park, but on days when he had a bag like today, he went to make cookies at his friends' place, which everyone called Powder House.

The driveway was clogged with an assortment of dented four-wheel-drive vehicles. On the front door someone had duct-taped a stand-up cardboard figure of Darth Vader. He was holding a snowboard, a giant weed version of the Canadian flag hanging off his lightsaber. POWDER HOUSE RULES, Darth Vader announced from a paper thought bubble.

The door was unlocked and the mud room was festooned with broken snowboards and bits of things that Jared didn't recognize.

The living room was wallpapered with posters of boarders on pristine mountain runs or jumping out of helicopters, bikinied chicks carving hills and dogs with hand-drawn dreads who were sitting on boards. Beanbag chairs and futons and blow-up furniture and camping cots cluttered the house, jumbled where they had been thrown or fallen. A tall blond guy in blue thermal underwear was passed out on a beanbag, his finger thoughtfully inserted in his ear.

"Hey," Jared said.

The guy didn't move.

No one else was home, which was unusual, but then Shames Mountain had a fresh layer of powder. Jared cleared a space on the kitchen counter and washed the double boiler and bowls he was going to need. A corner of the fridge was taped off with yellow crime scene tape. Someone had added a biological-hazard warning sign and a masking-tape label that was neatly Sharpie'd in hand-drawn block letters, WANT COOKIES?!? FFS <u>STOP</u> EATING THE BUTTER.

Jared's ingredients had been raided last time, so he'd toasted the weed on a cookie sheet and then added it to microwaved Cheez Whiz. The inhabitants of Powder House had grumbled as they dipped their Doritos, and Jared'd said they could damn well go out and buy him more ingredients if they wanted cookies. He usually gave them some free cookies for the use of their kitchen and they usually bought the rest of his cookies fresh from the oven. He wasn't sure how they kept their jobs. The guys said there was always a way when the work camps were short-staffed, but the amount of weed they went through in a week (even without his cookies) had to be turning their drug test urine samples radioactive green.

He shook the bag into a bowl. The weed was sticky and bland, a tasteless smoke but a decent edible once it was turned into pot butter.

The guys had a gas stove, which was underused. He thought he'd try baked pot s'mores if he could get the cookies the right amount of crispy and if someone would go get him marshmallows and chocolate. Or make a giant cookie pizza and put gummy bears and whatever candy they had on it and drizzle everything in chocolate. He was melting the butter in the double boiler when he heard the front door open. He gave the butter a stir with a wooden spoon and was turning to see who was coming into the kitchen when something like a frying pan whacked him on the side of the head.

"Hey, asshole."

The smoke alarm blared and the kitchen was filled with a dark grey fog and the reek of burnt butter and overheated metal. Jared rolled onto his side and upchucked pizza chunks. Every time he heaved, his temples throbbed, sending lightning bolts shivering across his scalp.

"Nice," the blond guy in blue thermal underwear said. "You're cleaning that up."

Blond Dude fanned a towel under the smoke alarm. The windows and door were open and the air rushing in was frigid. Jared tried to get up and failed, then slid back onto his butt.

"If you're too baked to stand, you're too baked to cook," Blond Dude said. "Asshole. Go burn down your own place."

"Cookies," Jared tried to explain. "I'm the—"

"We don't have any cookies. The guy who makes them is a spaz. He comes when he comes and he doesn't sell to assholes who barf all over other people's floors."

Jared looked down. Someone had taken his jacket. His shoes were missing. And his wallet. And his cellphone. The pot butter had either been scooped up or burned. He put the back of his hand to his mouth, hoping not to barf and failing, heaving into a pasta pot that Blond Dude shoved at him.

Could be worse, his inner voice said.

Jared didn't see how. He was out the pot, the money he'd have gotten for the pot, the cookie butter, his phone and his good jacket.

You're breathing.

He felt distant, at a distance, not entirely there. He pushed himself up the wall and stood, weaving. His head had ballooned to the size of a tree, too heavy to hold up, and he wanted to curl up on the floor and go night-night. He rummaged through his socks and found the key to his place in the basement. He thought, Time to go home.

"Hey, clean this up!" Blond Dude yelled at him as he started to make his way out. "I said clean this up, asshole!"

When he touched the sore spot on his head, his hand came away damp. He was expecting blood, but it was sweat. Not that bad, then. Once he got some painkillers, he would be fine. Fine and dandy. Candy. Holy crap, he thought. What the hell was I drinking?

Blond Dude grabbed him by the elbow and handed him paper towels. Jared listlessly mopped up his own vomit.

"That was a Paderno, asshole. You're going to reimburse us for the double boiler you wrecked. Got it?"

"My socks are wet," Jared said.

"Keep scrubbing. I'll tell you when you're done."

Jared emptied the vomit-filled pasta pot in the garburator, which nauseated him, and he was throwing up into the sink when the guys came home. Saul, he of the Jesus hair and the big, sad brown eyes, came up and patted him on the back. Kyle scratched his arms, tweaking.

Saul grinned. "Jared, man, how wasted are you?"

"Got rolled," Jared said. "Someone took my weed."

"He almost burned down the house!" Blond Dude said.

"Mel, chill. This is the Cookie Dude."

"Bullshit," Blond Dude said.

"Mel's helping us move. He's a big fan of your baking." Saul grabbed Jared's chin and turned his head. "Your pupils are dilated. Did you get clocked?"

"So clocked. Felt like an anvil."

"Here? In our house?"

"Yeah." Jared turned away, heaved and heaved and heaved over the sink, and the pizza gradually became a slurry of bile. Mel made a face and left the kitchen.

"We've got weed," Kyle said. "Make cookies with our stash."

"I'm going home," Jared said.

"Did you see who did it?" Saul said.

"No," Jared said.

"Hey, I want cookies, man," Kyle said. "This is bullshit."

"Go buy off someone else," Jared said.

"And after all the business we gave you, you disloyal asshole."

"Go to hell, Kyle. For all I know, you're the asshole that rolled me."

"Chill, chill," Saul said. "Guys, fucking chill."

"Hey, we're loyal customers and he's treating us like shit."

"He's a kid, Kyle. Fucking lay off the crank and rediscover your brains."

"Fuck you, Saul. Fuck you." Kyle stomped out of the kitchen.

"We got shitcanned," Saul said. "Everyone's bummed."

Jared coughed and waited, feeling the muscles in his stomach clench. "You're fired?"

Saul sighed and hopped up on the counter. "Yeah. The foreman's buddies showed up and our drug tests were suddenly relevant. He let us go. We'd stay, but it looks like we're blackballed."

Jared wanted to wash the taste out of his mouth, but he didn't want to start upchucking again.

"Squares," Saul said with a resigned shrug. "Whaddya gonna do?"

Jared used Kyle's stash to make the guys one last batch of cookies. Mel gave him a ski jacket and Kyle gave him a pair of boots. Saul paid him as if it was a normal cook and the guys started phoning their friends to have one last blowout before their finances forced them to move. Jared watched the snow coming down, sipping a beer while they ate their way through the cookies. Their first partiers wahooed as they banged the door open.

"You should come with us, Cookie Dude," Saul said.

People said all kinds of things when they were wasted, but it was the thought that counted, he guessed. "I hate snowboarding."

"No one's perfect," Saul said.

Saul gave him a muscle relaxer shaped like a little house and told him to go crash if he felt like it. Jared washed the pill down with a swig of beer, then wobbled towards Saul's bedroom, which was filled with cardboard boxes. He flopped on the bare mattress, turning over to stare at the ceiling. Music blared to life, a frantic, trippy trance tune, the subwoofers so loud the windows rattled. Jared considered the distance between Powder House and the nearest bus stop. He also considered calling his mom for a ride, but she'd bring Richie and they'd end up crashing the party and he wouldn't get home.

"Cookie Dude?"

A pretty girl with Smurf-blue hair smiled shyly from the doorway.

"Hey," Jared said, pushing himself up on his elbows. "Jared. Hi. I'm, yes, the Cookie Dude. And my name is Jared. Did I say that already?" Shut up, he told himself. Be cool.

"Murchadh," she said, pointing to herself.

She wore a short blue dress over tie-died leggings. She had her long hair braided into a crown. Her eyelids twinkled with pink glitter. She studied him, moving closer. Her contacts made her eyes intensely green. "I liked the magic in your baking."

"Thanks. It's a decent bud."

"I'm sensing loss in you." She sat on the side of the bed and touched his chest. "I'm sensing mourning."

He wanted to say something clever to make her laugh, but nothing witty would come. "My dog died."

"We're all going to die soon enough," she said.

"Glass half empty, huh?"

"We're in the Anthropocene. The human-driven extinction event." She shrugged. "But we're all information, so no one really dies."

Jared frowned, wondering if that made sense and he was too stoned to understand it, or if she was the one who was wasted and talking shit. "Is that the Mayan prophecy? Twenty-twelve, end-of-the-world stuff? 'Cause that was just a movie and not a—"

She kissed him. His lips tingled. She sat back, breathing hard. Her lips sparkled greenish white in the dim light, like glow-in-the-dark stars blinking. Whoa, Jared thought.

She touched her lips. "What are you?"

"So high," he said.

"My mother was a Selkie."

"Cool," Jared said, not sure which country that was.

"Magic calls to magic," she said. "I belong to the sea. Who do you belong to?"

"I'm not seeing anyone, if that's what you're asking."

"You have the moon in your eyes," she said.

Yup, she's stoned out of her gourd, Jared decided. "Yeah?"

"And I have the ocean in mine."

"Is that poetry?"

"Shh," she said, unbuttoning his shirt.

7

NORMAN ROCKWELL REDUX

Jared caught the 6 a.m. Skeena Connector bus to go visit his dad in Terrace. He rested his head against the window and tried to sleep. The bus was on the highway for forty-five minutes before it wound through Jack Pine Flats and came out in Thornhill. Jared got off at Walmart and walked the seven blocks to his father's apartment.

The chihuahuas barked at him as he came in the front door and his stepsister Destiny told them to hush and gave Jared a peck on the cheek. Her belly bulged under her pink Minnie Mouse sweatshirt.

"I made some oatmeal," she said.

"I'm good," Jared said.

They sat at the kitchen table and Destiny handed him a coffee. He could hear his father's new wife, Shirley, muttering in the bedroom, occasionally shouting along to her AC/DC songs. Destiny didn't like it when her mom cranked her music because the dogs went nuts. She must have gotten her mom to wear headphones. The dogs skittered through the kitchen, sniffing Jared's shoes and jeans.

"How's the baby?"

"He likes to kick," Destiny said. "I keep telling him to lay off my bladder, but he's got no ears."

"Is Dad here?" Jared said, hoping he wasn't on a tear.

"He's in the hospital," Destiny said. "His back again. The new meds aren't working. Or they aren't working together. Something like that."

Crap. "Why didn't you text me?"

Destiny shrugged.

"Do you know when he's getting out?" Jared said.

Destiny picked up one of the dogs and it licked her mouth. "Remembrance Day, I think. Isn't that right, Hoho? Isn't that right?"

Hoho barked.

"I got rolled," Jared said.

"Shit. We're almost caught up on back rent."

"I've got another sell in a week or so. That'll bring you guys up to date and then we'll just have to worry about January."

"Thank Christ," Destiny said. "The shelter won't take dogs."

"Did the insurance people get back to him about his disability claim?"

"I dunno."

"Did you call them? Did you ask if they got all the support papers?"

"Do I look like a secretary?"

"Destiny, this is important."

Destiny hugged Hoho, glaring at the table. "They don't listen to me."

Destiny was a year older than him but sometimes seemed five. "Can you get his papers from the bedroom?"

"Sure," she said, carrying Hoho with her.

Jared watched the other dogs meander through the kitchen. His head still ached from Wednesday's excitement. The coffee was watery. Destiny was probably rationing it or using the grounds again. He should have thought to stop at Walmart to grab a tin of Folgers before he came. He chugged the coffee and tried to remember everything about the woman handling his dad's file. Nana always said the foundation of charm was remembering the bullshit people wanted you to believe.

After they brought the rent to the office, Jared and Destiny went to Walmart. The taxi driver was not impressed with either their trip or their tip. Jared helped Destiny out of the cab. She forgot about having wanted to bring her dogs when Jared suggested she take one of the scooters. She zipped ahead of him to the baby section and they looked at really small clothes that made Destiny cry. Jared wasn't sure if the tears were happy or sad.

Once they were through looking at baby clothes, they groceried up. The wait for the taxi back was endless. Jared vowed to save enough to get a beater so he could take off whenever he wanted to. Destiny sat on the scooter until an old lady asked if she could use it, then the greeter brought Destiny a chair. Their taxi driver was a woman who recounted each of her births in graphic detail on the ride home. Jared carried the groceries into the apartment as the dogs went crazy, loving Destiny's ankles and knees with licks and tail wags.

Destiny made him lunch. Shirley staggered out, ran the tap and poured herself a glass of water then went back to her room, trailing booze fumes that made his eyes water. Jared had expected the woman who broke up his parents' marriage to be wildly hot, but she was mousy, with large, scared eyes. Jared ate his sandwich and drank his tea. Destiny hugged him for a long time when he left. She tried to get Hoho to kiss him and he said he had to go.

On the way to Mills Memorial Hospital, Jared bought his dad a twenty pack of old-fashioned plain Timbits and a coffee. He stopped at the front desk to ask what room his dad was in. His dad was alone when he got there. The entire afternoon Jared was his only visitor.

"You know what's ironic?" his dad said. "You're the backbone of your family until you crack your backbone."

His dad was trying to lighten the mood. Jared didn't know what to say or do. He held up a plastic cup with water and ice. His dad sipped. He shook quietly, his skin pale, the bones of his face jagged in the fluorescent light. Jared put the cup back on the table. The nurse came by with a wafer-thin strip of Suboxone for his dad.

"Who's this handsome guy?" she said.

"My son, Jared," his dad said.

"Your dad is one tough cookie, Jared," the nurse said.

When she left, his dad leaked tears. "If I could afford it, I'd go back on Oxy in a heartbeat. Damn hillbillies ruined it for everyone."

"Sorry," Jared said.

"Hallmark should make withdrawal cards. 'Deepest Sympathies on Being Cut Off Oxy,' haha."

"Yeah."

"How's your mom?"

"The same."

"Well, that's life with a witch, huh?"

Jared examined his fingers. "How long's Shirley been on the tear?"

"She's not good with stress."

"Sorry."

"Don't be sorry," his dad said. "Do me a favour and get a desk job. Won't pay as much, but it won't crack your vertebrae."

His dad drifted off to sleep. Jared ate one of the Timbits. The big issue in the divorce was the house. His dad's back was never going to be the same and the disability cheque was small. His dad had wanted to sell the house because he didn't think they'd be able to keep up the mortgage and the bills. His mom had dug in and refused, saying they had to fight for it. Jared watched his dad sleep, fitfully and in obvious pain, and he suspected that neither of his parents could stand to be reminded of his old dad, the strong one, the guy who'd once nicked his shin with a chainsaw and kept bucking wood.

And then, of course, there was Shirley.

Maybe his dad hadn't been fooling around with her while he was married like he claimed, but the second he met Shirley in physio, he started acting like his old self. He was protective of her, constantly wrapping his arm around her shoulders. Defending her against all slights. Asking if she was cold. Seconds after the divorce, they'd moved in together. Nana Sophia hadn't shown up for their wedding and, although invited, wouldn't go to any of Shirley's family pot-latches but expected her son to make an appearance at hers in Alert Bay. Nana didn't include Shirley in the invitation and only sent a plane ticket for Phil. When his dad didn't go, they'd stopped talk-ing. Nana said Shirley and her family were jumped-up commoners who didn't know how to potlatch properly. His dad said Nana was a stuck-up old coot who'd gotten her money by being a low-rent Elizabeth Taylor. As for his mom, Jared wasn't sure if it was being saddled with the mortgage or being unceremoniously dumped for someone dishwater plain that drove her to instant rage whenever someone mentioned Philip Martin's name. She had spent Shirley and Phil's wedding day burning every single photo of him she could find in an old carved bowl, eventually tossing in the jewellery he'd given her and bits of his clothes as she roundly cursed him and his whore.

After the whole mess with David, his dad had come to see Jared in the hospital. He had brought him sneakers and snacks, had sat with him watching TV, and Jared had wondered if he was trying to make up for running out on them. He had offered to take Jared in, but they both had known Jared wouldn't get along with Shirley, and that the idea would be supremely unpopular with his mom, who had sole custody. So Jared had asked his dad if he could stay with Mrs. Jaks while his mom was in mandatory anger management. His dad had said he'd talk to Mrs. Jaks and the social workers about giving her his child support while Jared stayed there. As he was leaving, his dad had stopped in the door, sad and serious.

"David was born mean," he'd said. "And he hid it good. Don't blame yourself, okay? None of this is your fault."

Just then Jared heard a commotion in the hallway, and then someone shouting in another language. Nurses and a security guard ran past. His dad woke, and they played cribbage until Jared had to leave to catch the last bus back to Kitimat.

"You can stay with us any time," his dad said.

"Thanks, Dad," Jared said. "See you next week."

"Don't be a stranger."

While he was waiting at the bus stop, his mom texted him: *Where u @?*

Hanging @ friends, Jared texted back.

Which friends?

Kelsey & Blake. CoD marathon.

R u home for pizza?

In the zone.

K. TTFN

He snorted. Her "Ta ta for now" was what she used to text when they ironically pretended to be normal. He texted back an equally ironic *TTYL*.

She was going to be so pissed if—when—she found out he was helping out his dad. Jared didn't want to live with his dad. He wasn't picking sides. God, no. He just didn't want his dad to be homeless. He didn't want to worry about her reaction, but it wiggled around the back of his mind like a melody that you hummed without thinking.

8

THE CHRISTMAS TREE HUNT

Jared studied his reflection in the cracked mirror above the utility sink. His hair was floppy. He couldn't remember the last time he'd had it cut. He took a pair of scissors and carefully cut as much of it off as he could manage then took a pair of clippers and buzzed his head. He left a layer of fuzz to camouflage the bump where he'd been clocked. The shape of his head was okay. He'd been worried he'd have some weird lumps. Nana Sophia said imitation was the sincerest form of flattery, so if Richie had a freaking crewcut, Jared now had one too. Lame-ass, but cheap.

Richie was watching football on TV and Jared went in and sat beside him.

"I got rolled," Jared said. "Someone stole my weed."

Richie glanced his way, did a double take and then stared at Jared's head as if he'd just noticed Jared had one. Jared had been expecting laughter or mocking, but got nothing. His mom's boyfriend turned back to the TV.

"Shocking," Richie said.

"Yeah," Jared said.

"Do you know who it was?"

"Party pals."

"Did you mess them up?"

"Uh, no."

"Your mom wants me to get you gear."

"I kind of like my feet without bullet holes."

Richie laughed. Jared couldn't believe he'd actually made Richie laugh.

"Don't tell Mom, okay? We don't need her beating up a bunch of high school kids."

"I like it when she gets o-rang-a-tang," Richie said.

"Ew," Jared said. "Dude. Scarred for life here."

"Mess them up," Richie said quietly, seriously. "Or they'll hit you again."

"I'm going to cool it with the cookies. I was shitty at sales anyways."

Jared went and got two beers from his mom's side of the fridge. He handed one to Richie. They drank and watched the Toronto Argonauts get hammered by the BC Lions. Jared pretended to be interested in the guys running around with a football, counting down the infinitely long period of time to the end of the game.

Over the next few days, Richie wasn't exactly his best bud. But he stopped calling him Useless and the threats to kick his ass into tomorrow went down and that was all Jared really wanted.

He woke in the dark to find his mom by his bed. She unzipped his sleeping bag and shone a flashlight in his eyes. She was wearing a fluffy pink snowsuit.

"Mom. Come on, it's cold."

"Get your shit together. We're off to the cabin."

Ugh. The hunting cabin. God, he'd thought he'd never have to endure it after the divorce. It wasn't really their cabin, but the guy who owned it used to be his dad's friend and had moved away, leaving them the keys. His dad used to take Jared hunting, but most of the time they were just riding around on ATVs and making s'mores. "Are we penguins? Who goes to their cabin in the middle of winter?"

"I'm going to count to ten," his mom said. "And then I'm going to kick your ass up the stairs."

Jared swung his legs over the side of the bed. He reached for the lamp, but nothing happened.

"Power's out, genius," she said.

"Awesome."

"Less bitching, more moving."

"We should get the generator going. I don't want the pipes to freeze."

"The guys are taking care of that."

"Can I stay here and make sure we have pipes? Please? You and Richie go have a honeymoon."

She slugged his shoulder and he rubbed it and stood up. He dug around in a tote for some clean socks and a sweater to go over his thermal underwear. His mom handed him a navy blue snowsuit with reflector tape on the cuffs. The suit was designed for someone taller and heavier. Jared jammed his feet into his boots, tucking the cuffs in.

Richie sat tall in a new truck he could never afford, a flame-hooded red Ford F-450 crew cab diesel Dually. Someone had decided the cab wasn't high enough and lifted it like a mud-bogging monster truck with fat, studded wheels. The amount of chrome decorating every edge could build a Transformer. The truck was loaded with matching red snowmobiles. Jared felt his stomach sink. He hoped all that crap wasn't stolen. Theft over five grand would get his mom in deep, deep trouble.

"Where'd you get that stuff?" he said.

"Where'd you get your boots?" she said.

Richie honked and the horn played "Dixie."

"I don't think we're rednecking it up enough," Jared said. "Why don't we tie some horns to the hood?"

"We'll try to run over something suitable on the way to the cabin," she said.

"Is all this shit hot?"

She laughed. "It's ours. Legit. Some numbnuts couldn't pay his debts, so we traded."

"Willingly?"

"You worry too much. Sometimes you just have to grab life by the throat and shake."

They barrelled down the whiteout like it was a sunny summer day, his mom and Richie growling along to George Thorogood's "One Bourbon, One Scotch, One Beer." Even the snowplows weren't stupid enough to be on the highway yet.

They pulled off at Onion Lake. Jared stubbornly stayed in the cab while Richie and his mom unloaded the snowmobiles. The snow stopped falling. The morning was grey. His breath steamed the window near his face. The clouds hung low, sunk down over the mountaintops. The trees were iced like Christmas cookies. His mom threw a snowball at his window.

"Move it," she warned him.

When he hopped down from the truck, she shoved a helmet at him. He had a choice to ride bitch seat with his mom or Richie. He clomped across the fresh snow and sat behind his mom, who revved enthusiastically. They took off across the highway and up a logging road. His mom laughed when Richie passed them, towing a little sled, then yelled something that was lost in the whine of the engine. His goggles fogged. The trees blurred past. He felt himself slowly going numb.

The cabin was waist-deep in snow and they hadn't brought snowshoes. His mom and Richie cheerfully waded to the door. Richie went back to the sled for a metal box that turned out to be full of an assortment of handguns and ammo. Jared usually was in charge of keeping the cabin warm, but his mom told him to go sit with Richie. She started the fire while Richie placed a revolver on the table.

"You're lazy and you'll never practise, so you're going to stick to revolvers. Got it?"

Jared blew into his hands.

"Short barrel for easy conceal. No fucking exposed hammer spurs, because they get caught on everything. And we didn't fucking cheap out. This is a titanium revolver. This is a fucking Smith & Wesson." Richie smacked him on the side of the head. "Are you listening, Fuckwad?"

"Ow," Jared said.

"I love you enough to steal the very best," his mom said, and they laughed.

Jared stared out the window while his mom stuck her tongue as far down Richie's throat as humanly possible. After that was over,

Richie took the revolver apart, naming the pieces. Jared reluctantly recited the names after him. Then he put the revolver back together and handed it to Jared.

"Fly at her," Richie said.

Jared fumbled and dropped the bits. He tucked his hands under his arms. His mom gave him a plastic cup of coffee from her Thermos. The coffee was thoroughly Baileyed. As the cabin warmed up, so did Jared's fingers, and he got the hang of the revolver. Next Richie slowly explained the different types of ammo.

His mom chopped kindling and then started throwing her axe at one of the posts. Richie stopped talking to watch her aim and throw, aim and throw. His mouth hung open and his eyes glazed. Jared mimed putting the revolver to his head and pulling the trigger.

Richie grinned. "You got a hot mom. You should be used to it by now."

In the afternoon, they stood on the back deck and shot at the snow on tree branches. Jared loaded and unloaded resentfully. His mom and Richie kissed. Then Richie disappeared into the cabin and came back carrying an AK-47. His mom squealed and clapped her hands. They took turns firing into the trunk of one of the target trees, which quivered until it creaked, cracked, then fell over.

"Tim-ber!" they yelled together.

"Normal people buy their trees from the Boy Scouts," Jared said. "Normal people don't hunt their Christmas trees down and kill them."

"Did my sweet'ums want to kill the tree?"

"How can you be grumpy on a day like this?" Richie said, opening his arms wide. "Man, I would have killed to have your life when I was a kid."

"I'm freezing my ass off," Jared said.

"Do you know what always makes me smile?" his mom said. "Grenades."

"No way!" Richie said.

"Way!" his mom said.

"Oh, good gravy," Jared said.

On Monday, his mom sold the new truck, the snowmobiles and the trailers and they went down to the bank and paid off the remainder of their mortgage.

"Free and clear," she said.

"Except for the bills," Jared said. "And taxes. And—"

"Okay, Buzzkill, this is a win. You celebrate wins. You don't shit on them."

"Sorry."

They bought pizza and beers and drove home in their shitty old truck with the sticky clutch and holes in the floorboard. They ate in the living room, his mom gazing around the room like she was seeing it for the first time.

"I was homeless," she said. "And now I own a home."

"When were you homeless?"

She sipped her beer, studying him. "I guess you're old enough."

Jared waited. She flipped on the TV. She pulled him into a snuggle and he pulled himself out.

"I'm sixteen," Jared said. "It's weird. That's why Richie gets all bent out of shape."

"You lived in my uterus," she said. "You came out my vagina."

"Ew. Mom. Boundaries."

"You use condoms, right?"

"Again. Boun-da-ries."

"I was your age when I was knocked up. I want you to live a bit before you settle down and give me grandkids."

Jared played with the tab on his beer can, bending it back and forth. "Sorry."

"I don't regret you."

"Gran doesn't like me," he said. "I remember that."

"My mom's messed up," his mom said. "The nuns messed her up. They made her think everything Indian was evil. And that includes you and me."

"Why did she think I was a Trickster?"

"Uh, hello? What part of 'messed up' did you not understand?"

"But why? What happened?"

Jared let her pull him down. She stroked his forehead like she used to when he was a kid with the flu staying home from school. *Wheel of Fortune* came on, and Jared wondered how Mrs. Jaks was doing.

"Your dad is dead to me," his mom whispered. "The blood in your veins is mine and only mine. He screwed us over. Mom screwed us over. So we forget them. We leave them in the past and we don't talk about them."

Jared swallowed. "But—"

"Jared, enough. You got a big heart, and if you let it lead you around, people are going to use that. Trust me on this, okay?"

9

COOKING WITH EBONY

Ebony Stewart's brand-name perfection was completely out of place in his basement pad, but she sat on his couch and accepted a beer as if they had remained friends since grade school. They hadn't. After she'd morphed into a hot chick and had started running with the cooler-than-you crowd, she'd pretended not to know him. He almost expected to see aliens landing or Elvis singing to signal that he was deep in a weird dream.

"Your cookies are good," Ebony said, smiling. "Not too hippie. Fresh, not frozen. Decent weed."

Jared considered telling her to go to the track team bake sale for cookies, but decided against it. Her sweater was soft. "Thanks."

She tucked her hair behind her ear. She'd flat-ironed it into a silky black sheet that shone even in the crappy basement light. "You've got a lot of loyal customers."

"I got rolled," Jared said. "I'm going to cool it with the cookies for a while."

Ebony sipped her beer, studying him. Her makeup made her face a pleasant mask. "I heard you're picky about your sales. If you sell to someone, they have to be fairly cool."

"No, it's trust issues. I need to not be narced on."

"Do you think I'd narc on you?"

"No," Jared said. "But I just got beat on and my head hurts. Not in the mood to bake."

"Are you going to make them pay?" Ebony said.

"I don't even know who it was. I got clocked from behind."

"I can find out," she said.

Maybe she could. Maybe she couldn't. But he suspected it was one of the Powder House guys, and would prefer not to know for sure. "Live and let live. Richie can sell you j if you want."

"I can get my own pot," she said.

"Do you want the recipe?"

Her brow furrowed. "You expect me to cook?"

"My kitchen crew got fired and run out of town," Jared said. "I can't bake here 'cause Mom and Richie will eat all the product."

"You can bake at my house," she said. "Mom and Dad are working out at Kemano for another week. I've got the place to myself and the neighbours aren't nosy."

Jared considered it. "How much?"

"I get half the cookies or half the sales."

"That's kind of steep."

"No one's going to jump you. No one's going to narc. I supply the weed and the kitchen and you give me an ingredient list. All you do is show up and bake."

Considering he was close to getting his dad out of debt, a little fleecing probably wouldn't kill him. "I'll try it. Once."

"You need to sell some to Dylan."

"Your boyfriend's an ass."

"You don't think my boyfriend is worthy of your cookies?"

"He is single-handedly responsible for every wedgie, swirly and locker pop I've ever gotten. If there is a bright spot in the universe, he's at the ass end farthest away from it."

"You hurt his feelings," Ebony said.

"Wait a minute—are you the one who told him my cookies are 'da bomb'?"

Ebony sneered. "Who talks like that? No one cool talks like that. I bet it was Greer."

"I would never sell to that stuck-up chick."

"Your ski bums resold your cookies to a bunch of kids for a big markup. Oh, relax. No one cares who you are as long as you keep them baked."

"Dylan runs his mouth. I just made peace with Richie. I'm not aggravating him again. No, thanks."

"Dylan will keep his mouth shut," Ebony said. "And high school is a much nicer place when you have the hockey team backing you up."

"Ebs, man. Not my circle. I'll just get stomped and have my product snitched."

"Cookie Dude," Ebony said. She put her hand on his knee and whispered in his ear, "Please? Pretty please?"

She was warm, her sweater was fuzzy and her chest moved in hot ways when she leaned into him.

"Okay," Jared said, blushing. "But if I end up in the hospital, it's on you."

She smiled and took her hand back. His thigh tingled where she'd touched it.

"You are about to become very, very popular," she said.

"Pinch me. It's like a dream come true."

"That's what gets you stomped," Ebony said, standing and chugging her beer. "Your snarky-ass attitude."

Ebony's house had been gutted and remodelled from a sixties bungalow into a glossy dark wood and granite, stainless steel–applianced open-concept pad. Her parents must be raking it in at the camps, Jared thought. The last time he'd been here, her house had been all broken windows fixed with duct tape, rusted-out appliances and wall-to-wall grungy shag carpeting.

All the ingredients were laid out on the table. Ebony's stash was brutally sticky, promising a gong-show kick. Ebony did her homework at the butcher's block island while he simmered the pot butter on the stove. She was taking correspondence courses on top of her regular classes so she could graduate early.

He picked up a bunch of fluffy pastel bags with pink and blue ribbons for ties.

"What's this?" Jared said.

"Those are the bags I want you to use for the cookies," she said.

"I brought my own."

"You have a great product," she said. "But your dollar-store Baggies are ghetto."

"So?"

"So if you're selling out of my house, you need to up your game."

"No one's buying my cookies for the girly packaging."

"This is about your brand, your image. That's local, grass-fed butter. That's unbleached, organic flour. That's medicinal-grade weed.

We're top-shelf. We're not some badly sewn Gucci knock-off."

"It's about getting baked."

"You're going to make triple the amount of money for half the amount of cookies," Ebony said.

"My buyers aren't going to buy a bunch of overpriced girly shit."

"That's why we're selling to my friends, not yours."

Watching Ebony curled over her books while he baked was a surreal way of spending his Friday night. She was carefully non-committal in class, never volunteering answers or participating much. Her grades were non–honour roll, but decent enough to get her a university spot. She was working hard not to look smarter than anyone else, because smarter rarely translated to popular. While the cookies were baking, Ebs showed him how to load the dishwasher and wipe down the counters.

Ebony gave him her old Samsung phone, preloaded with the numbers of the people she wanted him to sell to. Even her castoff was better than the phone he'd had stolen at Powder House. Dylan was the first person on the list.

And he soon arrived, smirking. "Hey, Walter White. Where's your fucking hair? Did you get lice?"

"I'm regretting this already," Jared said to Ebony.

"Touchy," Dylan said.

Ebony sold the rest of the cookies, swanning around like she'd done everything herself. Within the hour, her phone was ringing constantly and she made her voice sympathetic and pained as she explained that all the cookies were spoken for, but she'd put their name on her list for next time.

"It won't be a party unless we're invited," she said more to herself than him, smug.

"Livin' the dream," Jared said.

Ebony gave him the dates her kitchen would be free. Then Jared took the bus downtown and deposited his money in his account. He stared out the window on the bus ride home. He missed Powder House. Sure, he knew he'd been getting a little fleeced, but at least the guys didn't boot him out the door the second he was done like he was an ugly, beer-goggled booty call.

His cell buzzed. Message from Dylan: *So. Baaaaaaaked. I want all ʒ cooooookies. All ʒ cookies r mine. MINE. Hahhahahahaha. Wooooo.*

Lightweight, Jared thought.

Later that evening, someone banged on his door. Jared considered not answering, but they kept hammering away until he threw his blankets off and stomped up the steps. Dylan swayed in the doorway.

"Heeey," he said. "Cookies?"

"They're all gone." Jared tried to close the door, but Dylan held it open.

A truck in the driveway honked.

Dylan leaned in. "Are you shittin' me? You're shittin' me, right? Riiight?"

"Dude," Jared said, waving away Dylan's booze fumes.

Dylan shoved his way inside, stumbled down the steps and flopped on the couch. "You're, you are lying. You, *you* don't want to sell me shit. Right?"

"Go home, Dylan. You're fucking wasted."

"Holy crap," Dylan said, swinging his head around. "What a shit-hole. Do you live here?"

"My mansion's getting renos," Jared said. "This is my summer residence."

"What?"

"Get out."

"Dylan!" someone yelled. "Move your ass!"

"I can't go back to house league," Dylan muttered. "Dad's going to kill me if I go back to house."

"Whatever. Dude. Your friend's calling you," Jared said, grabbing Dylan's wrist and hauling him halfway off the couch.

He flopped back down, glum. "I want cookies."

"You've had enough cookies."

Dylan frowned. "You, you don't tell me what to do."

Jared went to his private entrance. A stocky white kid waited near the door.

"Where's Dylan?" he said.

"Inside," Jared said.

The kid stomped inside and down the stairs and stood in front of Dylan. "Get it together, man."

"You're a good guy, Bambam," Dylan said. "A good guy."

"Jesus," Bambam said. "I don't have time for this. I'm out."

"You can't leave him here. This isn't a flophouse."

"I'll pick him up in the morning. I'm not babysitting his lame ass all night."

"Hey!" Jared shouted at the guy's back. "Fuck. What a douche."

"MVP," Dylan said. "He da, deserves it. Bambam's a strong two-way centre."

"I have no idea what you're saying."

"I dunno. Anymore. I used to wannit. And now I can't even . . ." Dylan's head flopped back and he started snoring.

Perfect. Just peachy, Jared thought.

Come get ur damn boyfriend, he texted Ebony. *He's crashed @ my place.*

———

Jared woke to the sounds of Dylan puking in his toilet.

"What time is it?" Dylan said between heaves.

"It's time to shut up," Jared said.

"I've got practice. Can you drive me home? I have to pick up my shit."

"Dude, flush the can. You're stinking up the place."

Dylan stood and staggered over to the sink. He ran the tap and put his head under it. Water splashed all over the floor. Jared sat up. "Need a cab?"

"Can I borrow forty?"

"Jesus," Jared said. "I'm not your bank."

"Ebs paid you, man. I saw her pay you."

"I blew it on coke and hookers."

"You're funny," Dylan said, sounding surprised.

"Yeah, I'm a riot," Jared said.

"I'm gonna get benched if I miss practice," Dylan said. "Again."

"And?"

"And I have fifty bucks at my place. Drive me home and it's yours."

"You're wrecked, man."

"We'll get some coffee. I'll be fine."

Jared threw a jacket over his PJs. Dylan staggered up the stairs behind him. Jared went around to the front door, leaned in and took the truck keys hanging up in the hallway and warmed his mom's truck up, brushing off the snow and scraping the ice off the windows while Dylan held his temples. The road to the rez was freshly plowed and dark, closed in by tall trees. They caught up with the plow at the entrance to Kitamaat Village.

"Pass him, pass him, pass him," Dylan said.

"There's a bridge up ahead. Left or right?"

"Left."

Jared had been to the government docks to swim when he was younger, but he hadn't ever driven up the hill to the subdivision that overlooked the reserve and the Douglas Channel. Dylan's house was two storeys, light blue with white trim. A gold Toyota Sienna and a black Dodge Ram hogged the driveway. Jared parked on the street. Dylan hopped out and disappeared inside.

Someone loved Christmas. The trees and shrubs, eaves and windows were lit with white and blue lights. On the roof, Santa hefted a toy bag with his reindeer lined up at the peak. Jesus glowed in a manger on the front porch. Mary blinked spastically beside a very bearded Joseph. Dylan tiptoed out of the house, came back to the truck and handed him a twenty-dollar bill.

"The rest when you get me home after practice," he said.

"What? I didn't agree to that. Catch your own ride home."

"Shh. Go, go, go."

The outside lights went on and a chubby guy in grey thermal underwear came out on the porch. His short salt-and-pepper hair stuck up like a porcupine.

"Dylan!" he shouted.

"Fuck," Dylan said.

The guy went inside the door, stuffed his feet in some boots and then turned around and tromped down the steps. Dylan sighed, and walked towards him. When they met in the driveway, they spoke quietly, intensely, both crossing their arms. Jared reached over and shut the passenger-side door. The guy broke away and walked to the driver's side, gesturing at Jared to roll the window down.

"Do you have a licence?" he said. "Your learner's licence at least?"

"Hey," Jared said. "Don't drag me into your family crap. I was doing Dylan a solid."

"My son doesn't need help from the likes of you."

"Nice. You're welcome. Having your son pass out and puke in my place was so classy. You obviously raised a gentleman."

"Don't give me lip, you disrespectful little shit."

"Don't give me grief, you disrespectful old shit."

"Leave," Dylan's dad said, hitting the truck door. "Now."

"Yeah, you're all class," Jared said.

As he backed out, he caught Dylan's expression of stunned amusement. Dylan saluted him. His father's scowl was lit by the truck's headlights as Jared drove away.

Yikes, Jared thought. Normal people, man. So aggro.

At school on Monday, he noticed Ebony and Dylan too late to avoid acknowledging them, so he nodded. Ebony scowled back while her moron of a boyfriend just grinned. Dylan stopped in front of him and held his hand over Jared's head. "Don't leave me hanging, bro."

Ebony kept her arm around Dylan's waist, glaring at Jared. "His dad was super pissed. Dylan's grounded."

"Up high," Dylan insisted.

Jared high-fived Dylan to get him to stop waving his hand around. "He was already pissed," he said.

Her nostrils flared. "Yeah, thanks for making a bad situation worse, Mr. Sarcasm."

"Ebs," Dylan said. "Be cool."

She elbowed her boyfriend in the ribs. She pointed at Jared. "No going off on Mr. Wilkinson again or you find another kitchen."

"I think I should be a doctor," Jared said.

"What?" Ebs said.

"Doctor Sarcasm."

"Oh, my God," she said. "You are such a loser."

"Doctor Loser," Dylan said, making an L with his fingers and bouncing them on his forehead. "Paging Doctor Loooooser."

"You're Doctor Loooooser, you vomit specialist," Jared said.

"Said Doctor Sarcasm, leading specialist in head-in-ass disease."

As they snickered, Ebony flexed her hands in and out of fists. "I've got to start dating college guys."

After school, Mrs. Jaks told Jared she was going to see an oncologist at the Vancouver General Hospital and she needed help getting her house ready in case they started chemo right away. Jared spent Saturday afternoon shovelling the Jakses' driveway. Mr. Jaks came out to help dressed in his pyjamas and slippers. Jared asked him where the WD-40 was and they went into the garage. Jared brushed the snow off Mr. Jaks's pyjamas and was going inside to get Mrs. Jaks when the old dude roared, thrusting his fist in the air.

"The Russians are stealing my potatoes!" he yelled, looking out the back window of the garage. "They're all over my garden!"

"Your garden's under four feet of snow."

"They're mocking me! Look at them mocking me! Hurry! Get my shotgun!"

"No one's there, dude. No one's in your garden. Chill, Mr. Jaks. Just chill, okay?"

Mrs. Jaks opened the garage door and shook her head. "Petr, come have tea."

"The Russians are raiding my potato garden!"

"The police are going after the Russians," Mrs. Jaks said. "They'll bring our potatoes back."

"They won't!"

"I bribed them. They're coming later to collect their money. We'll get your potatoes back."

"Oh. Okay, then," Mr. Jaks said, and stomped inside.

"Humour him," Mrs. Jaks said to Jared.

"But no one's out there."

"You know that and I know that and my dear, sweet Petr knows that, deep, deep down. But you reminding him that he's hallucinating doesn't do any of us any good, does it?"

"Well, no."

"You're a decent boy, Jared." She patted his shoulder. "Will you visit him in respite while I'm in Vancouver?"

"Sure. I can get you some medicinal marijuana if you need it. I hear it helps with the side effects."

She laughed. "I'm too old to become a drooling pothead."

"Hey, never say never."

"When you finish the driveway, I have spaghetti with moose meatballs."

"You rule."

She kissed his cheek. She hesitated and seemed like she was going to say something else, but they heard a clatter from the kitchen and she rushed inside to see what her husband was doing.

Jared hoped she would pull through. She was nice. She deserved a lot better than getting shitcanned by leukemia.

Xmas moola in your account now, Nana had messaged Jared over Facebook. *Don't spend it on your father. Or your mother.*

She'd snapped a selfie wearing a red swimsuit and sunglasses, the wind lifting her hair like a black cloud. The background of the picture was a wooden deck and a sparkling blue ocean dotted with white sailboats.

You didn't have to, Jared messaged her. He scanned the feed, waiting to see if she was online.

The money is for YOU, she wrote. *I mean it.*

Destiny's having her baby soon.

My pretty, pretty enabler. Repeat after me: I'm not responsible for the crappy decisions of the grown-ups in my life.

Jared rolled his eyes. *Love you, Nana.*

Love you more, Cutie.

They chatted a bit longer, and then she had to sign off. He unpacked a fake tree he'd picked up in the second-hand store, but it listed to the side and failed to make the room any merrier. As he was throwing on some tinsel, Blake stopped by with some beers. His friend had a nasty shiner that Jared ignored. They sat on his couch and laughed at his tree, and then gamed until the beer ran out.

"Can I park here tonight?" Blake said.

"My couch is your couch."

"If Dad comes by, don't open the door," Blake said.

"'Kay," Jared said.

"Don't even go near it."

Jared opened the desk drawer and pulled out the handgun his mom had given him. He proved it, popping the chamber open to show it was empty, and then handed it to his friend, grip first.

"Ammo's in the nightstand," Jared said.

Blake stared at the gun in his hands, not moving. "He's such a tool."

"Yeah. There's always one in the family."

"I wish he'd just . . ."

They were quiet.

Jared showed him the basics, and Blake loaded it a couple of times but left it unloaded on the coffee table. Jared dug up a sleeping bag and gave it to him. They watched a DVD of *Independence Day*, which they hadn't done since they were kids. Every once in a while Blake's eyes drifted past the TV to the door. Jared remembered the dread he'd felt when his mom's ex David was in their lives. The constant bile at the back of his throat from his queasy stomach clenched in a knot.

The world is hard, his mom had said. *You have to be harder.*

10

ABANDONMENT ISSUES

Martina Yelan came up to him after their Math 10 final as he waited at the bus stop. She had thick, cat-eye liner and mile-high brown hair with chunks of blond streaks. While everyone else was in parkas and ski jackets, Martina wore a fluffy blue sweater over nude-coloured leggings. She stopped in front of him and asked for a light. She cupped his hand.

"Cookies?" she said.

"I'm out."

"Text me when you have more." She pulled a pen out of her purse and wrote a number on his hand. "I like to party."

Jared caught the bus downtown, took some money out of his bank account and then waited again for the bus to Terrace. A tall Native man in a black parka stood beside him. He was clean-shaven, had thick, well-groomed eyebrows and floppy, product-filled hair. The guy mimed shivering.

"Cold enough for you?" he said.

"Yup," Jared said, pulling out his phone.

Seventeen messages from Destiny. He sighed. She'd given birth to a boy a week ago, but the baby daddy went AWOL. He wasn't in camp.

He wasn't at his rented room. The money she'd been expecting from him hadn't come through. Jared planned on paying the last of his dad's back rent and taking off as soon as humanly possible. He felt bad for her, but she was driving him nuts. And burning through his cellphone minutes.

The bus arrived and Jared took a seat near the back doors. The Native guy sat beside him. Jared played Brick Breaker on his phone to avoid conversation as people filed onto the bus.

"Christmas shopping?" the Native guy said.

"Yup," Jared said.

"Are you finished school?" the guy said. "Is it finals?"

Jared glanced at him. He was smiling like they knew each other. He was about his mom's age, early thirties.

"Not interested," Jared said.

"Oh, hey," the guy said. "This is not a come-on. Just friendly conversation to pass the time."

"Dude," Jared said. "Way creepy, okay?"

"Geez," the guy muttered. "Try to be sociable and look what it gets you."

Jared stared out the window at the snow as they made their way to Terrace. His mom and Richie were off to Smithers, reason unknown. She'd told him it was a romantic weekend, but he suspected it was business. Unless you were big on skiing, Smithers in December was super cold and extra snowy. She'd left him two fifties to get takeout.

"Luke," the guy said. "I am your father."

Jared glared at him, wishing he'd go away.

"Philip Martin isn't your father, Jared," the guy said quietly. "I'm your real dad. My name is Wee'git. Your mother shot me in the head when—"

"Freak," Jared said. He stood, grabbed the pole and hopped over the guy.

"I'm not lying to you."

Jared pushed through the other passengers, right to the back of the bus, where he kept a wary eye on the freak until he got off the bus at the next stop, at the Mount Layton Hot Springs. Jared leaned down to check he was really gone in time to see a raven flap upwards. The guy was nowhere in sight. Jared scanned the bus in case he'd gotten back on, but couldn't see him. Christmas always brought out the crazies.

He got off at Walmart and walked to his dad's apartment building. He knocked a long time at the apartment office until the manager came to the door, looking sleepy. Jared gave her the last of his dad's back rent and got a receipt. She yawned as she wrote it out.

"So they're all caught up, right?" Jared said.

She shrugged. "See you January."

Jared took the receipt to his dad's apartment and tried to quietly slide it through the mail slot. Destiny opened the door as he was backing away.

"Hi," she said. Her eyes were swollen and red. Her nose was raw. Her ponytail was loose and skewed to one side. She had a towel over one shoulder that had the sour smell of puke. The dogs barked around her slippers as she stared at him.

"Didn't want to bug you," Jared said.

"Want to meet your nephew?"

No, he thought, he really didn't, but there was no way to back out of it without looking like a total douche. "I can't stay."

The baby was sleeping on the couch, wrapped tightly in a blue blanket like a baby burrito. He had a squishy, wrinkly face like an old man and frowned, pursing his lips as he slept.

"Want to hold him?" she said.

"No," Jared said.

"Scared?"

"Yup."

"Chickenshit." She lifted the baby carefully and held him out.

Jared shook his head, but she placed the baby in his arms. He weighed about as much as a watermelon, surprisingly heavy.

"Uncle Jared meet Ben," she said.

"Where's Dad?"

"One of Mom's brothers died," she said. "They said they're going to the funeral, but I think they just wanted to get away from us."

"Oh," Jared said.

"Yeah," Destiny said. "Want some coffee?"

"Sure."

She disappeared into the kitchen and came back with a mug. She put it on the coffee table. "I don't think they're coming back any time soon. Can you stay the night?"

Jared froze, horrified.

"Please?" Destiny said. "Pretty please? You don't have to do anything. I just . . . I just . . . I . . . Everyone's leaving me. Everyone's running away."

Jared said, "For a bit. I have to catch the last bus back. It doesn't run on the weekends."

"Okay," she said, wiping her nose.

They watched the news like an old couple. Native people round-danced in a mall in the opening news story. Another group danced at an intersection. Some were in regalia, but most were wearing T-shirts and jeans. The dancers were supporting a chief who was on a hunger strike. The chief was just about to be interviewed when the baby woke up, mewling, and Jared tried to hand him back.

"Just a sec," she said. "I have to make his formula."

She disappeared into the kitchen. The baby wailed, and Jared cringed as the dogs started barking. One of the neighbours banged on the wall. Destiny came back with a bottle and took the baby. As Ben started feeding, the dogs settled down, curling onto assorted blankets on the floor.

"You're a good uncle," she said.

Destiny showed him how to change Ben's diaper and then how to make a bottle. Jared burped the baby, who then puked.

"Nice," Jared said, checking out his shoulder.

They laughed and Ben sniffed then fell asleep. The clock ticked past the time when the last bus would leave and he was stuck at his dad's place for the weekend. Destiny made popcorn and they ate in front of the TV. Ben slept again.

Destiny turned the Christmas-tree lights on. They flickered as her dogs nosed around the base, sniffing the ornaments closest to the floor. She dug out an old deck of Uno cards. They played a couple of games while Ben pursed his lips, sucking like he was dreaming of boobs.

On Sunday after supper, Destiny went out for diapers and didn't come back. Midnight rolled around. Ben waved his arms in his bassinet, mewling.

Where r u? Jared texted her. *Fucking pissed ur pulling this shit.*

He peeked out the front window. The streets were snowy and empty. Hoho padded up to him and sniffed, wagging his tail.

"We're ditched, Hoho," Jared said.

The weekend hadn't been fun, but it hadn't been horrible. She was planning a turkey dinner for Christmas, but he now suspected she wanted to make dinner so she could tempt him over and then ditch him with Ben again. The baby broke into a full cry, and Jared found a bottle in the fridge, ready to be reheated. He took a deep breath. He nuked the bottle, shook it and tested it on his wrist the way Destiny had shown him. He sat on the couch, propping Ben up. The baby peered around the room as he drank.

Ben fussed, let out a nasty fart and then finished the bottle. The clock in the kitchen ticked. The dogs barked at something outside and Jared hoped it was Destiny coming home.

The next time Ben woke, Jared couldn't get the baby formula right. Ben wouldn't drink it. He took three tries to figure it out and the baby upchucked and pooped, upchucked and pooped, and then finally, finally fell asleep and woke up exactly three hours later, screaming like he was being murdered. Jared decided he was never having kids. The second he was old enough, he was getting himself snipped. They slept fitfully in the living room with the TV on, volume turned low. Destiny staggered home late the next morning, a package of diapers under her arm. Jared waited for her at the front door while she fumbled with the lock. She flinched when she saw him there.

"Got the diapers," she said.

"Not fucking funny," Jared said.

"What?" Destiny said. "What's the big deal?"

"You didn't even fucking ask. You just took off."

"Geez, you big baby, that was, like, what? Four hours? Five?" She pulled a twenty out of her pants pocket. "I'm going to pay you."

"I gave you that money," Jared said. "You want to pay me with my own money."

"Family helps you," she said. "We're family."

"That doesn't mean you get to dump your kid on me and take off to party. That's not cool."

"I'm going to bed."

"Whatever. I'm gone."

"Can you just watch him while I take a shower? A few more minutes?"

Jared put on his jacket. Destiny glared at him.

"You're just like everyone else," she said. "Taking off when things get hard."

"I'm not your sucker," Jared said, shoving his feet in his boots. "I don't like being played."

"I didn't play you, you fucking drama queen!" she shouted after him as he stomped down the sidewalk. "Some uncle you are!"

Blake was gone by the time Jared made it back to the house, but he'd left some thank-you beer in the mini-fridge. Jared flopped on his bed and slept. When he woke, he had eight texts from Destiny.

Luv u, Destiny texted him. *Ben misses his uncle.*

Not babysitting 4 u, he texted back. *Forget it.*

Jared went upstairs and made coffee. His mom came downstairs and fried him some eggs. She had her hair pulled back in a ponytail.

"You finished classes?" she said.

"Tomorrow."

"Lay off the partying for a while," she said. "You reek of puke."

"Thanks."

"I call 'em like I smell 'em." She bumped him playfully. "What's up?"

"Did you ever think of not having me?"

"Did you knock someone up?"

"Geez, Mom."

"Did you?"

"No. I have not knocked anyone up."

"I never regretted you," she said, pouring him a mug of coffee. "You little weirdo."

11

REQUIEM FOR THE TRILOBITES

252 million years ago on Earth in late May on a Monday, the trilobites were going out for Starbucks before work, la la la, near swampy Pangea, the single continent that stretched from pole to pole. The trilobites tended to avoid the weird, hippie mammals and reptiles that had decided to give land-dwelling a go and had descended into eating each other, their own young and whatever else they could chase down and swallow.

No accounting for taste, they told themselves. We'll stay here in the ocean doing exactly what we've been doing for the last 200 million years, thank you very much.

Not that the oceans were much safer. Still, the trilobites weren't much worried about sharks, who, at this point in their evolution, looked like truck-sized tadpoles, and who in turn were meat for the Dinotrodons, mammals who had developed flashy back fins and were always ready to show off their teeth and their newly hinged jaws. The trilobites had limped through an extinction event only eight million years earlier, which had pruned off all but the hardiest and luckiest of their species. Nevertheless, they were alive and looking forward to another 200 million years of avoiding being dinner for sea scorpions and the ancestors of crabs.

But the Earth had a bad case of gas from a lot of undigested trees. Asteroids were due to boom through the atmosphere like falling angels, wings afire. The area that would one day be Siberia was going to hurl lava like a frat boy upchucking during rush week. Pangea, the superest continent, was about to split like a tight pair of pants. The Permian Age was about to convulse, boil, then die, taking nine out of ten of all living species kicking and screaming into oblivion. The world would go dark. The ocean would become an airless acid bath. The clouds would rain death. But that was due to start tomorrow, the blackest of Tuesdays, and today was Monday.

The trilobites were blindsided by the end of their world. They were like, whoa, man. What the hell? What did we ever do to you? But no one answered and they had nowhere to hide. Nowhere was safe. Every last trilobite died. Their bodies were covered with mud and ash. As the eons passed, they were pressed into fossils that would, one day, make lovely bookends and paperweights.

Mass extinction sucks.

12

NEW YEAR'S WELTSCHMERZ

Jared woke on the first day of 2013 covered in a Buzz Lightyear comforter on an inflatable mattress. He was wearing a *Battlestar Galactica* Viper pilot T-shirt and matching boxer shorts. The ceiling was speckled with greenish-white stars that probably glowed in the dark. Model rockets lined the shelves. On the poster behind the TV, a guy in a dark suit with flippy hair emerged from a glowing blue phone booth: *Doctor Who Returns!* Framed, autographed pictures of assorted actors lined the walls. He didn't recognize any of them, but they all wore costumes of a shiny spacesuit variety. The TV was playing a DVD that looked like it was set in some historical time where a bunch of ratty-haired people were watching a blond chick eat a raw heart. The mattress squeaked like a beach ball as he got up on his elbows to check out the rest of the room.

A hefty Native kid leaned over from his perch on the nearby bed. He was wearing the same PJs as Jared, but in a larger size. "Hi."

"Hey," Jared said.

The kid paused the DVD as the blond chick tried not to upchuck. "You want breakfast?"

His stomach lurched. "No. But I could use some hair of the dog."

"Sorry, dude, dry household."

"Sucks to be you."

The guy laughed. "It really does. Thanks, by the way."

"My smartassitude is my gift to the universe. No thanks are necessary."

"No, dude. You know, for last night. At the New Year's Eve party. You saved me from getting snowbanked. You know, by Dylan. And his lame crew."

"Crap."

"You were awesome."

Ebs wouldn't be happy if he'd publicly embarrassed her boyfriend. "What the hell happened?"

"It was a pretty mellow party, and then you said, 'One, two, three, four—I declare a Cracker War,' and then you guys went in the backyard and played tag with firecrackers."

He didn't remember that, but it sounded like something he would do. "Yeah?"

"Dylan's sister didn't like it and she told me to stop you guys and Dylan was all pissed. He was ragging my ass and him and his buddies were going to heave me into the snowbank and you got all up in his face and you said, 'Dylan, for fuck's sake, that shit's not cool.' And he was all, 'You wanna piece of this?' And you were all, 'Settle down, Scarface.'"

"God."

"And everybody laughed and he was getting all 'roidy and said, 'Take your fat homo boyfriend home, loser.' And you were like, 'Wow. Who talks like that? Oh, no, it's Squidward! Someone get him a clarinet.' And he was like, 'Fuck you, shithead.' And everybody was like—"

"Okay, okay," Jared said. "I get it. I ran my mouth. Do you have any Aspirin?"

"I've got Junior Advil. Liquid form."

Jared groaned and flopped back against the mattress. Just once, he'd like to wake up from a blackout next to a hot chick with booze. Even waking up in Bangkok with a face tattoo would be more interesting than some random kid's room of Science Fiction Fandom.

"I'm George," the guy said.

"Jared," he said.

"There's a video," George said.

"Damn."

"I uploaded it to YouTube, if you want to watch it later. Search *Squidward Smackdown.*"

"No."

"HD."

"Can you take it down? Please?"

"One hundred and thirty-seven hits. And I just put it up this morning!"

The light burned his corneas and Jared put a hand over his eyes. "He's getting shitcanned from his hockey team. He hasn't told his parents yet."

"One time, he stole my pants and swirled me and waited for me outside the bathroom and filmed me all the way home and put it on YouTube."

"Dude, please take down the video."

"Fine," George said, sitting up and plunking his laptop on a pillow. "But only because I owe you. This makes us even. Forever."

"Um, where are my clothes?"

"Mom's washing them. You got a beer dump."

"A what?"

"They dumped a keg on your head."

Well, that explained the smell. "Nice."

"Everyone was mad because they wasted so much beer, though. But you kept going on about your destiny, so I didn't know where you lived and had to bring you home or you would have froze to death. Mom washed you with baby wipes. If you were, I dunno, worried about how you got clean."

"Sorry."

"Mom spent the whole time telling me this is what happens when you get blind drunk."

"I'm glad I could be your lesson in abstinence."

"Ha," George said. "I'm tweeting that."

"George, man, chill. It's too early in the year to be tweeting. Twitter down, man."

"Ha. Haha. Yeah, I'll put this on the Facebooks."

"Dude. Seriously? Who reads this shit?"

"Everybody!"

"Everyone posts. No one reads."

"We should meme you."

"Meme yourself."

"Hmm. I've got a picture of Darth Maul or a Dalek. Whaddya think?"

"I think I need a coffee."

"Mom won't let you have any. You're not old enough."

"How far is Tim Hortons from here?"

"They haven't plowed the village road yet."

"I'm still on the rez?"

"Dylan's two houses over."

"Shit."

"His sister invited me over to help set off her fireworks. She's cool. We're all Beaver clan. Dad's Fish."

"Yeah?"

"What's your clan?"

Jared shrugged. "Mom doesn't talk to her family."

"Clan fight?"

"General aggro."

"It happens. My aunt wanted Ma-oo's house when she died and hasn't talked to Mom since she got it."

"Who's Ma-oo?"

"My gran. My aunt has her own house, but she wants her daughter to move out of her house and there's no places in town or Terrace 'cause of all the out-of-towners renting everything."

Jared couldn't follow the twists of this and didn't really care. "Do you mind if I hit the shower?"

"I think Mom's going to insist," George said.

The bathroom down the hallway was painted like an undersea paradise. Happy dolphins balanced on their tails. Tropical fish formed bright clouds in the corners. The shower curtain had orcas breaching, framed by the setting sun. The towels were ripe peach with aqua waves and shells. The toilet was decked out in fuzzy blue shag. He hoped it was ironic, but it probably wasn't.

He had a bruise on his cheek, but it was light, slapped red with a touch of purple where someone's ring had made an imprint. Nausea came in waves. He flipped the lid up and dry-heaved in the toilet, whose water was bright blue and perfumed to smell like baby powder. He sat down and pulled off the T-shirt and boxers.

After the shower, he found his clothes and his jacket neatly folded on the closed toilet lid. He squeezed some toothpaste on his finger and scrubbed. George knocked on the door and brought in a ginger ale and a couple of Gravol. Jared knocked them back.

"Did I have a phone?" Jared said. Ebs would kill him if he lost her cast-off phone.

"On the desk."

"Thanks."

Happy New Year, Son, his mom had texted.

So hungover, Jared texted back.

U ok? a few seconds later.

In the village with friends.

Need a ride?

Going 2 hang. How was HNY?

Lots of fireworks.

Ew. Mom. TMI.

Hahahahahaha. Richie says HNY.

HNY back.

TTFN

TTYL

Seventeen messages from his stepsister Destiny. He'd told her he was going out, but, from the texts she'd sent, she'd assumed he was going to go out, stop over at his dad's place and babysit Ben so she could have her New Year's fun too.

All I wanted was 1 nite, her final text read. *U ruined it. U ruined everythin u selfish prick!*

Jared considered ignoring her but texted: *I told u I wouldn't babysit after u pulled that shit.*

A few seconds later her number popped up. *Jared. Im tired. So fckn tired. Can u just come?*

No. Ur going to dump him on me and disappear. Forget that shit.

Ur his uncle. Ur family.

Jared shut the phone off.

George had restarted the DVD while Jared was texting Destiny. The show had subtitles. Jared was too tired to read.

"Thanks for being my crash pad," he said.

"In *Battlestar Galactica*, there's this Viper pilot whose call sign is Crashdown."

"Uh, okay."

"Can you call me Crashpad?" George said.

"Seriously?" Jared said.

"It's cool," George said. "A Viper pilot call sign."

"You got it, Crashpad," Jared said. "I gotta go."

"Later."

"Later."

Jared searched the hallway for his boots. The air outside was damp and cold. The snowbanks were littered with the empty cardboard shells of fireworks. He had a vague memory of clouds of sparkling lights and cars honking. Dylan's house was quiet and littered with bottles, empty chip bags and wilted veggie trays. A couple of guys were passed out on the living room floor. Jared went down the hallway. He knocked on Dylan's door and cracked it open.

Dylan vomited into his trash can. Jared went to the bathroom and got a roll of toilet paper. Dylan swatted it away, glaring at him.

"Hey," Jared said.

"Get the fuck out."

"You okay?"

"Fuck you, shithead."

"Fair enough." Jared pulled a chair up to the bed.

"Do you want to die? Is that it?"

Jared shrugged. "My head feels like elephants tap-danced on it."

"Go to hell." Dylan heaved. "Straight to fucking hell."

"Sorry," Jared said. "I'm an asshole when I'm drunk."

"You're an asshole fucking period."

"Yeah. That's the general opinion."

"Mouthy, too."

"Dude, I'm not arguing."

"What the hell are you doing here?"

"If you're going to beat the shit out of me, let's get it over with."

Dylan eyed him like he didn't understand English. "What?"

"You heard me."

"Is this a set-up?"

Jared sighed. "Do you want some coffee?"

"Are you shitting me?"

"I shit you not."

Dylan threw up and Jared went to the kitchen and made coffee. He sat at the island and turned on his phone again.

Sorry, sorry, sorry, sorry, sorry, sorry, sorry, Destiny had texted.

I hate my life, Jared thought.

He checked his voice mail, erasing Destiny's messages as soon as he heard her voice. One of the messages began with a long pause.

"Jared?" Mrs. Jaks said. "I'm home. I need some help."

She'd phoned two days ago. After the holiday parties, he couldn't really remember what he was doing two days ago. Dylan wandered into the kitchen and poured himself a coffee. He sat beside Jared. They drank coffee and stared out the window. The snow had started again.

"I'm pretty fucking pissed at you," Dylan said.

"Crashpad has a sad, dry life. You've got a billion friends and chicks hanging off your arm."

"Who the fuck are you talking about?"

"That guy, George. He's calling himself Crashpad now."

"Holy fuck, what a loser. He's an embarrassment." Dylan ran a hand through his hair. "Like I'm going to be."

"Chill, man."

"He bugs me."

"He probably bugs himself."

Dylan yawned. He rubbed his eyes.

"Heads up," Jared said. "Crashpad made a video and posted it to YouTube."

Dylan clocked him. Jared's chair tipped over and he skittered across the floor and his coffee dripped down his freshly washed jacket.

"Ow," Jared said.

"Fuck," Dylan said. "I'm going to kill that fat bastard."

Jared pushed himself up, stood, then righted the stool.

"Fuck," Dylan said. "Fuck, fuck, fuck."

"He took it down."

Dylan whipped his mug against the wall. It thumped and shattered, spraying a brown starburst above the kitchen table.

Jared touched his eye. His headache thundered through his skull. "Are we good?"

Dylan sighed and rubbed his head. "I'm too hungover to kill you."

Jared studied the weather through the window. "Happy New Year."

———

On his way to pick up Ebony and her friends, Dylan dropped him off at Mrs. Jaks's. Dylan revved his Chevy and fishtailed out of the driveway and down the unplowed street. Mrs. Jaks's driveway was waist-deep with snow. Jared waded over to the garage. He shovelled a path from her porch to the road, pausing to catch his breath and watch the other people on their street shovel and snow-blow. Rain had crusted the top of the snow so it was as heavy as wet concrete.

Jared kicked the snow off his boots on the steps and knocked on her door. When there was no answer, he tried the handle, but it was locked and he didn't want to wake her if she was sleeping. He sat on the top step and pulled a half-empty mickey of vodka from his jacket. He'd lifted it from the coffee table at Dylan's house. His mom didn't like Mrs. Jaks. She said Mrs. Jaks was slaving him. But after all the shit that had gone down with his mom's psycho ex-boyfriend, David, Jared felt he owed Mrs. Jaks. So much so, he'd even gone to visit her husband in respite. Mr. Jaks had gone a little nuts when he saw Jared. The old dude had kept screaming things at him in Czech.

Jared's throat burned where the booze hit the raw spots in his throat. His hands steadied. The wind and icy rain stung pleasantly. He'd felt a little guilty about not going back, but not bad enough to actually visit Mr. Jaks again. One of the neighbours stopped shovelling to stare at him. Jared lifted his bottle in cheers. The woman shook her head and went in her house.

Squares, Jared thought.

He tucked his bottle back in his jacket and leaned the shovel against the porch. The sidewalk slush had frozen into a bumpy sheet.

Jared pushed off and slid down the street. The rain pellets simmered on the trees, whose branches complained in creaks as the ice thickened. A multitude of footprints had flattened a path to his house. The front door was open and the hall was quiet. The hallway was lined with coat racks, which were half full. Everyone sleeping it off or at work, triple-overtiming in the New Year. Jared flopped on the couch and turned on the TV. Most of the shows were lame repeats. He yawned.

"Nice shiner," his mom said, coming into the living room in her bathrobe. "That's going to be really black when the colour settles in."

"Hey," Jared said.

"Hey, yourself," she said. She kissed the top of his head. "KD?"

"You know it," he said.

They went into the kitchen and his mom pulled a box of Kraft macaroni and cheese out of the pantry. Jared grabbed a pot and handed it to her.

"Is there a story behind that eye?"

"Once upon a time there was a smartass," Jared said. "And his buddy was cut from the rep team. And the smartass tried to lighten the mood with some smartassedness and his buddy was not amused so the smartass got clocked. The end."

"What an amazing word picture," his mom said. "It's like I was there."

"Dylan's in a shitty mood. I should've stayed home."

"So he used your face to make himself feel better."

"We're good, Mom."

"Hugged it out? Had a heart-to-heart?"

"Yup. Oprah would have been proud."

"If this becomes a habit," his mom said, "he's going to get an ass full of buckshot."

Yeah, that'd do wonders for Jared's reputation. "Nothing says *muy macho* like having your mommy avenge your boo-boos."

"Nothing says *target* like letting himbos use you as their punching bag."

"Where's Richie?"

"Making his rounds."

They watched the water boil. His mom shook in the macaroni. She paused to light a menthol and blew the smoke towards the ceiling. He turned and hopped onto the counter. He offered her an empty beer bottle and she tapped her cigarette ash in it. After a bit, she tucked her cigarette into the corner of her mouth, used the lid to drain the macaroni and then shook the powdered cheese in the pot. She globbed in a generous spoonful of margarine and mixed until it was uniformly orange. She poured some in a cup, handing it to Jared. He squirted some ketchup on it. She poured herself a cup and they toasted.

"Same shit, different year," she said.

"You should write for Hallmark, Mom."

She grabbed his chin. "Damn shame this cute face has got such a smart mouth and weenie disposition. That crap you get from your dad."

But your talent for self-destruction is all your mom's, his inner voice said.

She let his chin go. "Only cheap booze and leaky condoms will get me grandchildren."

"You see? That's a Mother's Day poem right there. Hallmark doesn't know what they're missing."

13

OXYDIPAL COMPLEX

The next day, the bus was an hour late and filled with bargain hunters. To pass the time on the long ride between Kitimat and Terrace, Jared listened to the girls in the seat in front of him forming a plot. Someone named Danica had pissed them off. They were going to either lie about her boyfriend cheating or tell her mother about Danica stealing her antipsychotics.

Speaking of plotting, Ebs's cell number appeared on his phone: *We need 2 talk.*

No, Jared thought. We really don't.

Never one to let things go, Ebs added: *Now.*

Jared stuffed his phone in his back pocket. The queen could stew. He was sick of dealing with Ebs. His burnout friends could be violent and unpredictable, but they didn't grind on and on and on about who was more popular. If, every now and then, someone whacked him over the head and stole his stash, it would be worth the price as long as he never, ever had to hear Ebs's crap about whose purse was really a knock-off or whose mom was mowing the coach's lawn to get their darling off the bench.

By the time the bus got to Terrace, the windows were steamed and everyone was quiet. The walk to his dad's apartment was slushy. He knocked on the door and his dad answered, giving him a hug.

"Trouble?" his dad said, looking at Jared's shiner.

"Good time gone wrong," Jared said. "You know how it goes."

"Huh. Well, glad you made it," he said. "The landlord's up my ass about the rent."

"But we're paid up. Have you phoned the insurance company about cutting you off? Maybe we should talk to a lawyer."

"They rip you off," his dad said.

"I can't keep this up, Dad."

"I know, I know. I'm not asking you to."

Jared stepped inside but wasn't met with any barking. "Where's Destiny?"

"Around."

His dad sat and struggled to put on his shoes. Jared helped him.

"I'll call your case manager," Jared said.

"Already did. Still giving us the runaround."

"It'll only take a sec."

"Let's just get the rent paid." His dad watched his shoes, and then glanced up at Jared. The look was cagey, like a burnout trying to get a discount with a sob story, like a girl moving in to kiss you while giving your jacket a pat-down.

Jared's gut clenched. "You got a cheque, didn't you?"

"No," his dad said. "Your mom's got you all paranoid. I wouldn't do that."

"So if I call the insurance people and ask if you cashed a cheque, they'll say no."

In the long silence, his dad grew a goofy, sheepish smile.

"You're playing me," Jared said.

"I'm going to pay you back," his dad said. "Every single penny you gave me is coming back at you, son. With interest."

"Did you blow it? Your whole cheque? Had yourself a party? Had a good laugh?"

The smile faded and the sadness etched in his dad's face was real. Looked more real. Wasn't cagey. "I raised you."

"How long? How long have you been getting—" Jared decided he didn't really want to know. Until the booze and the drugs, his dad had been a decent guy. It was hard to look at him, but it was hard to leave him in the lurch, knowing Destiny and Ben needed a place too. If his dad got the boot, so did everyone else. He considered giving the rent to the manager so he could be sure it would be paid. But he hated this. Hated the way his dad was trying to hold it together but probably wouldn't. He hated that his dad couldn't meet his eye. He took out his wallet and gave him the rent money.

"Thank you," his dad said.

"I'm not coming back," Jared said.

"I know," his dad said.

He got himself a pepperoni pizza. While he was waiting, he scrolled through his messages. Ebs texted screen after screen in ALL CAPS mode. Nana Sophia had sent a picture of herself sitting in a gondola, legs demurely folded to the side, Venice glistening in the sunlight behind her. In the next picture, she posed in the bow, head thrown back. Her hair was loose and she was wearing oversized sunglasses.

Born-again virgin, she'd messaged him. *When he tells me. That he's go-ing. To take another pee. And he falls asleep. O-ooooh, uh-oh!*

Nana, he messaged back. *TMI.*

He ate, wandered around the mall and then waited for the bus. The plotting girls who'd caught the bus with him to Terrace were hogging the benches. They'd forgotten their plot and were laughing and comparing their finds.

U home 2nite? his mom texted.

Yup.

Luv ur guts.

She was probably drunk and lonely, but he read it and reread it, swallowing. *Back atcha.*

Sarcastic lil shit ur lucky I luv u nuff not to murder u in ur sleep.

Ya, ya.

Get ur rotten ass home b4 I hunt u down.

I have pizza.

Best son ever.

TTYL

TTFN

14

LOST

His dad had worked at Eurocan for eight years. They all knew the pulp-and-paper mill was closing for months before it did, but it didn't make it any easier for the 535 people laid off. His dad had sat at the dinner table, drinking beer after beer, staring at his walking papers. Jared could still feel the unease of those first weeks with his dad holed up in his bedroom and the steady flow of U-Hauls emptying their street.

His dad moved out a few months later. His mom started selling things and their house became hollow. His mom cried all the time and he'd never seen her cry before, so he knew things were bad. And then she met David.

David brought flowers. David paid bills. David made them dinner and they all washed the dishes together. His mom couldn't stop smiling and Jared resigned himself to having an uptight stepfather who helped him with homework and expected good grades. Jared couldn't focus, though. He started hanging out with Blake and Kelsey more, so he could lose himself in gaming and stolen booze. His marks drifted lower. And lower.

Jared hid his report card in the bottom drawer of his dresser under his socks. He came home from school and David was waiting in his bedroom.

Ribs bend. The little muscles between the ribs are ticklish up to a point. You never know how you're going to sound when you're in pain. Jared remembered the pores in David's forehead, the lines of concentration between his eyebrows while in the background someone squealed, the sound a dog would make if you stepped on it and kept stepping on it.

Neither of them had noticed when his mother came into the room. Jared heard a mechanical thud. David spasmed, and then there was another thud and David let go of Jared's arm, let go of Jared's ribs. David's knee came off Jared's legs. David reached for his own feet but couldn't bend that far.

His mom dragged Jared off the bed. She held a nail gun in front of her, and all the blood was gone from her face. David flailed and screamed, stuck standing with his feet nailed to the floor. He tore off the blankets, tore at the mattress, at the bed frame. The movie downstairs was loud. New sound system. Just like a theatre at home, David had said. Jared guessed that he'd had a plan even then. When they'd met, he was probably thinking he would need a sound system to cover up the screams. His mom checked Jared over. Jared cried and said he wanted to leave.

"He likes your fear," she said. "Guys like him don't know how to stop."

She put the nail gun down and whacked David with a chair until he fell over.

"I'm going to kill you, bitch!" he screamed, struggling to get up. "I'm going to kill you!"

She pinned David down with her knee on his throat so she could nail-gun the soft part of his underarm to the floor. David's mouth made an O of pain and then he thrashed and vibrated, the veins in his neck like worms crawling on his throat.

"Jared!" David said. "Jared! Jared!"

She pressed the nail gun into Jared's hands. "You have to show him you aren't afraid."

Jared shook his head and let the gun drop. She wiped his nose with her shirt and held him by the shoulders.

"The world is hard," she said. "You have to be harder."

He wouldn't nail-gun David and his mom wouldn't let him leave until he did, so they'd stayed in the room with the movie on replay downstairs. David screamed himself hoarse on the floor and the room went dark as the sun flared and died, and the street lights flickered to life. Jared held the nail gun, and his mom—tense and jumpy—told him David was going to never, ever let them go if he didn't—

Pop.

The thing he'd never told anyone, not a single soul, ever, was that in that moment, in a weird, weird dream, he'd popped out of his body. Jared found himself outside their house. But instead of being night, it was day and the sunlight was like an old picture with a bad filter. His body felt cold, like he'd been out sledding for a long time. He could hear the movie playing in the living room. Underneath it, he could hear David still screaming his name.

The sky was blue, but it sputtered like a TV with a bad connection. Sometimes, in the dark part of the sputter, the surrounding mountains were bare rock and the ground was waist-deep with swamp. Things moved in the darkness.

He felt fear like ants crawling in his spine.

Not far, but then very far, but then below and then beside him, Jared saw a glow surrounding the Jakses' house. He walked carefully towards it as the landscape guttered and shifted. His hand went through the doorknob and he wondered if he was dead, if his heart had stopped, because he couldn't hear it and he felt bad that he'd left his mother. He wondered if he could go through walls like Casper the Friendly Ghost and he tried and the door burned as he went through it, a little zap like static electricity.

Mr. Jaks was asleep in his chair and Mrs. Jaks was crocheting on the sofa. She looked up at him and frowned: "Khulhgha hoonzoo. Ndai la nyoozi'?"

In this dream, he understood she was asking his name.

"Lost—light—I—here—Jared." He stopped, confused. The words rumbled from his mouth, echoed and faded, and then went so loud they were nothing but sound.

"Jared," she said. "Laura le soozi'. Nts'e hoont'i?"

Where do you live? "House . . . next—bad man—hurt."

She sighed. She put her crocheting down.

Pop.

While her body stayed on the sofa, a glowing shape of her lifted up and came to stand beside him. She held out her hand. "Sulh tan'us?"

He took it and they walked outside. She sang a song he didn't understand, but he knew it was a lullaby and his footprints lit up and glowed behind them as they walked back to his house. An ambulance had parked in their driveway. His mother cried and kept saying his name, and he saw himself on the stretcher—his frozen face, his blank eyes—and Mrs. Jaks lifted him up and put him back in his body.

15

DESTINY KNOCKS

The party at his mom's house was more of a pre-bar soaker. People got a little hosed so they wouldn't have to drink a lot of overpriced hooch to get drunk. Plus, nothing interesting started until later. So they came to his mom's place and chatted as they drank, a low-key start to their evening out.

Alex Gunborg, the Goth from Jared's high school with the contact lenses that made him look like he had cataracts, huddled in the corner with his Goth buddies. They moodily drank their beers. Jared wasn't sure whether they were really miserable or whether it was a fashion statement that went with being a Goth. His mom made her way over to the Goths and Jared tensed, expecting trouble. She wouldn't put up with underage kids at her parties unless they were Jared's friends. When she told the Goths to leave, Alex wheedled and his friends took a long time to unpark their asses, so his mom called Richie. Herd instinct took over and they stood as one, trying to amble in an unintimidated way to the door while keeping a wary eye on Richie.

Jared said good night to his mom and left. Alex waited at the bottom of the porch and caught Jared's arm as he tried to go around him. "Can we hang in your room? We have our own booze."

Jared shrugged off his hand. "No."

"Need some me-time?" one of the Goths sneered.

"Later," Jared said, pushing off and sliding down the icy path. He wobbled a bit more than he expected, but he thought his exit was not too shabby.

"Aw, come on," Alex called.

Jared rounded the corner and slid towards his side entrance. One of the Goths sang out, "Asshole!"

His cell buzzed. *U ok? Were they waiting for you?*

Count von Count & his muppets of darkness strike fear in no1.

My brave lil Grover.

He slipped as he stepped inside, but caught himself on the banister. The room did a slow spin. He shut the door and changed into sweats. He couldn't focus enough to play any games and, beneath his buzz, he felt a headache gnawing at his brain.

Jared had been played before, but never by his dad. As far back as he could remember, his dad had been relentlessly honest—child support, fifteen percent tips, taxes and union dues. Jared didn't actually want to think about his dad, but his brain wouldn't listen and he found himself trying to spot the moment when his dad had decided Jared was a sucker.

He wanted to believe his dad and Shirley hadn't sat around the kitchen table after he left, quoting Bugs Bunny, *What a maroon.* But he could see it. Maybe a giggle. A knowing glance.

What he wanted was a drink, but the fridge was way over there and he was comfortable where he was.

Just a nip, he thought, and groaned, not really wanting to get up and getting up anyway.

He'd decorated his fake Christmas tree with assorted beer cans hanging by their tabs and the tree glittered and stank in the corner, an empty vodka bottle serving as an angel at the top, random wings from someone's kid sister's Fairy Barbie duct-taped to the back. Fairy Barbie was naked and hugging a bottle of mini-bar-sized Baileys. Some smartass had added a wad of white granny panties to the tree.

I hate Christmas, Jared decided, and found a garbage bag and started taking down the beer cans. Then, on a whim, he lifted the top of the tree off and chucked it outside. The bottom of the tree followed. Fairy Barbie smiled from the centre of the coffee table. He tossed her in the garbage.

Which felt good. He'd redecorated. Decluttered. Remove the stinking, fake Christmas tree from the corner of your room and happiness will flow.

"Knock, knock," Destiny said, stepping through the open door.

Jared blinked at her. "Hey."

"You okay?" She pointed to her own eye.

Ah, his shiner. "Yeah."

She came down the steps, hands stuffed in her jacket sleeves. She'd done her hair in soft curls that fell to her shoulders. He hadn't seen her in makeup for a long time and had forgotten how pretty she was. She eyed the room, lifting one of her sneakers when she hit a sticky spot.

"Maid's day off," Jared said.

"You have a maid?" Destiny said. "Dude, she sucks."

He never had the heart to tell her when he was being sarcastic. She stood, trying on a smile, letting it fade.

"Your dad told me. About . . . you know," she said.

"Did you know?"

She nodded, eyes flicking away from him. "He got the first cheque in December. They wanted to get me baby stuff. Your dad feels shitty."

"Where's Ben?"

"My aunt's got him for the night."

"Oh."

Jared rolled the idea of his dad feeling shitty around his brain, trying to fit it in with what he knew, wondering what it took to get from the dad he'd known to the dad who let his stepdaughter, Destiny, do his talking for him.

"How'd you get here?" Jared said.

"A friend. We're s'posed to go out, but—" Destiny shrugged. She rocked on her heels, and then something on the ceiling caught her attention: he'd taped up the cardboard Darth Vader and the weed-based Canadian flag and the thought bubble proclaiming POWDER HOUSE RULES. "Is that, like, one of the Star Wars dudes?"

"Yeah," Jared said.

"Didn't know you were into that."

"It was a going-away present from some friends."

"Do you mind if I close the door?"

"Um."

But Destiny was already up the steps, miming shivering and then closing the door. She started picking beer cans off the floor where they'd fallen from the tree.

"You don't have to do that," Jared said.

"You help me all the time. I don't mind."

"Destiny, man, it's okay. Chill."

She took the broom from the corner and Jared protested some more and she ignored him and told him to watch TV. The shock of her being there began to fade and his brain, mildly hammered as it was, began to register that his mother was upstairs and she would not be happy that her ex's whore's daughter was in her house. Jared felt his throat go dry and took a pull of his beer. She would, in fact, go to her unhappy place and bring back a little holiday shitstorm. Deck their halls with twirling cherries. Ambulances and cop cars for everybody. Crap, he thought. Crap, crap, crap.

"Destiny," Jared said. "We're cool. We're so cool."

She stopped sweeping and stared earnestly at him. "I'm sorry. I'm sorry, Jared."

"Yeah," Jared said. "Hey, we all have crap moments. Right? Yeah. Okay, here's the thing—my mom is upstairs."

Destiny frowned. "Okay."

"And she's, um—"

Irrational? his inner voice suggested. *Homicidally violent? Voted most likely to be locked in an institution for the criminally insane?*

"She violently hates you and your mom. Violently."

"Do you want me to talk to her?"

"No," Jared said. "No, no and more no. No to infinity."

"We could invite her for supper," Destiny said.

"She's, um, allergic to dogs."

"I sold them." Destiny swallowed, and swallowed again, and blinked hard and then sat with a thump on the couch. The broom clattered to the floor and Jared's eyes went up, but all he heard was muted laughter and general sounds of low-key party. No shotguns being loaded. No grenades rolling across the floor.

"Yeah," Jared said. "What? Wait, you sold your chihuahuas?"

"I was so happy when Scott bought them for me. I thought he loved me," she said. Her tears leaked and her face went red. He handed her a roll of toilet paper. She broke off a piece and blew her nose. "He doesn't want to do the paternity test. Called me, called me, called me a lying s-s-slut. His wife is so mad."

"His *wife?*"

"Yeah, he's married and he has a house in Prince George. They just had a baby too. I got his real home number from his co-worker. His wife answered," Destiny said.

"Holy crap," Jared said, suddenly feeling better about his life.

"He said he was divorced. But he's not. I'm so *stupid*," Destiny said. "I'm so fucking *stupid*."

She leaned over and cried into his shoulder, big, gasping, hurt sobs. Jared's guts clenched, and he patted her shoulder.

"It's okay, it's all going to be great, you'll see," Jared said. He racked his brain for the magic words that would make her calm and quiet. He tried to remember some of the *Oprah* he'd watched when he stayed home sick from school. "One door closes. Another one opens."

She cried harder and he could feel her tears and her snot on his neck. He looked up and Darth Vader swung his red lightsaber and Destiny kissed him.

After, she waited, eyes half closed, lips parted, breathing hard. He was aware, suddenly, of her body against his, of her warmth, of her hands. Her jacket creaked as she moved to rest her head against his shoulder.

"You were there when everyone else ran away," she said. "You're a good man."

A confusing tumble of thoughts held him still. She smelled good, clean, and her hair was soft. He could still feel where her lips had pressed against his, sticky with lip gloss. Beneath it all, she had a baby-powder smell, and he realized he was drunker than he thought and he was holding his stepsister and that was awful and she didn't seem to care and maybe she was only being friendly. He was a good man, she'd said. A word he wasn't expecting and couldn't put together with his image of himself. Words. *Good. Man.*

He heard an imaginary banjo twanging. *Step. Sister.*

"Who'd you sell them to?" Jared said.

She pulled away. "Got another beer?"

"Yeah."

He went to the fridge, cracked open a cold one and handed it to her. She took a swig and sighed.

"I thought he'd come back," she said.

"People are shitty," he said.

"You're not," she said.

He couldn't move under her stare. He liked her well enough. She was pretty and he felt sorry for her. But he didn't want to be her boyfriend. He didn't want to be Ben's stepdad. *Stepdad.* The word was big, bigger than he could handle, but she was watching him, expecting . . . them to hook up? Be together? God, his mom. He listened and for a long moment he didn't hear sounds from upstairs and his heart did a skip and then people burst out laughing, like they'd heard a joke.

She took a long swallow. "You wanna sit?"

He did. A part of him did. A sad, crappy part of him that was pretty hard to ignore wanted to screw his stepsister and he felt about as clean as his floor.

"I'm going to pass out soon," Jared said.

Destiny turned her head. "I'm fat. I'm a huge, fucking cow."

"You're my sister," Jared said. "It's, I dunno. Weird."

She slowly turned her head back. "We're not really."

"We are."

She considered him, considered the room and sighed. They sat and drank and the party went on above their heads. After they'd finished his beer, Jared shook the crumbs out of his sheets and offered her the bed. She kicked off her sneakers and told him to remember to lock the door. He did, and then dragged a sleeping bag from one of the totes and settled in on the couch. He reached over and clicked off the lamp.

"Night, bro," she said.

"Night," he said. "Sis."

She giggled. "Just like *The Waltons.*"

"The who?"

"Never mind."

16

ROCKSTAR

Jared spent the morning trying to scrub the last few days from his basement suite. Destiny had left a smiley-faced note thanking him for letting her crash. He had a fuzzy memory about almost making out with her, which made him anxious. He bagged and dragged his Christmas tree to the curb. Holidays, he thought. Once he got a job, he was going to spend them on sunny, drama-less beaches.

His cell beeped. Ebs ranting. She'd spent several e-mails accusing him of making Dylan look like an ass. Using a lot of words and a tone that bordered on psycho. He was glad his dad was back on his feet financially, because the kitchen was now truly closed and if Ebs had her way, she'd lock him inside and burn it down. He was mad that she was blaming him for Dylan acting like King Dork. From her reaction, you'd think he'd slaughtered her first-born and sacrificed it to the Yahtzee gods.

Jared decided to take the bus to the store to get some odour-killing powder, the stuff you shook on rugs and vacuumed up. He was too hungover to remember what it was called, but it had happy dogs and cats on the box. He'd dreamed about Baby Killer all night. Her wet-dog perfume was still all over the couch. Which made him lonely, so he could either get rid of the smell or mope around all emo and shit.

He went upstairs and knocked on his mom's bedroom door.

"Fuck off," his mom called.

"I'm going to the store," he said. "Need anything?"

"Ginger ale," she said. "And Rolaids."

"Got it."

"Money in my purse."

"Are you guys decent?"

"Get the fuck in here, you dumb shit," Richie said. "And stop talking! Jesus."

His mom and Richie were two lumps under her comforter. His mom reached a hand under her bed and pulled her purse out. Jared handed her the wallet and she gave him a twenty.

"Lots of Rolaids," she said.

"Got it. Richie?"

"Fuck off."

"Need the truck?" she said.

"Too many road checks," Jared said.

"Weenie," she said.

"Hey, if you want your truck impounded, I'll happily—"

Richie hucked a pillow at him. "Out."

If Jared hadn't been so hungover himself, he'd have stayed outside their door and sung something loud and cheerful to piss them off. But his coffee sloshed unhappily in his guts and his head was throbbing in a way that made his veins ache. He jammed his feet in his boots in the hallway and headed off to see Mrs. Jaks.

Someone had salted Mrs. Jaks's driveway in a haphazard, hopscotch pattern. Jared took the ice chipper from beside the shovel.

He cleared and widened the path to the sidewalk. The snowbanks were too crusty and deep to budge. You'd need a truck with some guts and a blade attachment to clear them. Or a snowplow.

"Are you Jared?"

He turned. Standing in the doorway was a girl with blue-black hair in Princess Leia buns. She wore a white bathrobe over a long white dress. She'd slept on her do, so it was fuzzy and the buns were crooked.

"Hey," Jared said, straightening.

"Is that a yes or a no?"

"I'm Jared," he said.

"From the way Gran talked," she said, "I thought you'd be older."

"Aren't you a little short for a stormtrooper?" Jared said.

"Cute," she said in a tone that meant she didn't think it was cute at all.

Her face was weird. Her cheekbones were sharp and her eyes slanted. She was dark, probably Native, and tall. Wiry. None of her face should add up to pretty, but it did, and he realized he was staring at her. As the awkward silence went on, her eyebrow cocked, Spock-like, distant and judge-y of all things hungover and illogical.

"Is Mrs. Jaks okay?" he said.

"Gran's in a mood," she said.

"Oh."

"The meat freezer conked out while she was getting chemo," she said. "Gran wanted me to go over today and ask you if you could help us. She doesn't want to bring Děda home until she gets the basement cleaned up."

"Who?"

"Gran's husband. Old Czech guy. Yay high. Kinda losing it."

"Oh." Maggoty meat disposal while hungover? Awesome. But Mrs. Jaks probably wasn't up to much. And she hated asking for help. Damn. They'd probably been smelling it since she phoned. He decided to add Gravol to his shopping list. "When I get back from the store, I'll get Mom's truck. I'll take the rest of it to the dump."

"The curb's fine."

"No garbage pickup tomorrow. All the neighbourhood critters will get at it if you leave the bags on the curb."

"Where's the store?"

"Downtown."

"Can I catch a ride?"

"I'm bussing it."

"I thought you had a truck."

"There's checkpoints in town during the holidays. I only have a learner's and if I get cau—"

"Sarah! Are you trying to heat the neighbourhood?" Mrs. Jaks yelled from inside. "Close the door!"

The girl rolled her eyes. She stepped back and waited. "Well? Are you in or out?"

"Oh," Jared said, realizing she was inviting him in. "I'll finish the walk first."

"Suit yourself," she said.

He watched her close the door. He stood for a long time. Then he stomped his feet to get the circulation going, wishing he'd scrubbed himself instead of the basement.

She probably won't notice your fumes since she's got a basement of rotting meat, Romeo, his inner voice pointed out.

Sometimes his inner voice surprised him. Sometimes he wondered if that's what crazy people heard, other voices in their head making smartass remarks. But he stood and he listened and didn't hear anyone in his head but himself.

Baby Killer shifted and Jared's arm fell asleep, tingling uncomfortably. Then he remembered they had put Baby down a few days before Halloween. He slowly realized that he was not alone. Light shone on his face. He blinked awake.

A girl with a tangle of blue-black hair was scrolling through an iTouch. She was naked, he was naked and their bodies were pressed together under his sleeping bag. Sarah, he remembered. Mrs. Jaks's granddaughter. They'd spent a few hours cleaning out Mrs. Jaks's freezer. Mrs. Jaks had wanted to cook, but he told her he'd come by another night. He vaguely remembered going to a party with Blake and doing round after round of Jell-O shots. He didn't remember seeing Sarah at the party. It seemed rude to ask how they'd ended up together.

"Hey," Jared said.

"You've got a lot of condoms in your nightstand," she said. "And you were really comfortable putting one on when you were hosed."

"Mom's a big believer in not being a grandma until she's forty. I get them in my stocking every Christmas."

"Ah. Glad you aren't a whore. I need the clap like I need a hole in the head," she said. She groaned. "I can't believe you have Nickelback on your playlist."

"Is that my iTouch?"

"Okay, the Black Eyed Peas I can live with, but Nickelback?"

"I gotta hurl," Jared said.

"My reaction exactly," Sarah said.

Jared felt around for the garbage can. His basement was dark. And cold. The windows were blacked out by the snowdrifts. Jared's head throbbed, making his skin feel too tight. Bile crept up the back of his throat. He put the back of his hand to his mouth. The girl flashed the light from the iTouch screen around, found the garbage can and passed it to him. He hurled.

Classy, his inner voice said.

Shut it, he told his inner voice.

He put the garbage can as far away as he could reach, then curled under the sleeping bag and waited for death. Sarah poked him in the ribs.

"Mmm," he said.

"This never happened," she said. "I don't want anyone to know I hooked up with someone who likes Nickelback."

"It's 'Rockstar,'" Jared said. "Everyone likes 'Rockstar.'"

"I've got to stop doing E," Sarah said.

Sarah left after noisily hunting down her clothes. Jared stayed in bed all day. He managed some water at suppertime and then felt the first stirring of hunger. He emptied his puke into the toilet and washed the garbage can. He wandered upstairs to see what everyone was doing, but they were mostly hungover and not wanting company. He made himself a coffee and watched TV, but it was all repeats. He threw his clothes in the washing machine. He dragged the garbage to the curb.

He turned to find Sarah on his front-porch stairs, watching him. From her snarky remarks about his playlist, he hadn't expected to see her back at his place. Her hair was in two ponytails that stuck straight out from her head. She'd given herself freckles and wore a little tiara. Her tights were black-and-white striped. She squinted, huddled into her parka.

"Hey," Jared said.

"Gran wants you to come for supper."

"I'm still hungover."

"Chicken soup with dumplings. Your call."

His stomach rumbled. "Are you okay if I . . . I mean, you know. After last night . . ."

Sarah snorted. "Somehow, my heart will go on."

"So you don't like Nickelback, but Celine's okay?"

"Sarcasm, numbnuts. Learn to read it."

"Wow," Jared said. "I haven't heard *numbnuts* since grade school."

"Rush me to the burn unit," Sarah said. "You got me."

"I'll be over in a few," Jared said. "I gotta brush my teeth."

"Don't ask about Děda at dinner, all right?"

"Is he okay?"

"He's still in respite and Gran feels pretty shitty about not bringing him home yet, but she's not doing so great."

"Oh. Okay. Thanks for the heads-up."

"Smell you later, alligator."

"Seriously?" Jared yelled at her as she walked away.

She lifted both her hands and, without looking back, gave him a double-fingered salute.

He realized he was still watching her as she disappeared around the corner, and gave his head a shake.

———

He'd never seen Mrs. Jaks wear makeup before. She'd laid it on thick, but it wasn't hiding her greyness. Jared lifted the pot from the stove for her and put it on the table. When he sat down, Sarah handed him a soup bowl and a spoon.

"That isn't how you set a table, young lady," Mrs. Jaks said.

"I wish you weren't so hung up on bourgeois rituals," Sarah said. "Decolonize, Gran."

"At my place, we eat in front of the TV," Jared said, ladling himself a serving. "Mom hates dinner conversations." He served Mrs. Jaks, but Sarah grabbed the ladle from him before he could fill her bowl.

"Big words don't compensate for laziness, Sarah Emilia Jaks," Mrs. Jaks said.

"Gran, I love you," Sarah said, "but your blind adherence to the dominant culture's values makes me want to scream."

"Blah, blah, blah," Mrs. Jaks said. "You aren't getting out of the dishes."

"The soup's good, Mrs. Jaks," Jared interrupted.

"Thank you, Jared. How refreshing to see good manners in a young person."

Sarah broke a roll and handed it to her gran. Mrs. Jaks buttered it and dipped it in her soup. They argued without raising their voices, and Jared could tell it was a familiar fight, one they'd had many times before.

They went into the living room after dinner and watched *Wheel of Fortune*. When Jared looked over, Mrs. Jaks was silently crying. Sarah held her gran's hand. Jared got up and did the dishes. As he was drying them and putting them away, Sarah came and stood beside him.

"Gran went to bed. I feel like shit," she said.

"I've got some Gravol," Jared said.

"Emotionally, dumb-ass."

"Oh."

She moved in and hugged him. He put the dishcloth down and patted her back.

"I don't want to be here," she whispered.

17

COOKIE DUDE

Jared began the second half of grade ten hugging a Thermos of coffee as his mom drove him to school. He felt wrecked. Raw. He needed a vacation from his Christmas vacation.

"We're here," his mom said, nudging him.

He opened his eyes and she waved a twenty in front of him.

"For lunch," she said. "And supper. I'll be back tomorrow."

Jared took the twenty. "Richie's a big boy now. He can sell his own drugs. You don't need to go with him."

"Later, loser," she said, rolling her eyes.

"Bye, Mom."

He watched her drive away.

"Cookie Duuuuuuude!" Alex Gunborg and his muppets of darkness shouted at him from the science wing steps.

Jared hunched into his coat, gave them a wave as they laughed.

"Cookie Dude!" his track teammate Teresa Anselmo de Carvalho shouted from the front office.

Crashpad came up to him in homeroom. Sat beside him, serious, and said, "Did you see it?"

"Cookie Dude!" two of the girls at the front said, laughing.

"Someone put up a video. On YouTube," Crashpad said. "Of you. Called *Cookie Dude*. Actually, it's called *Cookie Dude Dumb-Ass*."

"Awesome," Jared said.

"I'm sorry," Crashpad said. "This is all my fault."

"Crashpad, chill, okay?"

"Cookie Duuuuuuuude!"

"I'm sorry. Look, I'll put my video back up and—"

"Crashpad," Jared said. "Relax."

"It looks like a whole bunch of camera-phone video spliced together," Crashpad said. "Everyone else's faces are blurred. It's you . . . you know . . ."

"Is there nudity?"

"You're falling off shit. Throwing up on a trampoline. Failing at water-skiing. You know. Dumb shit."

Jared shrugged. "Hey, as long as I'm not boning a pie or some weird shit, you know, fuck it."

Crashpad blinked.

"Crashpad, dude, it's okay," Jared said. "I'm not running for prime minister. Right?"

"Dylan's an asshole," Crashpad said.

"Somehow, I'll survive."

The only way to play it was to be a good sport and laugh it off. Jared high-fived the guys who wanted to high-five. He smiled, and felt like a boob, and decided to lie low for a week, playing Xbox in the basement until everything blew over.

Dylan and Ebs were hanging out near the cafeteria and Jared didn't have it in him to deal with them. He smiled, gave them a nod and was about to go back to his locker when Greer tapped him on the shoulder.

"Hey," she said.

Considering that her perky blondness had never noticed him before, he was immediately suspicious. "Hey."

"How'd it feel being E-boned?" she said.

"What?"

Greer laughed and tossed her hair, glancing over at Ebs and Dylan. "You know it was Ebony, right? She put that video together to mess you up."

"Your point?"

She leaned in and whispered, "If you laugh like I said something funny, you'll drive her completely mental."

Wow, Jared thought. Girl grudges are intense. "Seriously?"

"Later," she said, giving him her girly wave. She caught up with her friends and ignored the searing hatred Ebs was sending with her eyes.

Jared went outside to hang with the burnouts and bummed a smoke off one of his regulars, who punched his shoulder, repeating, "Cookie Dude."

"Yeah, yeah," Jared said.

Martina Yelan reached over and took his cigarette from his mouth and lit one of her own with it. She blew a smoke ring at him, holding out his cigarette. "Cute show."

"Tip your waitress," he said. "I'm here all week."

She considered him. "You're not as boring as I thought."

"Thanks."

"We should hang."

"I would enjoy hanging," Jared said. "Too. As well. I mean, yeah. Let's hang."

"Cool," she said. "I'm having some friends over tonight. Are you in?"

Rather than say anything, he nodded, hoping it would come off as less geeky than babbling at her.

"Dude," one of his newly recruited cookie buyers said, putting a brotherly hand on Jared's shoulder as Martina walked away. "Never stop making cookies."

His minor blip of fame was fading by the end of the school day. At least, there were no more Cookie Dude shout-outs in the hallway. His messages were filled with tags to his Cookie Dude link, but he couldn't bring himself to watch it. He was considering what to wear to Martina's party when he saw Sarah coming out of the front office.

She was talking to one of the teachers, hugging a binder to her chest. Kids paused, checked her out and gave her a wide berth, decked out as she was in a getup that looked like a Saturday morning cartoon. She had tiny buns above her forehead that looked like ears, and she was wearing some weird, flouncy white shirt and a short plaid skirt. The white tights ended in a pair of cowboy boots.

". . . know, I think it's more an issue of the treaties not being honoured," Sarah said.

"I can't change the curriculum," the teacher said.

"But you don't agree with fracking, do you?"

"That's not the point."

"I don't see why we can't bring it up in class," Sarah said.

"Sarah, I've loved our chat, but I've got to pick up my kids," the teacher said. "We'll talk more tomorrow."

"Bye." Sarah frowned, staring intently at a spot in the distance.

"Hey," Jared said.

She snapped back to attention. "Hey."

"What's with the outfit?"

"I'm Sailor Jupiter."

"Okay."

"Do you have a black marker?"

"Not here."

"I need to make my boots black."

"Wouldn't it be easier to get black boots?"

"I've got time," she said. "Gran said to go amuse myself after school or she'd have to smother me with a pillow."

Jared laughed. "Yeah. Family. Are you coming to school here now?"

"Are you going to the Idle No More walk?"

"The what?"

"Seriously? Do you live under a rock? It's all over the news."

"Kinda busy lately."

"Wow. Just . . . wow. Dude, Native people are rising up. We're protesting the omnibus budget bills that are stomping all over the treaties and this oil company called Enbridge—"

"Oh, that."

"Oh, that?"

"It's pretty much a done deal," Jared said. "The environmental review is a dog-and-pony show to shut everyone up."

"Way to bend over."

"Capitalism is a heartless bitch."

"Which TV show did you steal that gem from?"

"I think it was a meme."

"Whatever. I'm going."

The after-school rush hit a peak and they moved to the side of the corridor, leaning against the wall as kids pressed to get out. They wandered back to Jared's locker and then Sarah's. On the way home, Jared picked up some chicken balls and chow mein from the nearby takeout. He liked their silence as they walked, the way it was comfortable, especially after faking his way through an embarrassing day.

If he thought about all the effort Ebony had gone to, making a video of his lamest moments, he was choked and flattered. Ebs only attacked when she felt threatened. She must have been more bent out of shape than he thought. When he felt up to it, he'd ask Crashpad to show him the *Squidward Smackdown* video of his New Year's Eve fight with Dylan. Lame, drunk arguing couldn't have been the whole reason she'd spent her precious time making a hate video. He was surprised she'd even thought about him that long, intent as she was on plotting world domination.

Sarah followed him around the corner and he unlocked his door. She pulled out her cell.

"Hey, what's your wi-fi password?"

"Ticats suck, Argos rule," Jared said. "One word, no caps, no spaces. It's really slow."

"Gran doesn't even have wi-fi," Sarah said. "They still have a land line and they don't even have call display. It's like stepping back in time."

He cleared off a spot on the couch for her and then rinsed a fork in the utility sink. Jared handed her the plastic fork that came with the takeout and gave his a shake. They checked their phones and took turns eating the chow mein.

"Ahhhh," Sarah said. "Interwebs, how I loves yous. I never leaves yous again."

Jared cleaned the crap messages off his phone. He texted Crashpad asking about the protest and Crashpad texted back that he was going to be a drummer at the walk.

U should come, Crashpad texted. *I got a spare drum. We need every1.*

"This is so frustrating," Sarah said. "The whole world is dancing and drumming and protesting, but I'm stuck here in the middle of nowhere."

"We're actually one town over from the middle of nowhere."

"Look!" She held up her phone. "Thousands of Native people marching. Thousands!"

"I'll introduce you to Crashpad," Jared said. "He has a spare drum."

"They've increased the police presence for the Vancouver protests," Sarah said. "They think it's going to be like the Riot at the Hyatt. Damn it. I'm missing everything."

Someone knocked at the door. Jared was expecting his mom, but Dylan was there, wearing a pinched expression.

"The video wasn't my idea," he said.

"Yeah," Jared said. "Kinda figured."

"Dude—"

"It's okay," Jared said. "Look, I've got company."

"Ebs was pissed. You didn't—"

"What have you got to drink?" Sarah said.

"There's some Coke," Jared said over his shoulder, "and a couple of beers in the fridge."

"Thanks."

Dylan peered around him. "Who's the chick?"

"Bye," he said, shutting the door.

Jared took the empty cartons and put them in the garbage. He went over to the laundry side. Someone had taken his clothes out of the dryer and put them on top of the machine. He gave them a quick fold and brought them back to his room, tucking them in the totes.

"Your couch smells like dog," Sarah said when he sat beside her again.

"Yeah," Jared said.

"Do you have one?"

"She died."

"Sorry."

"Yeah."

They surfed and when Jared looked up, it was dark. He looked over at Sarah, who stared intently at her screen. He considered going to Martina's party, but he was comfortable and tired.

"Wanna fool around?" Sarah said.

Jared stopped texting. "You serious?"

She shrugged. "You're here. You're warm. You're slightly better than masturbating."

He laughed. "Hey, who can resist a come-on like that?"

"You talk too much," Sarah said, sliding her hand up his shirt.

They took a breather from making out and Sarah turned on the speakers of her phone. Some high-voiced chick lisped breathy lyrics Jared couldn't understand.

"Is this Enya?"

"Grimes," Sarah said.

"Sounds like Enya."

"Whatever, Nickelback." Sarah said this without heat, and began dancing around the room, shirtless. She wore a white sports bra and her nipples poked the cups. She used his T-shirt to hold her hair back, stretching the neck like a headband, the shirt inside out, falling behind her like a nun's habit. Her skirt flared as she twirled. Jared wrapped himself in the sleeping bag, drowsy and horny.

"See you on a dark night," Sarah sang.

She had a spazzy way of dancing. She flung her arms, hopping up and down like a kid in a bouncy castle.

"La la la la la," she sang.

Sarah's cell rang.

"'Lo," she said. "Hi, Gran. Yeah. Yeah, I'm at Jared's. We're hanging. What? Gran, I own my sexuality. I own my body and I—"

Jared grabbed the phone. "Hi, Mrs. Jaks."

"Are you using protection?"

"Mrs. Jaks, come on. It's not like that."

"I thought you were a good boy," she said, abruptly hanging up.

"Your gran's pissed," Jared said, handing her phone back.

Sarah reached out and put on her shirt. "What's your deal with her?"

"What?"

"It's kind of weird, don't you think? How you hang with the oldies?" Sarah turned the lamp on.

"She's okay."

"Are you that broke?"

"Mom spent some mandatory time in rehab and anger management," Jared said, not sure if he should tell her about his mom's very short stint in the joint yet. From past experience, it was a mood killer. "I crashed on your gran's couch for a bit."

"Poor you."

"Better than a group home. I watched Mr. Jaks when she needed a break. A bit of gardening. Shit like that."

Sarah took a brush out of her backpack and started tugging at her hair. "Yeah, Gran's a slave driver."

"She's okay."

"Is your dad alive?"

Jared sighed. "How long are you staying in Kitimat?"

Sarah concentrated on the ends of her hair, working a knot. "I don't think Mom wants me back."

"Yeah. For a long time my mom was mad about Mrs. Jaks taking me in," Jared said. "I thought I was going to have to live with Nana Sophia."

"Is that your gran?"

"My dad's mom. We don't talk to my mom's family."

"Oh." She kissed him. "I should motor. Gran's wrath awaits no one."

He laughed. "I'll phone you tomorrow."

"Use my cell. Gran listens in on the land line when anyone calls me. You can hear her breathing. It's so disturbing."

"Text me, then."

She paused at the top of the step. "Digits?"

Jared gave her his cell number and she typed in the numbers. His phone rang. She'd texted: *C u @ the propaganda mill.*

L8r, Jared texted back.

She blew him a kiss and closed the door behind her.

He lay on the mattress with one arm under his head, reluctant to turn off the lamp. Vader's POWDER HOUSE RULES thought bubble was coming unstuck from the ceiling and a spiderweb hung off his toes.

David had been charged with assault for breaking Jared's ribs. But so was his mom, for nail-gunning David to the floor and leaving him there all night. Her assault charges would have been dropped, or at least her sentence would have been lighter, if she'd played the helpless young mother valiantly protecting her young, but every second David was in court, she radiated homicidal intentions.

"You shouldn't dwell on it," Mrs. Jaks had said. "Forgive him and you'll live without his shadow on your lives."

"The world is hard," his mom had said. "You need to be harder."

18

KFC & BEER
SOLVE EVERYTHING

Hey, Jared texted his mom in the morning. *Hello? R u alive?*

The cursor blinked, but his mom didn't answer. He willed her to type something, anything. He pictured her and Richie draped out of the truck's blasted-out windows like Bonnie and Clyde, mowed down by the cinematic hail of machine-gun fire. He pictured them in the burned-out husk of her truck off a logging road in the middle of nowhere, slowly rotting away until they were bones.

His mom came back a few days later. He heard her voice upstairs. He heard her laugh. Heard Richie's heavy footsteps. She'd dropped some weight and her hair was trimmed. She'd brought him a bucket of Kentucky Fried Chicken and some beer.

"Where were you?" Jared said.

"At the spa," she said. "Getting a fucking mani-pedi. Where do you think I was?"

"Dead."

"Jesus, stop being a bitch."

"I just want to know where you were."

"I have two words for you," she said. "Plausible deniability."

"God."

"Drama down, Jared. I'm here. You're here. We have a bucket of dead, fried birds and enough beer to kill all the brain cells that matter."

They ate and watched TV. She opened a packet of wipes and held it up. "Need me to wipe your ass?"

"Real funny, Mom."

"Well, you're the one acting like a big baby."

"You are a piece of work."

She laughed and wrapped her arms around him. "Missed you too, Jelly Bean."

"Get off me."

"I loooooove you," she said.

"Don't do anything death-inducing. Okay?"

She sighed. She pecked him on the cheek. "Who's the Hallmark card now?"

The next morning he scrubbed off in the utility sink and put on fresh jeans and a T-shirt. He went upstairs and checked the fridge. Their shelf was mostly empty. He'd have to do a bake sale soon if he could figure out a kitchen. Maybe he could buy a toaster oven second-hand. Block off the vents upstairs and duct-tape the windows so the smell would be less noticeable. Jared poured himself a bowl of cereal and ate it in front of the TV. He washed his dish and put it in the rack. He considered checking to see if his mom was still home, but if she wasn't up by now, she probably wouldn't appreciate being woken. Two of the new replacement tenants came home from work and he said hi and left. Coming down the steps, he saw Sarah walking up the street in a grey skirt and blazer, her hair up in a smooth, shiny swoop. She wore red lipstick and a single string of pearls.

"Mr. Martin," she said.

"Job interview, Ms. Jaks?"

"If you protest looking like an Indian, you get your head cracked and cool your heels in holding forever," she said. "But if you wear the clothes of the oppressor, they let you call a lawyer."

"Ah, the Idle No More protest."

"Coming?"

"Okay."

They caught the bus to the Kitamaat Village Road entrance, then transferred to the bus to the reserve. Sarah held his hand. She'd cut her nails short and painted them to match her lipstick. Her hand was warm. The day was sunny. The road hugged the shore. The rough ocean reflected ripples of light on the bus ceiling and lit the dust motes gold. Sarah's lipstick glistened when she smiled at him. Funny, they hadn't known each other more than a week and he'd already forgotten what life was like without her.

There were other people at the Rec Centre. There were speeches. There were songs. Jared only remembered Sarah's face, excited and happy. The tips of her fingers searching out his.

When Jared got home, he found his door kicked in. His clothes were tossed around the room and most of the furniture was broken. The mattress had been slashed. The wall that separated his space from the laundry room was full of punches. They'd taken apart the toilet tank. Jared shut off the water. It drained into the hole in the concrete, but his clothes were crumpled and muddy. He sorted out the clothes that were salvageable and wrung them out in the utility sink. His cellphone buzzed.

U mite want 2 stay wit Blake for a few dayʒ, Richie texted him. *Ur momʒ pissed.*

He went upstairs and found his mom covered in drywall dust, her knuckles bleeding. She stood in front of the fridge holding the door open. Richie was nowhere in sight.

"Hi," Jared said.

She kept looking in the fridge, then grabbed a beer and cracked it open. She closed the door and turned to him.

She lowered her head, glaring. "Have you been helping your dad?"

Jared shrugged.

"Care to explain?" she said.

He backed up a step.

"Your dumb-ass stepsister brought me up to speed," his mom said. "Destiny wanted to tell me what a peach you are. Helping the fucktard and his whore and her dumb-ass."

"So you redecorated my room," Jared said.

She hurled her beer can at his head. He ducked. She shoved him and, when he didn't shove back, shoved him again.

"Fuck you," she said. "You goddamn fucking disloyal piece of shit. I'm the one taking care of you! And you go and help that lying, whoring son of a bitch! Fuck you!"

He walked out and down the street. He expected her to follow him, expected to hear her truck. Expected her to scream shit and throw things, but she didn't bother.

19

ADVENTURES AT
THE ALL NATIVE

Jared woke up on the floor in a motel. The room was a bunkhouse of guys, sprawled in various states of passed out. Beer cans, vodka mickeys and assorted empty booze bottles littered the place. He heard the toilet flush and Bambam, one of Dylan's hockey teammates, wandered out and flopped on the pull-out couch.

"Hey," Jared said. "Where are we?"

"Motel," Bambam mumbled into his pillow.

"Where?"

"Prince Rupert."

"Crap," Jared said. "Where's Dylan?"

"Shut up already."

Jared still had his wallet, his phone and his shoes but couldn't find his jacket. He had seven-fifty to his name. His battery was dead and he didn't have his charger. He went into the bathroom. In the mirror, he saw someone had drawn a large black *L* on his forehead. Nice, he thought, wetting his thumb and rubbing it to see if it would come off.

The past came back to him. He'd parked at Blake's for a week and a bit, and then with Kelsey for a few nights before going back to Blake's. When he wore out his welcome, he asked Dylan if he could couchsurf, but Dylan said his dad still held a grudge against Jared for mouthing off at him, and besides, Dylan was going to take a few days off school to go watch the All Native Basketball Tournament and they should go. Jared had said he didn't have any money. Dylan fronted him some and they'd watched a couple of games then went to a party. After that, things got fuzzy.

Jared recognized the name of the motel and realized it was the one he had been conceived in. His dad had been playing on the intermediate men's team for the Lax Kw'alaams. Nana Sophia loathed sports and never went, even though she loved Prince Rupert—mostly, Jared thought, because she had loved her husband, his grandfather. His parents had hooked up at an after-party. When they were still married, his mom said she'd never seen anyone as handsome as his dad and she knew the second she saw him that he was the one. Nine months later, Jared was born. Two months after that, his parents had gotten married.

He found his shoes and stuffed his feet in them. Dylan wasn't in the room. Dylan's truck was in the parking lot and a stunned red-haired girl was sitting in it, buttoning her shirt. Dylan and Ebony were standing in front of it, and as Jared got closer, he could hear them arguing. Ebony was crying, her face leaking even as her expression remained stubbornly pleasant, waiting out Dylan's explanation about why she had just caught him with another girl. When he stopped talking, she bitch-slapped him with her purse. They both stood shocked, and then Ebony really laid in while Dylan shielded his face. Jared backed away. More drama he did not need.

Since none of the guys looked like they were going anywhere soon, Jared decided to hitch home. He swiped a toque and a sweater. The motel was near a McDonald's, so he bought a large coffee and a small cheeseburger. He ate and then walked to the highway, sipping his coffee.

Jared had made it to the industrial park at the edge of town by lunchtime, but no one had even slowed down. A light drizzle started. The last sips of his coffee were cold. Crows played in an updraft. The highway was still. Mist wound up the trees. Humps of grey snow huddled in the ditches. He decided to keep walking. If he got to the turnoff to Port Edward and no one picked him up, he'd go back to the motel, maybe borrow someone's charger and call Richie to come pick him up.

His mom couldn't stay mad at him forever, could she? How long could she hold a grudge? How long could he stay away from the house? Nana was always an option, but one with tie-cutting consequences. That relationship-ending move wasn't something he wanted to do. Yet. His mom was trying to teach him a lesson. All he had to do was chill.

An older burgundy Caddy passed him and then pulled onto the shoulder. Jared jogged to catch up with it. He opened the door and stopped. An old Native woman smiled at him, her giant glasses dusting her cheeks.

"Where you heading?" she said.

Beneath her face, Jared could see something twisting. Crap, he thought, I must have done acid last night. The old woman was plump and smiling, perfectly respectable in a flowered dress, work jacket and square orthotic shoes, but Jared saw something in her that was as dark as cedar bark, with large yellowed fangs and knobby, twisted knuckles. 'Shrooms. He could have done magic mushrooms. That would do it too.

"Kitimat," he said, willing himself to get in the car.

"Oh, I'm not going that far," she said. "I'm going to Terrace. Is that all right?"

"That's perfect," Jared said, still not moving.

The thing he was seeing drooled. The old lady raised an eyebrow. This is why we don't do 'shrooms or acid, he told himself. The psychedelics lingered and lingered and he had to deal with shit like this when in reality he had lucked out and gotten someone to stop. He couldn't make himself lift his feet.

"I'm catching a chill, dear," she said.

"You shouldn't be picking up hitchhikers," Jared said.

"I have a good feeling about you," she said. "You look familiar. Who's your mother?"

"Maggie Moody."

"I don't know who that is. Where's she from?"

"Bella Bella. Dad's a Martin from Alert Bay."

"Well I'll be," she said. "Do you know Sadie Cranmer?"

"Sorry."

"I hate idling. It's bad for the environment."

"I think I forgot my phone. Back in the motel. Damn it. Thanks—"

"Which motel? I can drive you back if you like."

"I wouldn't want to put you out."

"You look cold, dear. You shouldn't be out without a jacket in February! I would feel terrible if you caught your death."

Jared shut the car door and backed up, smiling, smiling, and watching the thing underneath the Grandma-skin start to snarl.

Get in the car, you moron, he told himself.

Run, his inner voice told him. *Run now.*

A logging truck rounded the distant curve, coming towards them. The old woman shrugged and signalled, then drove off. The wake of the logging truck chilled him. He saw the car pause at the crest of a hill. A couple of trucks coming from Rupert bombed past him. The Caddy disappeared and Jared headed back to the motel. The rain started to squall, gusting and driving sideways.

When he got there, Dylan was drinking in his truck in the motel parking lot. He honked. Jared's feet were sore, his clothes were drenched and his teeth were chattering. He was already weirded out and he didn't really want to deal with Dylan in a mood.

"Hey," Dylan said, powering the driver's-side window down.

"H-h-hey," Jared said.

"Those assholes won't let me in the room."

"Y-y-yeah?"

"Yeah."

"Wan-na-na g-g-o home?"

Dylan nodded, taking another pull.

"M-maybe I-I sh-should drive?"

"Get in the fucking truck."

"H-how much booze—"

"Don't be a little bitch, Jared. Get in and shut up."

The mystery of why the guys wouldn't let Dylan in the room deepened, Jared thought, coughing. Jared said, "S-s-ee you."

"Jared, wait," Dylan said. He slid over to the passenger's side.

Jared hopped in, cranking the heat. When his shakes stopped, he pulled his seat belt on. Dylan didn't put his on. Jared's skin burned as it thawed out. The sky was darkening early because of the low clouds. He glanced at the gas gauge.

"I've got three bucks. We need gas."

"I've got money," Dylan said.

Jared drove to the Indian gas station. Dylan told the attendant to stuff the tank. Jared went in and bought another coffee and a chocolate bar. Dylan bought a two-litre Coke and a country music CD. Jared got the key for the can and used the hand dryer to get the cold out of his shirt. He wrung his jeans out in the sink. When he got back to the truck, Dylan poured out half the Coke and refilled it with the vodka, giving it a shake.

"Did I do acid last night?" Jared said.

"How the fuck should I know? What am I, your mommy?"

Awesome, Jared thought, starting the truck. Just awesome.

Dylan spent a long time taking the plastic wrapper off the CD. He frowned, squinting hard as he worked to get the disc in the slot. He flipped through the first few songs and settled on "You and Tequila."

"Ebs and Tequila," he sang at the chorus.

About the millionth time Dylan repeated the song, Jared noticed the burgundy Caddy pulled into a rest stop. He had no intention of stopping, but he still pulled the truck over and parked behind it. The car was dark, but the back windows were fogged. The rest stop was unlit. The truck's headlights picked up the rain bouncing off the car's rear window.

You should check on the old broad, one of his voices said. *She probably fell down and broke her hip. Come on, hero. Go see.*

"I gotta piss," Dylan said.

Jared couldn't say, hey, that's a really shitty idea. He wanted to, but couldn't. He scanned the stop. Two outhouses were off in the darkness, gravel paths leading through the bushes. Dylan stumbled out of the truck and whizzed over the embankment. Jared shut off the CD. The windshield wipers thunk-thunked like a heartbeat.

The engine hummed. The leaves fluttered in the pounding rain. The nearby ocean sucked at the rocks as the waves rose and fell.

Dylan climbed back in and said, "Hey, put the tunes back on."

"Give it a rest," Jared said, then found himself getting out of the truck, while his mind played him a montage of movie idiots in horror stories who went up into the attic to investigate with flashlights that blinked out moments before they were hacked to death. He looked into the car. A bag of knitting was open in the back seat. The doors were locked. Maybe she was hurt. Maybe she'd fallen down and couldn't get up.

"Hello!" Jared called. "Are you okay?"

The truck horn bleated, loud and long.

"Hey, moron!" Dylan said, hitting the roof of the truck. "Let's roll!"

The tunes roared back to life.

Across the highway were railroad tracks. Past the tracks, there was a cliff. Between the cliff and the tracks were bushes that moved in the wind and the rain. He had a weird moment where he pictured himself from the vantage point of someone in the bush, seeing himself lit by the headlights, staring back.

Then he was back in his own head and Dylan was singing. He was tired, bone-tired, and didn't want to go back to Dylan's place. He didn't want to couchsurf anymore. He wanted to go home, but he didn't think he had it in him to deal anymore. Maybe it was time to stay with Nana. Maybe it was time to leave.

When they pulled into his mom's driveway, the house was dark. If she'd really wanted to hunt him down, she would have, Jared thought.

Dylan was a problem. He didn't want to hang out with him, fresh as he was off a breakup, but Jared couldn't just let him drive off. But Jared didn't know if his mom was going to kill him and then Dylan as collateral damage.

"Stay here," Jared said. "I'm going to call you a cab."

"You drive me home," Dylan slurred. "Now."

"I'm not dropping you off and then hitching home."

"You owe me, asshole."

"Dude, you are not the only fucktard in the world who messed up, okay? I've got my own shit to deal with."

"I'm, uh, not sleeping in your shithole. No way."

"God, just stay here. I'll call you a cab."

"No. No, I don't, I, no cabs. No fucking cabs."

"Then sleep in your truck."

"Assssshole."

Dylan staggered after Jared along the path, holding himself upright by keeping an arm on the wall, the other arm curled protectively around the Coke bottle. Someone had fixed the door. The broken furniture was gone. The punched-out holes were patched, but not painted. He had a new TV, but the Xbox was missing. Baby's squeak toy was on a chair. His friend swayed on the landing, stumbling down the last three steps and careening into the wall.

"Shithole," Dylan said, flopping onto the mattress.

"Hey," Jared said. "Be my guest. Take my bed."

Jared threw his damp shirt in the corner. He rummaged through a tote for a thick sweatshirt and some dry pants. Someone had cleaned his sleeping bags and put them neatly in the other tote. Jared threw one to Dylan.

"It shouldn't count if I don't 'member," Dylan mumbled.

Jared brushed his teeth. He gave his face a scrub, but the black
L was still not coming off. He had an urge to write on Dylan's fore-
head. Golden boy had rejoined the God squad. Ebs had been happy.
Until today.

"Hello?" Dylan said into his cellphone. "Pick up. Okay, then.
You're the one I lo-ove. You're—you're the one I love. I don't even
think I—I don't even think I slept with her, Ebony."

"For the love of God, hang up," Jared said.

"You, you shut up. You."

"Dude, Ebs is not going to appreciate being drunk-dialed right
now."

"I know that." Dylan took a long time to shut the phone off and sit
up, lifting the Coke bottle and gulping like a kid. He pulled the sleeping
bag over his legs. "I feel bad for you. Living. Living in this shithole."

"Thanks, Mother Teresa."

"I—I . . ." He burped and upchucked onto the floor halfway
through the burp.

Jared pulled his blanket over his head and willed Dylan to pass
out. He ached from too many nights on too many couches and he just
wanted to sleep.

"Sorry," Dylan said.

"Forget it."

"Can you—can—that stinks. I—I don't think I can . . .
I need . . ."

"Dylan, for fuck's sake, go to sleep."

Dylan lay back down. Jared considered turning off the desk lamp,
but it had been a weird day and he felt weird. He actually didn't mind
the distraction of Dylan explaining to no one that he was entirely
innocent and had probably been tricked into bed.

Sometimes Jared wondered if he wasn't, sort of, a little, wacka-doodle. Like today. Getting all freaked out over an old lady.

Maybe you should cut back on the hooch, genius, his inner voice said.

Is that me? Did I think that? Am I mental? Did I imagine all that?

"'Cause I love you," Dylan said. "I love you and that—that means we—we forgive. We forgive. 'Cause we're meant. We are meant."

Ebs was not going to stand by her man. Ebs was going to have a good cry and then go for the jugular and she would not give up until Dylan was in about ten times the pain he'd put her through. Dylan had as much hope of convincing Ebs to take him back as Jared had of convincing his mother that he was a good son.

Jared woke late. Dylan had left without cleaning up his vomit. The stew-like puddle stank beside the mattress. As much as Jared liked hanging with Dylan, sometimes the dude was too spoiled for words. Who didn't clean up their own vomit? God, Jared thought, holding his breath and using old socks to mop up the chunkier bits, followed by a vigorous scrub with cleaning stuff he mooched from the laundry room.

He checked his messages.

Bored, Sarah had texted him around suppertime yesterday. *Can I come over?*

I'm back, Jared texted her.

Thank the neutral-gendered deity, Sarah texted him. *Your mom still pissed?*

Yup.

The draaaaaaaama of it all. Throwing on some clothes. See u in a sec.
K.

Jared unlocked his door and shook the sheets clean. He didn't bother with music because Sarah hated everything he liked, calling him her Top of Pops lay.

Sarah knocked and then let herself in. She swished down the stairs in a vintage peach dress with white lace trim. Her hair was Bride-of-Frankenstein high with tiny white flowers tucked in the curls. She must have been super bored today. She brought a slice of Mrs. Jaks's moose-meat pie on a paper plate, plopping on the couch beside him.

"What's with the *L?*" she said, pointing to her forehead.

He touched his head. "Don't pass out at the party."

"Dylan?"

"Probably."

"He's a shit."

"Is your gran going to Van for more treatments?"

"Nice deflect."

"Nice what?"

"Dylan's a jerk. Why do you hang out with him?"

"Free booze."

She laughed. "Booze slut."

"I prefer the more politically correct Hooch Whore."

"You look like hell."

"I see charm school paid off."

"Hey," she said, wrapping her arms around him. "I had a rough couple of weeks, you know. Come on. Ask me what happened. I dare you."

"When it gets gnarly, you can stay here. Even if I'm not home."

She let go of him. "No offence, but it's pretty damn bleak here without you."

"I missed you too."

Sarah rolled her eyes. "Can the corn, dude."

"Tell me did you ever," Jared sang, imitating Bryan Adams, "ever, ever, eh-ver, love a gender-fluid person."

"You're such an ass."

20

THE HUMAN MANUAL

Humans come with an instruction manual, some twenty-four thousand genes, which, given the innumerable ways we malfunction, would appear to have been written by a dyslexic drunk on a bender. We're biological machines with consciousness, builders of empires, creators and destroyers of worlds, singers of sagas and dirges, able to envision the pearly gates of heaven and the fiery depths of hell, able to bounce around the moon, but unable to walk a couple of steps to put our water bottle in the recycling bin.

The difference between us, between one human and another, is probably one DNA base pair in every thousand. What does that mean? I can say with great certainty that you and I, we were born from women. We look up at the night sky and see the same stars, the same moon. Breathe and sleep and pray and work and daydream and sing and cry and fight and love, but in the end our bodies are meat. They rot in the ground or burn in the fire or are pickled in their own casings, displayed like waxed fruit for family and friends to weep over. Our bodies are transitory vessels built from recycled carbon like every other living being on this planet. Bits and parts of you have probably been a cricket or a dinosaur or a single blade of grass on the prairies.

With all the power of technology and science in the world, I would bet you dollars to doughnuts that you still trust a human face to be a human. But come closer and let me speak to the creatures that swim in your ancient oceans, the old ones that sing to you in your dreams. Encoded memories so frayed you think they're extinct, but they wait, coiled and unblinking, in your blood and your bones.

21

HOME ALONE

In May, with a little over a month left in school, Jared found final notices in the mail. He sold the living room TV. He waited on hold for BC Hydro. He gave the number of the bank receipt to the bored man who answered. Power would remain on. His mom's part of the fridge was down to pickle juice and ketchup. Her room was empty. The bed was stripped down to the mattress, with no clues showing how long it had been since she'd been home.

Guess if you're going to ditch your life, you just go and you don't need to tell anyone where you're going, he thought. He hesitated before phoning his dad. Jared had helped Destiny move into a shelter with Ben. Shirley had cried and cried on the couch. His dad had offered her money. Destiny had reluctantly taken it. She didn't answer his texts anymore, but she posted Instagram pictures of Ben in his new room. Ben scooting across a kitchen floor. Ben smiling hard with his first tooth.

Shirley answered his dad's phone. "You're a piece of shit."

Click.

He went over to see Sarah. Mrs. Jaks's face was puffed up like someone had punched her around. The women from her church were helping her clean and she was pointedly silent when he asked if Sarah was around.

He considered his options and then went on Facebook.

Hey, Nana, Jared messaged. *Can I stay with you this summer?*

A half-hour later, she messaged, *Why wait? We can be in Canada in a week.*

School shit.

Ah, well. Tell me when you finish and I'll send plane tickets. Do you have ID?

Yup. Thanks, Nana.

Love you, Cutie. Can't wait!

Love you, Nana.

Well, that was that. If his mom had hated him for helping his dad, she was going to disown him for running off to Nana's. But she was gone anyway. She wasn't answering her messages and she wasn't home. If he couldn't come up with money to keep the house going, he'd ditch it.

That afternoon, the power went out. Jared phoned BC Hydro and was told the cut-off had been scheduled and no one had cancelled it. Because he'd made a partial payment, they wouldn't be charged for reconnection, but it would take a day or two.

One of the tenants packed out.

"Tell your mom she owes me," Joseph said. "I'm taking the band saw, but she still owes me fourteen hundred. And she's not getting any more coke until I get paid."

The other tenants told him they'd give it another day or two, and then they were packing out too.

"I'm not paying your fucking bills," one of them said. "I've got my own fucking bills to pay. You're on your own."

He wondered if Sarah would consider coming to visit him on Salt Spring. He was sure he could get Nana to agree to her staying a week, though the idea of the two of them under one roof made him nervous.

Normally, this was the time of year when he and the Jakses turned the soil in the garden and got it ready for the potatoes. All bets were off this year. Everything felt shaky, and planning felt dangerous.

Jared went to school early and showered there, scrubbing the last few days off his skin. He loved hot water. Hot water ruled. He hadn't showered at school since he quit track. He stayed in until his skin was pruney.

Science had a pop quiz. French had homework due he hadn't done. At lunch, he ate a stale croissant with no-name margarine that he'd scored from the food bank. Spring had sprung. The grass needed cutting, the fridge was making noises and he had no idea how he was going to make the bills. He thought that was probably part of the punishment. If he was going to pay his dad's bills, then he was going to pay his mom's. She had a Biblical sense of justice. Eye for an eye, bill for a bill.

He was sitting on the steps near the science wing when he saw Sarah in the distance, coming down the sidewalk. She wore a dress that came down to her shins, covered in metal cones that clinked when she walked. Her moccasins were soggy from the rain. Her hair was sternly braided.

"Hadih," she said.

"What?"

"Hello. That's as far as I've gotten decolonizing my language."

"Oh. Yo, esto qua."

She sat beside him on the steps. "Can I stay with you tonight?"

"Power's out."

"Gran's in a mood."

"Park as long as you want."

She leaned her head against his shoulder. They sat on the steps and watched the rain. The buzzer rang. Kids streamed by them.

"We had Grandpa for a week," she said. "And he almost killed himself in the garage. He's back in respite. Gran's wrecked."

"Holy crap."

"Wanna skip?" Sarah said.

"Sure."

They wandered over to a nearby park and sat on the swings. Sarah pushed him and then he pushed her. She lifted her dress and climbed on top of the monkey bars. He laughed as he followed her and they sat on top. Her hair sparkled with rain.

She kissed him. Her lips were soft. She had the puffy-eyed look of someone who'd been crying and had covered it up with makeup that caked. Rain dewed on her lashes. Her breath was warm on his cheek.

"Let's go home," she said.

They built a fort from a dining room table with three legs, a chair and some blankets. They took the cushions off the couch and laid them down as a mattress. Sarah turned a battery-powered lantern on that she'd taken from Mr. Jaks's emergency kit. She flicked on her iPhone speakers and it started with drums, a synth and then Cree singers, their voices high and fast.

"This is my new favourite A Tribe Called Red song," she said. "'Red Skin Girl.'"

Jared pulled off his T-shirt and she stripped down to a wife beater and a pair of his undies. He lit a j while she put a blot on her tongue, leaning in to kiss him. He turned his head.

"I have shitty trips," Jared said.

"This is a good batch," Sarah said.

"You fly the friendly skies. I'm gonna float."

She put his hand on her ass, pressed his fingers against her cheek, warm and smooth. "Spank me."

Jared squeezed and she sucked in a breath. When he didn't do anything else, she lifted his hand and smacked it against her own ass. Jared took his hand back and coughed, tapping the j on the ashtray on the chair. "Not my thing."

He flopped on his back, breathing out, watching the smoke and then hacking.

"Stoner," she said, taking the j out of his hand and putting it in the ashtray. "What the hell are you good for?"

Jared shrugged.

She straddled him. She took his wrists and pinned them above his head. She smiled down at him, a big, wicked smile. "I could tie you up."

"No," Jared said.

"Come on," she said. "I'm bored of making out."

Jared reached out and traced the fine web of lines on her inner thighs. She put her hand over his.

"Stop it," she said.

"Who did that?" he said.

"I did."

The high came in mellow waves, like zooming down a water-slide. Whee, he thought. He took her hand and put it on his ribs. "My mom dated this douche named David. He didn't like my grades, so he broke a couple of my ribs. Slowly. He got a boner when I started screaming."

Sarah flinched. "That's messed up."

After a bit she kissed him, then took her hand back and reached up for the j. She inhaled deep before she curled into his side.

"I feel numb," she said, "all the time, like I took sleeping pills and can't wake up. I just want to feel something."

"I don't want to hurt you," Jared said. "And I don't want to be hurt."

"What happened to him?"

"Mom nail-gunned his feet to the floor."

Sarah laughed. She turned her head and kissed his cheek. She put the j in his mouth. "I like your mom."

Jared inhaled and held his breath, a tickle in his throat, the bland smoke of Mrs. Brantford's wheelchair weed filling their blanket fort. The paper route was the only money he had coming in, but still he bought her bag of weed. Maybe he'd do a sell, just to get some food. His old customers were still loyal. The j burned down to Jared's fingers and he put it in the ashtray, let it smoke like incense. Sarah hummed along as the chorus came in.

"Have you ever stood under northern lights?" she said.

"Yeah."

"I like how they crackle. That's how you sound right now."

"Cool."

"I'm serious," she said.

"You're wasted. I'm wasted. We are was-ted."

"You hum, real loud, like an electric guitar being tuned, or power lines on a hot day. I hear you all the time. I know where you are."

Jared giggled and then Sarah giggled and they bumped their heads together.

"Wooooah," Sarah said. "You're glowing."

"Yeah?"

"I can see your bones. Look at your bones. You're an X-ray."

Jared looked down at himself but didn't see what she saw. Sarah made sounds like a lightsaber. He giggled.

"Vader," Sarah said. "Vader on the ceiling."

"Powder House Rules," Jared said.

Sarah straddled him, lifting her arm and showing him her new cuts, presenting them like Vanna. He wasn't sure how he was supposed to react, so he played it cool, nodding. She hadn't had them last night. She must have done them while he was asleep.

She used an X-acto knife on herself in front of him. She met his eye, as if daring him to say something. As long as she didn't cut him, he was fine with it. Well. Maybe not fine. Maybe weirded out. She got lost in the cutting and he became a piece of furniture, something she sat on.

"What are you?" he said. "Eleven? No hickies."

She blew a raspberry against his neck. "Come on."

"No."

"You let Dylan mark you."

"Ew. Way to perv up my life, Sarah."

"I wanna tie you up."

"No."

"Not with actual rope." She presented a black headband. "We'll pretend. Okay?"

"No. I told you why. Go *Fifty Shades* someone else."

She rested her chin on his collarbone. "I can pull a zipper down with my teeth."

Jared's breath hitched. He felt his sudden erection press against his jeans. "Yeah?"

Sarah reached over for the X-acto knife and cut into the cushion.

"Hey," Jared said.

She threaded the headband through and then lifted one of his wrists and then the other. "'As an apple tree among the trees of the wood, so is my beloved among young men. With great delight I sat in his shadow and his fruit was sweet to my taste.'"

"Is that poetry?"

She kissed him with lots of tongue. The headband was springy and he didn't like it, but she licked and nibbled her way down his throat, her hand on his crotch. She licked his rib. The erection sagged. He stared at the ceiling and Vader had lost his thought bubble. Powder House didn't rule. She kissed each of his ribs, light presses, her breath on his skin. She tongued his belly button.

"Ew," he said.

"'His speech is most sweet, and he is altogether desirable.'"

She unzipped his jeans with her teeth, holding his eyes with hers. He lifted his hips so she could pull his pants off. He sprang free, hello, and she brought his jeans down to his knees. Kissed, slow, up his thighs. He wanted the jeans off, he wanted them off. Her tongue, soft, warm and wet, her tongue, her teeth, the slippery perfection of her mouth. He sighed. She held his hips, her fingers, she, she, the tip of her tongue, the soft underside of his cock, his wrists.

The world is hard.

He laughed as his erection became painful, thumped like a hope-ful dog's tail, and then he moaned as she lowered her mouth. A sharp thread of pleasure made the world warm, made the sheets against his skin feel like silk, made his head go back, and he heard himself and it was embarrassing to sound like that but her mouth.

"I don't know, Sarah," he said. "I don't know."

She popped up, leaning on an elbow, and they panted. She leaned in to kiss him and he turned his head. She puckered and made kissy noises.

"It's all you, dumb-ass," she said.

"Get off me. Get. Goddamn it, Sarah. No."

"That's right, baby. Say my name."

He laughed and he was about to say something but lost it as her hands stroked, with exactly the right amount of pressure.

"God," he said. "Mmm, God."

"Goddess," she said.

"The great-uncles are threatening to drive down," she said.

"Yeah?"

"Mom never talks about them. We're supposed to tell people we're Spanish."

"Wow."

"I know, right? She says I'm mostly white. My dad's white. She's half-white. Gran lost her status when she married a white guy—"

"Your grandfather."

"He never liked me. Even before he went senile."

"He's okay."

"He sees a brown cunt like everyone else." She sat up.

Jared wasn't sure what to say.

"Dad works all the time. Mom works. A lot. She said she wasn't meant to be a mom. We're all supposed to pretend that we're okay, that we don't, secretly, hate ourselves."

"Mom thinks I'm weak. I don't know if she's coming back."

"She'll be back."

He didn't know if that was a good thing anymore.

"She's colonized," Sarah said. "She's unthinkingly accepted her oppression and it's fucked her up."

"Don't ever say that to her face. Seriously. It will not end well."

She bent over and kissed his cheek. "I'll be right back."

He put his arm under his head. The sun was going down. He reached over and lit a candle, which smelled like cookies, which made him hungry. He ate a stale cracker, searching through the food bag he'd gotten from the food bank for things that didn't require cooking. He washed it down with a juice box. Sarah came back in a flowered dress. She'd brought a can of vanilla frosting and some Sesame Street cake decorations. She told him to close his eyes. He could hear her getting undressed and getting on the mattress. She giggled.

"Ready," she said.

She was naked on the cushions with her legs open. Her crotch was frosted and she'd placed a Cookie Monster decoration over her clit. Jared collapsed in helpless laughter while she sang, "*C* Is for Cookie."

"I think I love you," Jared said.

She made a face. "You'd say anything to get laid."

22

RAGGED-ASS ROAD

Jared put his last twenty dollars on his pay-and-talk plan so he could still text people and then he emptied out his secret savings account to pay off hydro. The last tenant, Matt, had handed him rent but given Jared notice he was moving. He said he'd been ditched by his parents too, and he was sure it would all work out for Jared, but he was sick of living ghetto. Seeing the pity in his eyes was like getting an acid bath. Late May. Four months since his mom had talked to Jared and five weeks since she'd been home. If it wasn't for Sarah, he'd be at Nana's already.

Matt walked into the kitchen and handed Jared a plastic bag with groceries.

"I got a pot roast," Matt said.

Jared looked in the bag and saw a chunk of meat with some potatoes and carrots. "I have no idea what to do with this."

"Me neither," Matt said. "But I gotta go to work. Figure it out and we can have pot roast tonight."

Jared couldn't find a cookbook. He poked the roast. He couldn't remember ever eating one, much less having seen anyone cook one. His mom liked steaks, greasy fried steaks, and Jared could feel his stomach growling. He wouldn't mind something other than food bank pastries and macaroni, but his Internet was out and he was sure his mom didn't have any cookbooks. He dialed Sarah.

"Hey," he said. "Do you know how to cook a pot roast?"

"Yeah," she said. "Because I'm secretly a housewife from the fifties."

"Do you have a cookbook?"

"Gran!" Sarah shouted. "Do we have a cookbook?"

"Of course we have a cookbook!" Mrs. Jaks shouted in the background. "Why? Are you getting off your lazy ass?"

"Yup, we gots one. Just a sec. Okay. Got it. Thanks, Gran."

"What's it say?"

"Pot roast . . . pot roast . . . Here we go. Preheat oven. Sear the flesh of a traumatized cow that spent its entire life in a factory farm. Throw—"

"Wait. Sear? What's sear?"

"Would it kill you to put the milk back in the fridge?" Mrs. Jaks shouted.

"I'll bring it over. Gran's being a bourgeois goon this morning."

"I asked you to sweep! How does that make me bad?"

"Proletariat should stick together! Not keep each other oppressed in eternal serfdom."

"Babies have a right to live!"

"Pro*letariat*! Not pro-choice, Gran. Marx says—"

Click.

Interwebs, Jared thought. I miss you.

Jared thought Sarah was at the door, but it was Dylan. Jared hadn't really hung out with him since Rupert. Ebony had moved on, but

Dylan hadn't, and Jared was sick of listening to him grind on about her. Dylan was easy to avoid. They didn't have any classes together and they hung with different crowds. Since he was here, his team-mates were probably sick of the moping too.

"Hey," Dylan said, stepping inside.

"Hey."

"Come on. Road trip. Get your shit."

Jared cleared his throat. "I got stuff to do."

"So? We're here for the party, man."

They stood in the hallway. Jared sighed.

"What?" Dylan said. "I'll front you some money."

"I'm going to hang."

Dylan fidgeted. "So you scammed some money off me and that's it? Fuck off, sucker?"

"You drew on my face, asshole."

"It was a joke. Fuck, did I hurt your feelings? Are you gonna cry?"

"You sang country music all the way back from Rupert. You threw up on my floor and left without cleaning it up, and, last but certainly not least, you grind on about the girl you—"

"Don't blame me for your shithole life."

"I'm tired of you making yourself feel better by looking down on me. Go slum around with someone else."

"Whatever. Ebs was right. You're an ungrateful, whiny bitch."

"Wow. You go run right back to Ebs and tell her she was right."

"Fuck you, you fucking loser."

"I'll pay you back what I owe you."

"Keep your money. I wouldn't want you to go without baloney."

"Yeah," Jared said. "Must be nice having Mommy and Daddy

wipe your ass all the time. Must be nice having everyone else take the blame for your spoilt, fucked-up messes."

"You're one to talk, you fucking alky."

"Knock, knock," Sarah said. She stood near the door, hugging the cookbook to her chest. Her skirt was stiff blue with a dark blue poodle on the hem. Her sweater was tight and splattered with fake blood.

"Go fuck yourself and your weird-ass girlfriend," Dylan said, stomping past her out the door.

"Go to hell, you big fucking baby," Jared said.

They stood in the hallway listening to Dylan clomp down the front steps. His truck squealed out of the driveway.

"Okay," Sarah said.

"Don't start," Jared said.

"Hey, he's the asshole. I come bearing gifts."

Jared took the cookbook. She'd earmarked the pot roast recipe with a condom. "Sorry."

She kissed his cheek. "Come on. Let's bake the flesh of an intelligent animal that spent its life shackled in its own feces so we can have cheap meat."

"You should have your own cooking show."

"Play nice," she said.

They went into the kitchen and Sarah hopped up on the counter, swinging her legs. Jared couldn't concentrate on the words. He thought of other things he could have said, and wished he'd said them sooner. The dude was an epic dipshit.

"He likes you," Sarah said.

Jared ignored her.

"I think he's two Es away from pulling your zipper down with his teeth."

"God."

"I think Ebs was jeal—"

"Can you not be a perv right now? Please?"

"I have no idea how we ended up in bed."

"I was drunk. You were high. Shit happens."

"No, you don't understand. I'm not regretting it. I'm saying I don't believe in monogamy, but I don't fall in the sack with just anyone. And I certainly don't believe in gender the way you do, and you've made it clear that you find my ways 'pervy.'"

"What?"

"I'm normally attracted to people willing to push heteronormative boundaries."

Jared felt his eye twitching. "So you're gay?"

"There you go," Sarah said. "Thinking in Western binaries again."

"So you're not gay."

"It's like talking to a wall," Sarah said through gritted teeth. "Do you even listen to anything I say?"

"But what does that mean? For us?"

"It means you confuse the hell out of me. I'm frustrated."

"Well, that's a big ditto."

"You're so retro. How can I be with someone who still defines himself as strictly male?"

"So you like chicks? Or guys . . . or both? Is that, like, the trans one or the bi?"

Sarah stopped swinging her legs and coolly considered him. She hopped down. "You're so not getting laid tonight."

The house was quiet after she left. He felt his life stretching in front of him like a highway at night. If he just left. If he left the house, no one would miss him.

Well, that's enough moping, he told himself. Time to roast some cow.

Jared heard a truck door slam and went to poke his head out his door. Richie was leading a gang of shouting, high party buddies towards the house. Jared heard his mother laughing upstairs and then wet smacks of a couple having sex in the laundry room. The music cranked into a crushing jet engine rumble. He put on his noise-cancelling headphones, relieved and nervous.

He woke later to find his mother standing at the foot of his bed. She swayed. She shook like it was winter, her pupils so wide her brown eyes were black. He pushed the headphones off.

"Mom?"

She stared at him, saying nothing. He sat up. He pushed the sleeping bag off.

"I'm sorry," he said.

"Liar."

"I'm not lying."

"You aren't sorry," she said. "But you will be."

23

DOCTOR WHO MARATHON

"This one's pretty good too," Crashpad said, holding up a boxed set. "These brothers hunt monsters and they drive around the country in this Impala and the tall one has demon blood but he—"

"Crashpad, chill, okay?" Jared said. "I don't care. Put anything on." God, shut up.

"I've got all the *Doctor Who*s."

"Yeah, that sounds good."

"Yeah?"

"Yeah."

Jared could hear Crashpad's mom in the hallway, vacuuming. She'd given him the stink eye, but George was practically bouncing when he'd shown up on their doorstep. Crashpad flipped through the menu choices and the show started.

"You can stay the whole weekend," Crashpad said. "We can do marathons until our eyes pop out of our heads. I've got all Blu-ray."

"That sounds"—awful—"cool."

"Okay, okay, I'll go get snacks."

Crashpad paused the show then wandered out of the room. Jared checked his messages. Zippo. Crashpad's mom stood in the open doorway, watching him. Jared straightened. She stepped into the room.

"I know all the change in Georgie's piggy bank." Crashpad's mom made a V of her fingers, pointing to her eyes and then to Jared. She stepped back and wound the cord around the vacuum cleaner, rolling it away.

What did you say to that? On the one hand, it was hilarious. On the other, how craptastic was your life when all old ladies felt the need to threaten you with movie gangsterisms?

Somewhere around series three of *Doctor Who*, Jared began to shift in and out of sleep. Crashpad would laugh and reach down to nudge him, that was funny, right? Right? Haha. And then Jared would watch TV and start to drift again. TV calmed his brain. TV made the questions about his life lie down and be quiet. His mom wouldn't leave his room and she wouldn't talk. She'd stood and stared at him and he couldn't go back to sleep with her all spaced out and weird and stalker-y, so he packed some things and hitched here.

Banging, someone banging on the door, and Jared popped awake. Crashpad was curled around his pillow, solidly out.

"Go home! You're drunk!" Crashpad's mom shouted.

"Ebs and Te-quiiiiila," Dylan sang.

"I'm calling your mom!"

"Poison . . . blood . . . tequiiila . . ."

Jared went downstairs and shoved his feet in his runners. Pulled his hoodie over his head. Crashpad's mom smacked Dylan with a magazine and he giggled and held up an arm.

"I got this," Jared said.

She glared at him but stomped inside, slamming the door behind her.

"Hey," Jared said.

"You're—you're a shitty fren."

"Takes one to know one."

"You're shit. Tee. Shitty."

"You got to stop watching *Sesame Street*, man."

"You thin—you think you're funny. You are not. Funny."

Dylan weaved around the porch, at one point looking entirely the wrong way. Jared took him by the elbow and sat him on the front steps.

"You've got to stop laying your crap on me, man," Jared said. "I have enough crap of my own."

"I'm—I'm . . . You don't get to tell me . . . what to do. Shithead. You're the shithead. Shithead."

Down the street, the lights went on at Dylan's house. Jared stuck his hands up his sleeves as the porch lights went on, making him and Dylan squint. Jared wished Crashpad's mom would chill.

"Ebs is dating Bambam," Dylan said.

Jared tried to remember which of Dylan's friends was Bambam. He vaguely remembered a stocky white guy. "Isn't he your team-mate?"

"Yup."

Dylan swallowed loudly. Jared was afraid Dylan was going to cry. Dylan's dad stepped outside, dressed in baggy sweats and a windbreaker. He paused on their porch, cupped his hand and lit a cigarette. Jared and Dylan sat in silence, watching his dad smoke as he crossed the street, ambling towards them, orange under the street light and then shadowed in the rainy night, bobbing red dot marking his hand like a sniper sight.

"Dylan," his dad said. "Home time."

"I'm—I am talking to my fren here, Jared. He's my fren."

Dylan's dad sighed. "Jared'll be here in the morning."

"I love her, Dad. No one believes me. No one."

"Dylan. Bed. Now."

"Night," Jared said.

"Come over," Dylan said. "You're my fren and I wanna talk to you."

Spending the night listening to Dylan drunk-dial Ebs was not something he wanted to do. "Dude, go home. We'll talk in the morning, okay?"

"'Kay," Dylan said.

His dad helped Dylan to his feet and they staggered home. Jared turned around to go back inside and found George's mom at the door.

"That boy's spiralling," she said.

"We're all spiralling," Jared said.

"He picks on George."

"I won't let him."

She squinted suspiciously at him, but held the door open and waited until he was inside and then locked it behind them.

In the morning, George's mom got three winter spring salmon delivered to her front door in a blue tote. She struggled to lift the tote off the porch. Jared wanted to stay in the breakfast nook eating cereal, but the golden rule of couchsurfing was the more useful you were, the longer people tolerated you. He chugged his orange juice. He walked over and took the tote from her.

"Where do you want them?" Jared said.

"Out back," she said.

She cheerfully gathered her knives, some black garbage bags and a sharpening stone. He stopped to jam his feet in his runners and followed her to a plastic folding table near the bottom of the stairs.

"Fillets or steaks?" Jared said.

"Fillets," she said. "I'm going to barbecue them in the pit. We can have some for lunch and freeze the rest."

"'Kay," he said.

"Do you want an apron?"

"I'm good."

He picked up the stone and put the edge on the knives before he started. His dad had been an avid fisherman back in the day. They used to hang out on his dad's speedboat, zipping around all weekend, catching and gutting fish and eating and camping on the shore. The winter springs were as fresh as fish could be and not be swimming around. He rolled up his sleeves. The first was long and heavy. He took the fins off, then the head, and then reached in and dragged out the guts in a neat pull. He dumped them in the bucket George's mom set up beside him. She watched him nervously until he started filleting the firm flesh and then she went inside. A young crow landed in the budding apple tree, tilting its head to study the gut bucket. It cawed, and more crows arrived. They watched him silently, their feathers rustling in the morning breeze.

George's mom returned with a large pot. She took the fish fillets and put them in the pot. Jared started working on the second salmon.

She disappeared around the house and came back a few minutes later with a hose.

When he finished cutting up the fish, she put the rest of the fillets in the pot and then brought out a dull axe and started making kindling. Jared took the axe from her and worked on the blade until it had a decent edge while she went inside again. Jared made his way through the cedar blocks until he had a good armful of kindling, then he worked on splitting the firewood. His mom liked the taste of cottonwood, but George's mom had stacks of alder that looked like they'd come from the beach, weathered pale grey and denuded of bark. George wandered over, watching him chop.

"Morning," George said.

"Hey," Jared said.

"Need help?"

"Does your mom have a lighter? Dry paper?"

"On it." George trundled off.

George's mom stacked the wood in a cinder-block firepit, and then George greased the racks. George started the fire and his mom split the fish heads in half. She washed and then salted the fish pieces. They stood around the fire as the fish sizzled and his mom cleaned the gutting table.

"I'm brainless until my third coffee! Tongs," his mom said. "George, take the guts to the curb before the crows get at them and I'll grab some tongs. And oven mitts. And a clean bowl."

They went back into the house. Jared stretched, watching the fire.

"That's a lot of fish," someone said.

Jared looked around, trying to find the person who was talking.

"You can't eat all of that by yourselves."

Slowly, Jared raised his head and the crows were watching him.

"Have a heart," one of them said. "We're hungry."

Jared's breath came fast.

"We'd be happy with the guts," another of them said to him. "You don't even have to give us the bellies."

Jared stood, stunned frozen.

"Typical raven," one of the crows said to his pals. "Greedy and selfish."

"Human lover," another spat.

They shot into the air as one, an angry black cloud of wings and beaks and talons, dive-bombing his head before they sped off into the trees. Some of the fish were missing from the barbecue rack.

Jared pinched himself. It hurt. The fire crackled and a piece of alder snapped as it tumbled lower, sending sparks twirling upwards. Okay, he told himself. Definitely laying off the hooch and the weed for a few days.

24

KISS & MAKE UP

The school bus to town went momentarily quiet as they hit the sweet spot on Suicide Hill where the cellphone service became reliable.

Hey, Sarah had texted him yesterday.

Hey, Jared texted back.

U mad?

R u?

Missed u this weekend.

Family drama. Nothing 2 do wit u.

Whatz wit da radio silence then?

In the rez. No cell towers.

Ah. R u wit Crashpad?

On bus on way 2 skool.

George leaned over and nudged him. "We're going to Lakelse Lake this weekend. Wanna come?"

"Sure."

Wanna hang @ lunch?

Kk.

C u soon.

C u.

At lunch, he sat with George and Sarah, who got into a long, convoluted argument about who they thought were the best companions in *Doctor Who*.

"Rose is hot," Jared offered.

They both paused, exchanged a look and then ignored him. George's mom had made Jared a beef and cheese sandwich and had given him an apple juice box. She'd also included four Wagon Wheels. He gave two of them to Sarah. He didn't see George or Sarah for the rest of the day, but he met up with George at the bus stop after school. Someone honked, loud and continuously.

His mom sat in her truck. Jared said he had to go. His mom rolled down her window as he walked up. Jared stopped out of reach.

"Get in," she said.

He stopped in front of the truck, waiting, and she squinted at him, annoyed. He cracked open the door, listening to it squeal on its hinges. He left his seat belt off.

"I've never touched you," she said. "I don't deserve this."

Kids streamed home on the sidewalks. Buses. Lines of cars waiting for their turn at the four-way. Low clouds. Snow retreating on the mountains.

"What the fuck is wrong with you?" she said. "Talk to me, dumb-ass."

"Do you remember the shit you said? In my room?"

No answer.

They drove in silence all the way to the house. Jared got out and headed for his room, but she snagged his arm.

"Are you hungry?" she said.

Jared carefully pulled his arm away.

"Bacon and eggs," his mom said. "Take it leave it."

Richie came into the kitchen as his mom was scrambling eggs. He paused when he saw them, then turned around and went back out. Jared sat on the counter, eating bacon slices as his mom finished frying them. She slid the eggs onto his plate.

"Dad's got his disability again," Jared said. "They'd cut him off. I didn't want him homeless."

"He left us." His mom cracked her eggs into the pan, two sunny-side-ups.

"I know," Jared said.

She met his eye, furious but cold. "I hate him."

"He's kinda sad."

She took a deep breath, held it and then let it out slowly. "God."

"He is." The eggs were dry and overcooked. He ate them, waiting for his mom to ream him out.

"He's playing you," she said. "That's what he does."

Jared looked at his feet. "So you ditched me. For months. And we pretend that didn't just happen?"

She stared at him, silent.

"Okay," Jared said. "Denial it is."

"I would have never married Phil if I wasn't knocked up. And my family . . . my family . . ." She sighed. "You have no idea what I did to keep you."

"Glad you're over that."

"Are you still helping him?"

"No."

"Then why'd you pawn the TV?"

"You took off, but we still had bills."

She took another deep, slow breath. "I was pissed. You have no idea what it took not to strangle you."

"Yeah," Jared said. "That's love."

She side-eyed him. "That's the only thing that kept you from being mulch."

"What did you say to Destiny?" he said.

His mom's eyebrow went up. She shook her eggs out of the pan and onto her plate. She took her toast out of the toaster and broke one of the yolks, sopping it up and taking a bite over her plate.

Well, that explained Destiny's lack of messaging. Jared'd thought she was pissed at him 'cause he wouldn't fool around and she was, well, hurt? Offended? Embarrassed? Who knew? If his mom had had a talk with her, he'd probably never know.

They ate and Sarah popped in while his mom was doing dishes and Jared was drying them and putting them away. Sometime after school, she'd painted her face so she looked like a cat, and she was dressed in a tight black suit, a black rope dangling from her butt.

"Hey, Miss M," Sarah said.

"Sarah," his mom said.

"I invented a joke. Wanna hear it?"

Jared gave his head a little shake, but Sarah said, "What does a sarcastic cow say?"

His mom stopped washing dishes.

"Moo, bitch," Sarah said, slapping her leg, laughing at her own joke.

"Are you calling me a cow?" his mom said.

"Geez Louise," Sarah said. "I'm saying if cows could talk, and one of them was sarcastic, it would say, 'Moo, bitch.'"

"She's not calling you anything," Jared said.

His mom wiped her hands on his dishtowel. "I'm going to do some laundry."

"Need help?" Sarah said.

"No. I know how to do laundry."

"Okay," Sarah said. "Gran wants her cookbook back."

Jared dug it out of the drawer and handed it over to her. She pecked his cheek. "See you, Miss M!"

When Sarah was gone, his mom turned to him. "You'd better be using condoms."

"You make her nervous."

"That wasn't nervous. That was cracked."

"Her mom kicked her out like yours did. Give her a break, okay?"

"I was alone in Rupert. *Working* at the cannery. Making my own fucking rent and my own fucking bills. I wasn't mooching off my gran."

"Who's dying."

"Don't fuck someone because you feel sorry for them."

"I'm not. She's got issues. Who doesn't?"

His mom came up to him and pressed her forehead against his.

He wanted to say same goes for Richie, but that wasn't going to go anywhere productive. "Where were you?"

She gave him a fierce hug but didn't spill.

They had two new tenants by the next day. Dinner turned into a party, and when the selfie patrol brought out cameras, Jared went downstairs. He didn't feel like faking a good time, but he didn't want to be pixelly accused of moping.

His phone beeped. His mom had sent him a picture of himself. *Kill n die*, she'd captioned it.

25

HUNT WITH THE NOBLE ORCA

Jared was dreaming about killer whales. Orcas flying through the ocean. He wasn't sure if he was an orca too, because he was behind a pod, listening to them click and gurgle and chirp as they chased seals to the shore.

And then he suddenly wasn't in the water. He was on a fishing boat.

"Hello, young man," someone said.

He turned and saw the little old woman/monster who had tried to pick him up outside Prince Rupert. She sat at a table with a cup of tea and a plate of Peek Freans cookies, the fruit ones with the red jelly centre. Her dress fluttered in the sea breeze. She waved her hand and a chair appeared.

The orcas circled the boat, their dorsal fins slicing the water.

"Hi," Jared said.

"Please sit," the old lady said.

"What's with your face?"

"Oh, that's a little rude, don't you think?" she said.

"You kinda got some monster showing through."

"It's not a monster," she said. "It's magic."

An orca breached, hovering in the air for a long time, like it was in a movie that had been paused.

"I don't let it out," she said. "And it gets frustrated."

"Your monster gets frustrated."

"Yes. I'm in Prince George right now, visiting some family," Monster Gran said. "But I'd like to drive back so we can talk. How does that sound?"

"Can't we talk now?"

"It's a little rude to be inside your head. I barely know you. I'm assuming you're one of us, but you don't know it yet."

"One of who?"

"Do you want to talk to me? Do you want answers?"

Jared shrugged. "As long as your monster stays away from me."

"I don't ever let my magic loose," she said.

The seals barked on the rocks, humping themselves higher up the shore as the orcas continued circling, studying them.

"I need to visit a few people, my dear boy, and then I'll see you in a day or so."

"'Kay," Jared said, wanting to get this part of the dream over with.

She smiled, but the monster underneath her face snarled at him. "I'll see you soon, Jared."

"Later," Jared said.

He expected the dream to change, to shift or end, but it didn't. He got up and leaned on the railing, watching the orcas. He saw his own reflection in the water, shivering in the waves, and the orcas, luminous patches of white and shadowed black, swimming beneath the surface. He could taste the sea salt and smell the funky, dead fish air from the orcas' blowholes when they surfaced to spout.

"This is so creepy," Jared said.

"Do you mind?" one of the orcas said. "We're hunting here."

"I don't know if I'm going crazy or not."

"It's not all about you," the orca said. "I have mouths to feed, you know."

"Yeah," another one said. "We don't come and mess up your hunt."

"Wake up," a third one said.

"I had the weirdest dream," Jared said to George and Sarah at lunch.

"I'm going to stop you right there," Sarah said. "I'm not that kind of girlfriend. I don't listen quietly while you blather on about the hot actress you fantasy-banged."

"So you admit you're my girlfriend," Jared said.

"Um, duh," she said. "Until someone less politically vacant comes along."

George said, "Come on, guys. Let's just have a nice lunch."

Jared frowned. "Are you talking about Idle No More? The Native protest thing? I thought that was done."

Sarah and George gave him cool, lethal stares.

"I am this close to perpetrating some lateral violence on your ass," she said.

"Dude," George said. "That's cold."

"What?" Jared said. "What?"

26

SPIRAL

The main floor of his mom's house was clean, shiny clean like it hadn't been in years. Everything smelled like bleach and soap. Jared stopped in the front doorway and wondered if one of the new tenants was a neat freak.

"Hello!" Jared said.

His mom's favourite leather jacket was on a hook in the hallway. Her boots were beneath it. The kitchen sparkled.

"Mom?"

The stairs had been washed and the cleaner had left white water marks on the wood. He knocked and waited a few minutes before cracking her bedroom door open. She was sitting on her bed. The shade was off the lamp and she had Richie's shaving mirror in front of her face.

"Hey," Jared said. "It's just me."

She'd plucked her eyebrows into the thinnest of lines, and was concentrating on plucking hairs on her face that Jared couldn't even see.

"Mom? Where's Richie?"

She glanced at him. Jared sat on the edge of her bed.

"I'm busy," she said.

"Okay. What're you doing?"

"Building a fucking nuclear bomb," she said. "What does it look like I'm doing?"

"I think that's enough," Jared said. "I think if you pluck any more, you're going to start pulling your skin out."

"It's itchy," she said. "My hair is itchy."

"Maybe you need a Benadryl."

"I can feel things crawling in the roots."

"Mom, I don't think there's anything there. What're you on? What did you take?"

"It's all good," she said.

He reached to take the tweezers from her and she stabbed at his hand. He whipped his hand back and she went back to plucking, ignoring him as she focused on her face. The back of his hand had scratches where she'd gotten him. Tiny, parallel lines of blood.

Jared sat with her until he couldn't watch anymore, and then he went out, walked, with no destination in mind. He stopped at a bench and listened to the birds, to the traffic, to the blood coursing through his body and his own heartbeat, loud in his ears.

27

WHEN THE VOICE IN YOUR HEAD IS A MONSTER

Jared was conjugating verbs in French class when he was hit by a sudden need for pizza. *We should have pizza for supper*, his inner voice said. *Let's go to the Pizzarama.*

He didn't want to bump into his mom's old friend from high school, though. He didn't want to talk to her about his mom. He didn't want to let his mind go there. He wanted to get through grade ten and then go stay with Nana.

Go on. Treat yourself.

Which was a weird thing to think. He didn't have any money. He'd tanked his savings paying off their hydro. He didn't want to ask Mrs. Brantford to front him the pot with a promise to pay her back. He didn't think that was going to fly, so he was trying to figure out who he could borrow money off, or what he could sell, or what job he could get, and pizza was the last thing he wanted.

Trust the universe. Trust that everything is going to work out.

He left school and his feet took him to the Pizzarama like they were walking on their own. Jared wanted to go home, but he didn't. He saw the burgundy Cadillac before he saw the little old Native lady with the monster hiding beneath her skin. She perched on a stool, smiling and giving him a wave through the front window like dream communication was normal and what they were doing wasn't insane.

"Hello, Jared," she said. "What a pleasant surprise."

The monster underneath her skin snarled.

"Hey," Jared said.

"Did I tell you my name the last time we met? I don't think I did. How forgetful I'm getting. I'm known as Mrs. Georgina Smith," she said. "But my old name is Jwasins."

Jared didn't want to sit at her table, but he did. He slid onto the stool feeling stoned, even though he wasn't.

"I don't normally share dreams with humans," she said. "You must be very special."

"If you aren't human," Jared said, "what are you?"

"Are you hungry? I bought a half-pepperoni and half-Hawaiian pizza. I'm not a fan of soda pop—so many preservatives and additives—but I thought you might like a root beer. Please, help yourself."

Jared studied the pizza and root beer, wondering if it had any "additives."

Her smile twitched. "I'm not a witch, if that's what you're thinking. I don't generally go around poisoning people."

Jared blushed. "Are you reading my mind?"

"Oh, heavens, no. It's all over your face. But you do get very noisy when you're upset or excited. I heard you for miles before I saw you."

"So you heard my thoughts."

"Can you read mine?"

"No."

"But you can see something under my skin."

The thing vibrated, shaking so fast it blurred.

She reached over and touched his hand. "I would like to tell you a story, dear. Would that be all right?"

Jared shrugged.

"Once upon a time," she said, "there was a shaman with two sons. The oldest son wanted to be a shaman in the worst way. To become a shaman, you must be able to communicate with the dead. The oldest son went into the forest and cleansed himself. He ate no food and only drank tea made from the bark of devil's club. He prayed and he pleaded for a spirit guide. He hit himself with spikes of devil's club and he poisoned himself until he puked blood. But he was alone in the forest. No spirits came to him.

"His younger brother wanted nothing to do with magic or magical creatures. He was in love with a woman who wanted high status and a strong warrior for a husband. His village was at war and he wanted to fight. He didn't want his father's lonely life. His father was regarded with suspicion, resentment and hatred by everyone, even his own clan, who all blamed the shaman when someone fell sick. His son saw the fasting, and the time alone in the wilderness, and the lack of friends and decided that being a shaman wasn't for him. But the spirits flocked to him like mosquitoes, torturing him until he gave in and became a powerful, powerful shaman."

Jared picked at a slice of pepperoni. "I didn't want to come here."

"Your curiosity brought you here," she said. "Not me. I don't use my magic. Ever."

"I stopped believing in magic around the same time I stopped believing in Santa."

"That fat bastard. God, he's annoying."

Wow. "You know . . . Santa?"

"Never accept any of his dinner invitations. He's a whiny perfectionist with a Jesus complex and a barely closeted Glogg addiction."

"Um, okay."

She sighed. "I'm sorry. I find him disagreeable. But that's neither here nor there. We're here to answer your questions."

Jared wished his life wasn't so weird. He wished he didn't attract so many weirdos. But who could be afraid of someone who still believed in Santa?

"So do you see spirits, my dear?" she said.

"No," Jared said.

"Never? Not once? Not even a ghostly brush or a spooky feeling?"

"Uh, no. 'Cause they aren't real."

"Well, that's . . . reassuring."

"What happened to him?"

"Who, dear?"

"The older son. The guy who wanted to be a shaman."

"He fasted until he starved to death."

"Whoa. That's grim."

"Then he haunted his brother until they had a magical battle that sent him to another universe and weakened his brother enough that a rival shaman managed to kill him with a poison that made him shit out his guts."

"Yeah. Okay. Sorry I asked."

"Well, I have a long drive ahead of me. Here's my phone number. Call me if you ever see a ghost. Remember, I can help you. I can be your guide."

"You're leaving?"

She pushed herself to her feet, taking a long time to straighten up. "I have a large, close family and they're always getting in trouble.

Children to yell at. Grandchildren to get out of messes. Goodbye, dear. It was lovely meeting you."

"Later."

He watched her hobble out to her car and slowly lower herself inside. She honked her horn, waving at him, and then backed out of her parking space without looking behind her. A blue SUV swerved to avoid her Caddy.

Jared felt dizzy, like he'd been under water, holding his breath too long. His heart sped up and his hands went clammy. *How did I know she'd be here? Did we agree to meet?*

You wanted pizza, his inner voice said. *You happened to bump into each other.*

He didn't, though. He didn't want to go to the Pizzarama. The idea of going to the Pizzarama got stuck in his head and he couldn't shake it.

You were going to see one of your friends and you saw her. You dropped in to chat.

I didn't, Jared thought. *That's not the way it happened.*

You're tired and you're not thinking clearly. Let's go home and have a nice rest. We're going to remember this as one of those strange coincidences. Life? Isn't it funny? You must be hungry. You should eat.

Jared studied the pizza. He stood, fighting the urge to sit back down. Pepperoni was his favourite kind of pizza, but he didn't want this pizza. He expected his inner voice to have an opinion about it, but after a few minutes he could move his feet. He left the untouched pizza on the table. As soon as he was out the door, he remembered he'd left his homework in his locker.

His thoughts tangled, but what was clear was that she had been in his dream and then had come to him to find out if he saw ghosts.

But what that meant was bizarre and unsettling. He wanted to forget what had happened. A little fading voice in his head wanted him to forget too, but another part of him watched everything with a cold eye.

You played her just right, it said.

28

ALWAYS THE BRIDESMAID

Jared was hungry when he got home, and weirded out. He was hoping for a text from Sarah, but the message on his Facebook was from Nana Sophia.

Finally ending this wretched honeymoon, Nana messaged him. *London for a few days and then home. When are you out of school?*

She'd posted a lot of pictures of her and her old dude eating at swanky restaurants—lots of food porn. Her new Facebook profile pic was a plate of squiggly food stacked like a bonfire before it was lit. Arty swirls of sauce filled in the white plate.

June-ish, Jared messaged back. *Depending on when my finals are.*

Wonderful! I'm counting the days. I'll have a room ready for you. What is your preferred colour palette?

Oh, good gravy, Jared thought. *Nana, don't go overboard, okay?*

Simple, masculine colours, she texted. *Got it.*

Love you.

Love you more.

No texts from his mother. No phone calls. He hadn't gone upstairs in days. He'd break the news to her after he was on the plane. If she noticed he was gone. He'd been through this with his dad already. Her time apart from him had most likely been filled with new and exciting drug experiences. She hadn't been mad at him. She'd forgotten he existed. Jared didn't think he was that high on her give-a-fuck list anymore. He was running a distant second to whatever she was using, so far back it was like they weren't even running in the same race.

The next morning, Jared watched Mr. Jaks wander down the street in his pyjamas. He hesitated at the sidewalk, surprised to see the old guy back. He really wanted a quiet day. But Mr. Jaks's pyjamas hung off him, and his face was hollow, shadowed. His feet were bare and the ground was slick with rain. Jared carefully approached.

"Dobrý den," Jared said, which was the limit of his Czech, other than *ahoj*.

"Dobrý den," Mr. Jaks responded.

"Mrs. Jaks?" Jared said.

Mr. Jaks nodded and they walked together. Mr. Jaks seemed puzzled and nervous, tugging at the bottom of his nightshirt, scanning the streets, the mountains, like everything was new and threatening.

As they went up the Jakses' walkway, Sarah waited on the porch, hugging herself. "Hey, Děda."

Mr. Jaks frowned at Sarah. He said a few things in Czech and she rolled her eyes.

"Everyone's a critic," she said.

"Hey," Jared said.

"Hadih."

Mrs. Jaks was asleep on the couch, curled under a quilt. Jared took Mr. Jaks to their bathroom and gave him a quick shave. He gave

Mr. Jaks's dentures a rinse and handed them to him. Then they went to the bedroom and Jared helped him into a diaper and then his clothes.

Sarah had coffee on, so Jared scrambled eggs and fried sausages. He spooned sugar into Mr. Jaks's coffee and then took a cup himself. The table was covered with two plastic trays of wilting seedlings. They ate quietly.

Later, Jared put a rain jacket on Mr. Jaks and then his gardening boots. They went out back and turned the soil over in the raised beds. Mr. Jaks planted haphazardly, but he was calmer outside. After gardening, they went into the garage and Mr. Jaks picked things up and carried them around, humming. Jared started up the lawn mower and Mr. Jaks trimmed the front yard before getting tired and sitting on the steps. Jared put the mower away and they went to wash up. Mrs. Jaks was still a lump. Jared turned the TV to the news. Mr. Jaks fell asleep in the recliner.

Sarah came and tucked herself into his side. "Blurg. Mainstream media."

"Want the remote?"

"Nah."

He put his arm around her shoulders. She sighed.

"Gran's going to Van for another round next week. Gramps is going back into respite and I'm going to be here alone," Sarah said. "I haven't slept in days."

"You could sleep now."

"I can't nap."

"I'll sing you some Nickelback."

She slugged his shoulder and he laughed. He changed to the Weather Channel. After a while her breathing steadied and then she started snoring. The rain hit the window as the wind picked up. He felt his eyes going heavy, but he fought sleep. He wanted to stay here, in the quiet moment, when everything was calm and everyone was safe.

Zombie apocalypse of hangovers, his mom texted him. *Happening right now @ a bathroom near u.*

He didn't want to care about her anymore. He wanted to keep a minimum safe distance.

Did I hurt u? she texted.

He got up and put the cellphone on the coffee table. He made his way to the bathroom without turning on any of the lights. He heard Mrs. Jaks talking Mr. Jaks back into bed. Jared splashed his face and went back to the couch. Sarah was still passed out cold. He didn't want to pick up the phone.

Cold turkeyin it over here wit no eyebrows. Im gonna paint on some sarcasm lines so u no when I dont mean shit.

Txt ur mom, Richie texted him. *NOW.*

Jared shut off the phone. He wanted to stay with Sarah, but watching Mr. and Mrs. Jaks slowly dying was brutal. He wanted to believe his mom was sorry, but his dad was always sorry and he still kept doing crap he had to say sorry for. He didn't want to be a sucker, but he didn't want to be alone. Everything ached and all the choices felt wrong.

My mom used 2 clean like this. I sobered up n thot she was here. I was possessed by Mom. So weird, Jared's mom had texted him.

My brotherʒ a tweaker, Richie had texted him at the same time. *He shot me 4 my $.*

Jared sat at the kitchen table and wished he had a smoke as he scrolled down and down and down, trying to find an end to the texts.

Mom went 2 St. Mike's residential school until she got TB. They sent her 2 a sanatorium. None of the native kids there got penicillin just the staff. They put her in a body cast n starved her. Rows of kids coughing n choking in a dorm. Each morning they wheeled her . . .

Shithead came 2 me in the hospital n stole my sneakers. Wallet. Juice box. Wearing my sneakers tellin me Im paranoid. Fuckin h8d him so hard. U think ur mom҂ bad shes not.

. . . in2 a room in the basement n shone a purple light on her chest. Kids disappeared. She҂ only alive cause they lost funding n had 2 shut down. She married Dad cause he wanted a punching bag. He left cause she stepped out on him but I dont blame her . . .

My family thinks I called the cops on him. I didnt. He was hidin from cops. Some1 threw him out a hotel window.

. . . Met the cunt n he tried 2 smack me quiet. After he left Mom lost it tho. If I sniffled she had the bleach out. Cleaned n baked my dishes after I 8. I thot Dettol was wat every1 bathed in.

Dont leave it this way.

Mom went full God happy. Praying n kneeling n virtue n cleaning. My sis left the 2nd she turned 16. Me n Mom alone. Nothing ever good enuff. Nothing ever rite. She decided I was a whore n nothing was gonna change her mind.

Hey, Nana, Jared texted. *Mom has a sis?*

Never wanted 2 do that 2 u Jelly Bean. Never wanted 2 make u feel u had 2 run from me.

You're up early, Cutie. Morning! Here's a link to an article re: your aunt, Mavis Moody. Be forewarned, she's a writer. She published an essay

*in a magazine about searching the Downtown Eastside of Vancouver for
your mother. Words were spoken. I wondered if you knew about her. She's
one of your mother's triggers, so I hesitated to bring her up.*

*U fuckin useless shit 4 brains I no ur reading this I can see the check-
marks. Shez barely holdin her shit 2gether the least u can do is fuckin
say hey.*

Luv u, Jelly Bean. Luv u, luv u, luv u.

"Anything that turns me into my mom is big-*E* Evil," Jared's mom
said. "From now on, nothing but good old-fashioned booze and coke
for this broad."

She looked weird without her eyebrows, like she was massively
surprised. She'd shaped her forehead into a perfect square. It didn't
look like she had any nose hair left either. They lay together in her
bed. She shook even though she was under a mountain of blankets.

"Stop staring at my forehead."

"Sorry."

"Light me up."

Jared shook a cigarette out of the pack on the nightstand and
lit a menthol for her. The bed was pockmarked with tiny black cra-
ters. Her hands shook and she sucked in half the cigarette in one long
breath. She exhaled slowly. The ash fell in the bed. They were going
to have to ditch the mattress when she was done. Her sweat smelled
metallic. She'd started a pee bucket beside the bed that was a mix of
piss and puke. Her teeth clenched and she squinted, convulsing for a
few seconds before biting back a moan.

"Where's Richie?" Jared said.

"Booze run."

"Good. Good."

Richie came back and opened a bottle of whiskey for her. She chugged from the bottle and made a face.

"It's like masturbating after you've had your first orgasm," she said. "You're ruined for it. You know you can do better."

"I can take a hint," Richie said, unbuttoning his shirt.

"That wasn't a come-on, shithead. That was a metaphor."

"Dudes, I'm right here."

"You just said I'm better than meth. You can't take shit like that back."

"Richie, I'm this close to puking on you."

"Whatever turns your crank, baby."

"I'm going to give you guys some privacy," Jared said.

His mom caught his arm. "Are you staying here tonight?"

"Not in this room."

She managed a weak smile. "Love you, Jared. You know that, right?"

"Love you too, Mom."

"Now get out," Richie said. "So we can bang."

29

FIREFLY

"The uncles. The uncles are here," Sarah said, her phone call waking him from a dead sleep.

"Now?" Jared said. He was tempted to put the phone down and roll back into bed.

"In Terrace. At Denny's. Getting Grand Slams."

"Oh," Jared said. She sounded like she was in the middle of a hiccup attack. "Okay."

"Can you . . . come over?"

Jared sighed. "Do you have coffee on?"

"Yeah."

"Okay."

"I owe you," Sarah said.

"Just don't bogart the coffee."

He threw on some jeans and a T-shirt. He tasted his mouth, then took the time to brush his teeth. He'd be amazed if he passed grade ten. But Sarah sounded shaky, and maybe once the uncles came they could just go to school without further drama.

The morning was patched with fog that blurred some streets but not others, like random splats of Cool Whip. Light framed the mountains as the sun brightened the sky blue. The neighbourhood was silent in the early morning, aside from the guy at the end of the street who played non-stop Slayer in his garage. Rumour had it he was not signing his divorce papers and the thirty days was almost up. Everyone wanted someone else to go have a talk with him, make sure he wasn't planning on taking a car nap with the engine running, but no one really wanted to get involved. He had a lot of guns.

Mrs. Jaks was covering the kitchen table in black plastic garbage bags. Sarah gripped her coffee mug, stripped down to a pair of jeans and a plaid shirt, her hair tamed into a simple ponytail. Mrs. Jaks glanced up when he came in.

"The knives are in the block," she said to him.

"I don't think I can do this," Sarah said.

Mrs. Jaks paused, not sneering, but close.

"I never. Chopped. Up. I never . . ."

"You wanted to decolonize your diet," Jared said. "This is as decolonized as you get."

He went to the knife block, took the sharpening stone out of the drawer and started putting an edge on Mrs. Jaks's knives. Mr. Jaks used to be a fiend about proper maintenance. And moose. Mrs. Jaks used to joke he'd married her so he could always have fresh moose meat. Now Mr. Jaks watched TV, oblivious.

"Is it?" Sarah said.

"He lived free," Jared said. "He died free. He was owned by no one."

"It's a moose," Mrs. Jaks said.

"A wild moose living free," Jared said.

Mrs. Jaks rolled her eyes. She wanted her vacuum sealer from the top shelf. Jared took the chair from her and got it down. She wanted her smoker from the basement. Jared let her carry the wood chips, but not the machine. He put it outside on the deck and unrolled the extension cord.

"I'm not helpless," she said.

"You're supposed to limit your activity."

"Ah," she said in disgust. "Good work is medicine."

"Light activity."

"Hadih," Sarah murmured into her coffee. "Hadih, hadih."

"You don't tell me what to do," Mrs. Jaks said.

"Your doctor is telling you what to do," Jared said. "I'm reminding you if you overdo it, you're going to end up in Emergency."

"Ah."

Mrs. Jaks ran out of steam then and went to sit in the recliner, where she soon fell asleep. Sarah paced. When he came close, she grabbed his hand.

"No one in my family likes me," Sarah whispered. "I'm too white. I'm not white enough. I'm too weird."

"If they don't like you," Jared said, "they can go fuck themselves."

She blinked, rapidly. Then she curled into him, arms around his waist, her breath steadying on his neck. "We have to wake Gran for her pills."

"Let her sleep a little longer."

"I love it when you're butch." She kissed him.

He laughed into her mouth as her tongue made swirlies. She tasted like morning breath and coffee. She sucked his lower lip. Nibbled. Her hands travelled.

"Hey," he said.

"She's asleep."

"Noisy things," Mrs. Jaks said. "Who can sleep through your noise?"

"Sorry," Jared said.

"You gotta take your pills, Gran."

"Ah."

Sunlight sparkled through the lace curtains. Mrs. Jaks struggled to get out of the recliner. Jared was helping her up when they heard a diesel engine rumble down the street and cut off in the driveway. Sarah went to the front window. Heavy doors creaked open and slammed shut, echoing through the living room. Mrs. Jaks finally made it to standing.

Sarah opened the front door. In walked a tall, chubby Native guy with a shiny black pompadour, mutton chops, oversized sunglasses and a fringed buckskin jacket with sequins spelling out *Heartbreak Hotel* across the front. Native Elvis caught her up in a bear hug. Sarah squeaked and then laughed as he spun her around.

"Hadih!" she said.

"Well, hadih to you, little lady. Laura. You're so skinny! Stop dieting, you crazy thing. You're old and married and no one cares if you still fit your high school dresses."

"Ah, shut up, Doug. You aren't funny."

"Still telling me what to do," Doug said mournfully. "Bossy old woman."

"Knock, knock," another Native guy said as he poked his head in the door, this one with a similar large nose but in a cowboy hat.

Mr. Jaks stared at his wife's brothers, dazed. "Laura?"

Mrs. Jaks opened her arms and started crying, silently. Both guys walked over to her, bent down and patted her back. Sarah hugged herself. The Native Elvis, Doug, broke away from the big hug first.

"Can you give me a hand, kids? The moose ain't going to unload itself."

"Sure," Jared said.

Two Native women in jeans and work jackets were lifting the tarp off a skinned moose in the back of the crew cab truck. It was big. The neighbours' curtains started to flick.

"The missus and her sister," Native Elvis said. "Carrie! Dawn! This is Sarah!"

"Sarah?" the first woman said. "My, my, my. How pretty you are!"

"Get your lazy ass over here and help us, Doug," the second woman said.

"Guess which one I married," Doug said.

After everyone was asleep that night, Sarah knocked on his door. When he answered, she reached for his sweatshirt and pulled it over his head. She kissed him.

"Hi," Jared said.

"Hadih," Sarah said. "I brought magic mushrooms. Let's fly."

"Seriously? That shit's awful."

"It's way better than acid. It's natural."

"No, thanks. I'll stick to booze and weed."

She undid his belt. He stopped her from pulling down his pants.

"Are your uncles going to come over and shoot me?"

"Nah," Sarah said. "They like the way you handle your knife. 'He's a keeper,' they said. 'He knows his way around a moose carcass.'"

"They said that, huh?"

"I'm paraphrasing."

"You're what?"

"Shut up, Jared."

———

Sarah lay on top of him, her ear pressed against his chest. They caught their breath. Her weight was warm. She ran her fingers along his scalp stubble.

"Can I shave your head?"

He laughed. "Whatever cranks your motor."

She propped her chin up with her hands. "The uncles want us to come live with them."

Jared swallowed. "Yeah?"

"Would you visit us?"

"Sure."

"Mom's not going to let me go," Sarah said. "She hates the rez."

"I don't think she gets a vote."

"You've got fireflies around you," Sarah said.

"No, I don't."

"Whoa. They're big. Lots of them. A swarm."

"Cool."

"They're in a pattern. They're flying together."

"Yeah? I'm going to grab a beer." He carefully rolled her off him and she sprawled on her back, limp, eyes tracking invisible things on the ceiling.

"I like fireflies," Sarah said.

"I've never seen any," Jared said. He was down to a couple of beers.

"We lived too far north for real ones. I used to see them when I was falling asleep. Mom sent me to a shrink. But he said it was just a . . . just a . . . wow. They're making a river. A glowing river. They're travelling through time."

"Time, huh?"

"Time and space. They're going to bring us to the door."

"Wanna beer?"

"Shh. They're singing. I want to hear what they're singing."

Jared took a tube of Polysporin and covered the fresh cuts on her arm in a layer of ointment. One of them was deep and might need butterfly stitches. He lay beside her. Darth Vader was gone. A couple of ribbons of dusty duct tape marked the spot on the ceiling he used to occupy. Jared wondered how he'd missed Darth Vader vanishing. Assholes, he thought.

"Mobius," she said. "The fireflies say the fractal patterns are the clue. There is no end. Time eats itself."

"Who's Mobius?"

"The shape of the snake."

"Okay." He slipped his arm under her head. He took a tug of his beer. She sighed, snuggling into him.

"You should see this," she said.

"No, thanks. I have nasty trips," Jared said. "And I have enough shit in my life."

"I want you here. With me."

"I'm right here."

"I want you to see what I see." She pressed her palm to his forehead.

"Uh, Sarah?" Jared took her hand off and held it away from his head. She yanked back, but he held on. One of her cuts had opened up and dripped blood on his face. "Cool it, okay? You're getting intense again. Chill."

"Give me the knife."

"Not while you're wasted. No cutting." He wiped her blood off his face, tasting salt. His hand came away red.

"No cutting," Sarah agreed.

Jared let her go. She traced his face with her fingertip.

"Blood," she said.

"Your blood."

"You're mine. Now and forever."

"Awesome," Jared said. He wished people could make undying declarations of love and loyalty to him when they weren't half-cut or stoned out of their gourds. Or sorry.

"Fireflies dancing like auroras, rivers of light," Sarah said.

"Cool," Jared said.

"See what I see," Sarah said.

She covered his eyes with her hands and he was about to say something, about to make a smartass comment, but she took her hands away and the ceiling was gone. The sky above them was splattered with stars as bright as light bulbs, and in the high centre a swarm of fireflies flew in a figure eight. They buzzed, but not like bees, repeating a word Jared didn't know. The land beneath, the land they were lying on, was not his basement, but a wasteland with boulders and hard-packed mud, cracked dry. Dust swirled in small tornadoes of hot wind. The darkness was lit by the stars and the fireflies.

"Holy crap," Jared said.

He got up on his elbows. Sweat popped out all over his body in the dry desert heat. The land stretched out endless in all directions, warm as an oven. Something flickered in the corners of his eyes. He turned his head. A dark figure ducked behind one of the boulders.

"Can you hear them?" Sarah said. "I've heard this song before."

"I'm asleep," Jared said. "I'm dreaming."

His chest burned. He felt light-headed. He couldn't catch his breath. Sarah wheezed. He took great gulps of breath, but his head throbbed like he'd been under water too long.

"Wake up," Jared told himself.

He heard something clack like dice and turned to see a man squatting behind them. A naked man with his head cocked at a weird angle. He studied them, his forehead deeply sloped, skin smooth and stretched over his bony body, mouth falling open, teeth sharpened to points. He drooled. His necklace of finger bones clacked as he moved.

"God," Jared said.

"Singing."

The man crept along the ground like an ape, bony knuckles supporting his wide-chested body. He hissed.

"Wake up," Jared said, closing his eyes. "Wake up, wake up."

The fireflies sank until the swarm was above their heads, a hum like an amplifier waiting for the electric guitar to kick in. Low. Sarah sat, and then stood, lifting her arms. Blood streamed down her skin. The man darted forward and licked it. The firefly swarm sank lower. Shadows moved in the distance, more men like the man crouching below Sarah. More hissing.

"Get away," Jared said. "Get!"

The man circled, trying to approach Jared from behind. When the fireflies touched Sarah's hand, she started to shred, her hand going wispy like she was made of smoke.

"No!" Jared shouted.

The men with pointed teeth galloped towards them, grunting. Sarah drifted upwards into the swarm. Jared willed himself awake, willed Sarah awake, wanted them home, now.

30

WELCOME TO THE JUNGLE

Jared's mom still looked like death warmed over. Richie was wherever Richie went. She wasn't in the mood for company, so he parked himself on the couch. Turned on the TV. Sarah was busy with the uncles, who were going to take Mr. Jaks to Fort Fraser tomorrow. Mrs. Jaks was going to Vancouver with her sister-in-law, Dawn.

Jared was avoiding the basement.

Because. Because. Because of the wonderful things he does, his inner voice said.

I'm sane, he told himself. I had a bad trip and that makes your thinking—

You didn't do any mushrooms, his inner voice reminded him. *Only Sarah did.*

He clicked until he found the Weather Network. Nice, safe, boring Weather Channel. Light rain for Paris. Overcast in Amsterdam.

He could sleep on the couch here tonight. His mom and Richie weren't that loud. The tenants would probably be home soon and he could hang with them.

A hand came through the floor.

It's not real, Jared told himself. It's in my head.

The necklace of finger bones clacked as the man with the severely slanted forehead and pointed teeth pulled himself up from the basement, eyes boggling in horror as he stared around the living room.

Look at that, Jared thought. Who in their right mind films tornadoes from their porch? Get in the basement, dummy.

The ape man leaned on his knuckles, sniffing the air. His head swung back and forth. He bent down and sniffed the floor. Jared lifted his feet onto the couch. There goes the neighbour's house. Off to Kansas.

The guy filming was saying, "Whoa! Whoa, do you see this? Are you seeing this?"

The ape man carefully knuckled closer and closer to Jared, pausing at the couch, sniffing his way up. He hissed, showing all his teeth. If he was real, Jared thought, you'd be able to smell his breath, like a dog that had been eating rotten moose meat from a conked-out freezer.

Other hands scrabbled through the floor, their nails clicking on the linoleum.

I'm here, Jared thought. Alone in the living room. I'm watching TV. Nothing else is real. I know the difference between real and not, and this isn't real.

You have to calm down, his inner voice told him. *You're being too loud. Being this loud is dangerous when you don't know what you're doing.*

The ape man with the necklace swiped, but his hand went through Jared.

Because he's not real, Jared thought. None of this is real.

The hissing got louder as the other men filled the living room, blocking his view of the TV. You couldn't tell them to get lost because they weren't there.

They'd kissed, he and Sarah, and maybe she had mushrooms in her mouth when they kissed. They'd shared a beer. Sarah had eaten a lot of magic mushrooms and then bled in his face. That's all this was. They were figments of 'shrooms, a shared delusion. They were not real. He was having a 'shroom flashback. He'd altered his brain chemistry so his brain saw crap that wasn't there. It would wear off.

He heard them, hooting, one of them wailing like it was frightened, while the others gathered around him, waiting. Something banged the living room picture window and Jared jumped along with the ape men. He got to the window in time to see a raccoon or a cat, something dark, small and quick, skittering into the bushes. The ape men went silent. They drew close together and climbed carefully back through the floor.

When your scary hallucinations are scared, Jared thought, that's not a good sign at all.

"Jared," someone whispered. "Your mom's hurt."

Jared snapped awake. The basement was dark. Squares of orange light from the street lit the corner of the room where the ape men were huddled together, the window bars striping their skin with shadows. God, no more weirdness, he thought. Please. I need to wake up from this.

"She's hurt," the voice said again.

He couldn't tell where it was coming from or who was speaking to him—man or woman, young or old. He closed his eyes but held his breath, waiting. Even if his mom didn't want company, even if she was wrecked, even if she thought he was a big, whiny baby, he wanted to go upstairs and check on her. He wanted to reach into the nightstand and take out his gun. He wanted to move, but every instinct told him to be very, very still.

When he couldn't hold his breath anymore, he inhaled slowly, quietly, straining to hear. He was aware of his sleeping bag, of the chill from the concrete at his back, of the ape men shifting, lifting their heads to look around, but also being quiet.

A dog barked and Jared would have known that bark anywhere. Baby gave a joyful yelp, the kind she gave when she was tearing after a ball. Jared saw a shadow, and then her squashed-in face pressing through the bars of the basement window, her bark booming through the glass. Jared got off the bed and went to stand under her. Baby took off, and after a few minutes he could hear her pawing at the door.

Jared put his hand on the banister but stayed at the bottom of the steps, listening to her whine. Because that couldn't be Baby. He'd held her body. He'd buried her himself. She had spent the winter under the ground. But here she was, pawing and barking at the door, wanting him to let her in.

He knew he was awake. And he wanted, more than anything, to go up the stairs and see her looking up at him, tail wagging so hard her butt wiggled. But it wasn't Baby. It wasn't. He picked up his cellphone.

Mom? U ok?

Baby's squeaky squirrel was still in his sock drawer. He sat on the bed and held it. The ape men watched the door, and then their heads swivelled like sunflowers following the sun. Baby reappeared at the window. She barked. She ran back and forth between the two windows that looked into his room.

She was here, and he never thought he'd see her again, never thought he'd hear her bark or watch her crazy, crazy head shake.

Seeing her caused a spreading pain in his chest, like when a limb warmed up after it had gone numb. And as much as she wanted him to open the door, he wouldn't move.

When light brightened the sky pearl-grey and the street lights clicked off, Baby stopped barking. Jared stayed where he was until the sun rose and the light flooded through his room.

He opened the door slowly and stepped outside. The morning was chilly, but the sky promised a warm spring day. The ground was muddy around the house and Jared's footsteps were clear behind him. Baby's paw prints were obscured by smaller, clawed paw prints, patterning the mud around the basement windows like a dirty carpet.

Jared made a pot of coffee and brought his mother a mug. He hesitated before he opened her bedroom door. She leaned into her dresser mirror, giving herself bangs with small scissors. She fluffed the hair over her forehead. The bangs were long and covered her lack of eyebrows.

"Whaddya think?" she said.

Her hair was greasy, but what worried him was her painful scrawniness. Her collarbones jutted out and he could see the tendons and muscles moving under her skin. Her face had a zombie-yellow tinge with a rotting pimple high on her cheekbone.

"It's cool," he said.

"Your poker face needs work," she said, examining herself in the mirror.

"Did you hear a dog last night?" Jared said.

"No," she said. "But Richie gave me some Ambien. Why, did one of the neighbours' mutts get loose?"

"Yeah. They were barking around the neighbourhood."

"What day is it?"

"Thursday."

"What month?"

"May."

She blanked out, staring far, far into the distance. The ape men joined them, circling through the bedroom, wandering close to him. Since the weird-fest of last night, they'd stopped howling and shouting. They now used a system of hand signals that reminded Jared of the hunting signals his dad had taught him. It was like being stalked by mimes.

"You're packing," his mom said.

Jared felt instantly self-conscious, his hand going to the gun where he'd tucked it into his belt.

She studied him. "What's up?"

Jared shrugged.

"You never want to be that obvious. There's a holster in my bra drawer," she said. "Don't take off your coat in school and no one will notice."

He hesitated.

"Oh, for fuck's sake," she said, bending over and rummaging through her drawer. "What are you? Five? Ew, my mom's bras have cooties."

She helped him strap the holster on. They covered it with a loose dark T-shirt and then the jacket. She showed him the best way to reach under his shirt for a quick draw. She turned him to look in the mirror. She rested her chin on his shoulder, giving him a hug.

"Don't hesitate," she said, meeting his eye in the mirror. "If it's them or you, go with you."

31

THE UNIVERSE IS A
LONELY HUNTER

Did you ever pour a little Elmer's glue onto your hand, spread it around, wait for it to dry and then peel it off? Once it dries, the glue holds a clear imprint of the lines of your palms. Imagine our universe is the dried glue. All the beings on earth and in the sky, all the endless blackness of space, all the heavens in their great spinning chaos, everything we know exists in this thin copy of a completely different layer of reality.

Our universe is a membrane, a hologram, a soap bubble. We don't go through the looking glass. We are the looking glass. Some cultures imagine our world is on the back of a turtle, which, you would think, is not literal. But our universe rides a creature so strange, we don't have the senses to detect it or the math to explain it. Maybe we do live in a layer of mud on the back of a giant, multi-dimensional turtle.

Consider the dark star at the centre of our galaxy. Our Kali, our Odin-eating wolf at the end of days, this massive black hole shapes our galaxy into a maypole of stars pinwheeling around its gravity well. As we approach this cosmic

Charybdis, consider the violence necessary to shred the matter of suns into its swirling accretion disc, where the broken stars scream radiation before they're funnelled into the heart of the black hole. This gravitational meat grinder forces space and time into a gristly singularity.

This is a door not only in time, but in dimensions.

Consider roadkill. Consider the bloody pancake of a body now a shadow on a road. Your three-dimensional body made two-dimensional by the mass and velocity of cars. Now consider your three-dimensional body in nine dimensions: imagine pouring a glass of apple juice into the ocean. When you shift out of our dimensions, you run the risk of dispersion so profound, even the memory of you is obliterated. Universes are stubbornly separate.

Unless you are a Trickster.

32

DYLAN QUITS HOCKEY

At lunch, Dylan came and sat with him, so George wouldn't come near them. Jared motioned for him to come over, but George turned and disappeared. The ape men followed George around the corner, but came back.

Dylan sighed. "Mom says she doesn't care," he said. "As long as I'm happy."

"That's good," Jared said, having lost the conversational thread.

"It's bullshit. Him and Mom are moping around like someone died. They spent a buttload of money on my equipment. Hockey camps. Private coaching. Driving me to practices. Driving me to games. Tournaments. Fees."

Ah, the hockey thing. Jared wondered if Dylan hadn't quit because Ebony had started dating Bambam. Which was an awkward conversation he'd rather avoid. "Dude, it's okay."

"They're so disappointed."

"Pfft. So you don't play hockey. Are you holding up gas stations or torturing cats or burning down neighbourhood garages? You are not. They'll get over it."

"You're a weird little dude, you know that?"

"Pot, this is kettle."

"Fuck you, weirdo."

Dylan handed him his sandwich, a ham and cheese with loads of lettuce and sprouts. The bread was a gritty gluten-free variety flecked with seeds as hard as beetles. The cheese had the telltale plastic texture of a soy imitation. You could always tell when Dylan's mom made his lunch. Dylan tended to pack things of the sour-gummy-bear and Monster-drink variety. Jared ate the sandwich while Dylan picked at his non-GMO vegan protein bar.

"I don't know what I'm going to do with my life," Dylan said.

"You should take up crocheting," Jared said. "Make a nice little afghan to keep you warm in your rocker."

Dylan lunged at him and got him in a headlock.

"Adopt a cat," Jared continued. "I hear bingo is all the rage in— Ack!"

The ape guys hovered nervously, watching Dylan noogie him.

"All right, all right, all right, uncle," Jared said.

"Got any cookies?" Dylan said, letting him up.

"I'm out," Jared said.

"Seriously?"

"Seriously."

"You're not just saying that."

"I'm taking a party break. I had a craptastic trip that almost melted my brains."

"I don't think anyone would notice if you did."

"They'd notice if you grew some."

Dylan whipped the protein bar at his head.

Jared ducked, laughing.

"Where's your weirdo girlfriend?" Dylan said.

"Where's yours?"

"Everyone thinks she's cracked."

"Once you go cracked, you never go back."

"Come on, dude. She's so fucking ghetto."

"Why do you care what other people think?"

"What?"

"People talk. It's nothing but noise."

"Okay, Yoda."

"The party is strong in this one."

Dylan laughed, shaking his head. "Whatever, Darth Doofus. Dad's dragging me on a fishing trip this weekend. Want in?"

"Hell, no. You keep that nightmare to yourself."

"Come on. Fish. Open ocean. A tiny, rocking, confined space with my dad and his temper."

"Take George."

"You really don't give a shit what anyone thinks, do you?"

"Sure I do. But only on days with an x in them."

They paused as Ebony and Bambam strolled past. Ebony pointedly ignored them both, making a big show of being happy. Dylan's face became a careful study of indifference.

"I should motor," he said, standing.

"Later," Jared said.

"Later."

The ape men sniffed around the protein bar on the ground, hooting mournfully.

"You're not missing anything," Jared said, then realized he was talking to the air. He drank more water. He worried that he'd wrecked his brains for good. That his new reality included figments of his imagination looking longingly at tossed hippie food.

———

When he got back from school, his room smelled like burnt sweet-grass and cedar. Little red packets hung in the corners with fresh boughs of cedar. Jared hadn't seen that since he was a kid. His dad had laughed at his mom for hanging them up, but that hadn't stopped her.

Any news on your exam schedule? Nana Sophia texted him.

Not yet, he texted back.

Your room, my cutie. You like?

The picture showed a blue and brown bedroom with patio doors that opened to a deck overlooking a rocky beach and a sunlit ocean.

Cool. I like, Jared texted, feeling his guts clench. He didn't want to go now. Things were going better. She was off meth. He knew that didn't mean the drama was over; he wasn't a complete idiot. But he wanted to believe his mom would step back from the hard drugs, even though his dad hadn't.

The ape guys weren't bad. They were kind of sad. Maybe they were just a reflection of what he was feeling. Maybe that's all they meant.

He felt slimy for going behind his mom's back, but maybe if he waited until she was more stable to tell her, she wouldn't freak out. Or maybe she'd fall off the wagon and everything would be moot.

My Neanderthal is less dull these days. Travel doesn't agree with him but his own bed does.

Ew.

Love you, my prude-y cutie.

Love you, Nana.

His mom made tomato crouton Cup-a-Soup for supper and they ate in front of the new TV that Richie had bought. They were down to the free channels, so they watched the news. She'd bathed and her bangs didn't look that bad. Jared brought his cup and hers back to the kitchen and left them in the sink. His mom was in the recliner, her eyes closed.

"I'm going over to see Sarah," Jared said.

"Say hi to the freak for me."

"Mom."

"What?"

"Can you not call her that?"

"Huh," she said. "I thought I raised you honest."

"I don't rain on your date parade."

"Oh, I call bullshit. You whine like a chainsaw, Jelly Bean." She made her voice high and nasal: *"Richie's psycho. Death Threat's going to get you killed by bikers. Dad's addicted to painkillers."*

In the pause, Jared remembered the thwack of the nail gun.

"I never liked David either," he said.

There was a silence, then, "Are you blaming me?"

"No, no. God, no. I just . . . I . . ."

Jared remembered David screaming his name over and over. The horizon flickering. The cold of his dream. Waking up back in his body and seeing Mrs. Jaks walk back to her house, invisible to everyone but him.

"Did David try that shit with you?" Jared said.

"He wanted a little woman," she said. "I thought he just wanted to be Daddy."

She looked far away, lost in thought, and Jared knew then that David had spread his mean around. And she'd put up with it, until that night.

"I never thanked you," Jared said. "For David. For stopping him. You know. That night. So . . . thank you. For that."

"I deal with my messes," she said.

33

THE SHADOW OF
YOUR EXISTENCE

The ape men got excited when he went near Sarah. Not because of Sarah, but because of the fireflies.

A FOR SALE sign hung on the Jakses' front lawn near the sidewalk. Jared swallowed as he walked past it.

Jared heard the fireflies humming as he climbed the front stairs. The ape men galloped through the door before he opened it. He could hear Sarah and Mrs. Jaks talking in the living room.

"Hey," Jared said.

Sarah patted the seat beside her. The ape men stared and hooted at the cloud of fireflies above her head. Jared refused to look at them in the same way he refused to look at the ape men. The fireflies buzzed and flickered, slowly churning, lightning sparking between them in feathery silver forks. Jared concentrated on Sarah's smile, on the way she wrapped her arms around his waist. Her T-shirt shifted and he could see a new patch of Band-Aids.

"Are you selling your house?" Jared said.

"Good afternoon, how are you?" Mrs. Jaks said. "Oh, I'm fine, and how are you? See? That's how we greet each other."

"Gran got offers already," Sarah said. "Ten grand above asking is the top so far."

"You're leaving?"

Sarah squeezed him. "We told you. We're moving in with the uncles."

"But not forever."

"The news is not good," Mrs. Jaks said. "I want my husband taken care of."

And then Jared was crying. It was sudden and he couldn't stop it and the ache of everything, everything, everything, the sadness of it, the unfairness of it. Sarah pulled him closer and they held each other. Her chest hitched.

"God, stop it," she said. "Jared, stop."

"We need tea," Mrs. Jaks said, pushing herself up.

That set Sarah off, and then Jared joined back in and they leaned their foreheads against each other and bawled. Mrs. Jaks stomped into the kitchen and they heard her banging cupboards.

"I should help her," Sarah said, hiccuping.

"I'll do it," Jared said.

"Stay where you are!" Mrs. Jaks yelled from the kitchen. "I can lift a damn teakettle!"

"I love you, Gran," Sarah called.

Mrs. Jaks muttered and banged the saucers and cups onto the table. Sarah giggled. Jared wiped his nose on his shirt.

"It's that kind of day," Sarah said. "We've got strangers poking into all the corners of the house and me melting down every hour or so. Glad you could join the fun."

"When are you leaving?" Jared said.

"Soon," Sarah said.

"D'où venons-nous?" the fireflies said, their voices vibrating through the living room like church bells ringing slightly out of turn, echoing and answering each other. "Que sommes-nous? Où allons-nous?"

The ape men howled at the fireflies. Jared knew how they felt, though he was momentarily shocked that his hallucination spoke French and seemed to be conjugating verbs. Sarah was waiting for him to say something.

"I'm going to miss you," he said.

"Don't," she said. "Just chill with the end credits, okay?"

"The shadow suggests the object," the fireflies said. "Your existence suggests birth and, inevitably, death. Whereas the shadow of infinity suggests the divine. Or God, to use your crude terminology."

"Tea's ready," Mrs. Jaks called.

Jared and Sarah held hands as they walked into the kitchen. Mrs. Jaks served tea in her best china, roses and gilt. She brought out saran-wrapped plates of cookies and bars that her church group had been dropping off. The leader of the ape men stuck his spear in the middle of the fireflies. They shifted out of the way.

"In the same way a pure poem could not be made of words," the fireflies said, "reducing the universe to a single formula, however complex, highlights the limits of human reliance on the tangible. Transcendence requires more than simple mathematical manipulation."

When Richie was grinding on about football, Jared hadn't thought there could be anything more boring. He was wrong. So wrong. Wrong times infinity. If he was going to have hallucinations, he preferred the ape men, who puttered around Mrs. Jaks's kitchen, bending over to sniff some things and glare suspiciously at other things.

"Jared?" Mrs. Jaks said. She held up the sugar bowl.

"Thanks," he said.

"You are words," the fireflies said. "Your soul is the poem. The struggle to make mortal words say the infinite unsayable is the struggle that defines sentience."

Oh, dear God, Jared thought. Poetry. Come on. I'm already suffering. Maybe if I shove this spoon through my ear, I won't hear them anymore.

"It's like talking to algae," the fireflies said.

"Knock, knock," a woman's voice said from the hallway.

"I can't deal with this," Sarah said. "I'll be in my room."

The fireflies followed her as she left the kitchen. The ape men took off after the fireflies. The real estate agent and a couple came into the kitchen. Mrs. Jaks offered everyone cookies and they chatted, and then the agent asked if the couple wanted to see the upstairs rooms first.

When Jared and Mrs. Jaks were alone again, she sank into the kitchen chair, running her hand over the table.

"Petr made this," she said. "He hates tables that wobble."

He had always wanted to ask her, and now he was afraid this would be his last chance. The timing was awful.

"Mom and I were talking about David," Jared said. "I never told her about . . . you know, us. In that weird place."

"Whuloh te nutiéne duché duhúdíyaíh," she said. "Dreamers sometimes walk in their sleep."

"Was I sleepwalking?"

She lifted her teacup and took a sip. "You were."

"Did I . . . did I do anything weird?"

"I'm glad you came to me when you were lost," she said, putting her cup down carefully. "I would have been lost without you."

He couldn't meet her eye. She touched his hand, lightly squeezed it and let it go.

"I hope they keep the garden," she said. "Petr loves his garden."

The house sold by the end of the day. A couple with twins were going to pay just the asking price because Mrs. Jaks had liked them.

"They let their girls play in the backyard before they looked at the house," she said. "And the wife started weeding the lettuce patch."

Later, as they were getting ready for bed, Mrs. Jaks's daughter-in-law, Dawn, drove in from Prince George to help Mrs. Jaks get ready for the move. Dawn was dressed in a heavy floral dress and workboots. She had a kerchief tying back her greying hair. She hugged everyone and squished Sarah's cheeks before kissing her.

"Can Doug bring Petr down?" Mrs. Jaks said. "To say goodbye to the house before we start packing?"

Dawn's lips went narrow and her eyes spilled over. She nodded.

"Good, good," Mrs. Jaks said. She patted Dawn's shoulder.

Mrs. Jaks suffered through Dawn and then Sarah giving her more teary hugs, her face pinched. The Jakses were not huggy. Dawn followed her down the hallway to help her get ready for bed. Sarah curled around him on the couch, resting her head on his shoulder.

"I love you," Jared said.

The longer the silence went on, the more awkward their hug became.

"You don't have to say it back," he said.

"Are you saying it 'cause Gran's dying and you feel sorry for me and you think that's what I want to hear?"

"Oh, good gravy."

"Don't roll your eyes at me."

"You seriously overthink everything."

"I feel like my guts are being ripped out slowly. I . . . I . . . you . . ."

"Okay, okay. Let's pretend I didn't say anything."

She sighed. "You're not the worst boyfriend in the world."

"Wow. Maybe we should just not talk."

"Maybe you should go home."

"Maybe I should."

"This is the part where you stomp home, asshole."

"Buh-bye."

He really, really, really wanted to slam the door and it took every ounce of self-restraint to close it normally. He did stomp down the steps, though. He stomped down the walkway and he stomped down the dark street lit by street lights and the full moon, then he started to feel silly about stomping around like a five-year-old pretending to be a dinosaur. Then he remembered Sarah saying he wasn't the worst boyfriend in the world after his declaration of love and he stomped up the path to his house and around the corner to his door.

And saw Baby waiting for him in the moonlight.

He got down on his knee and patted his thighs. Baby galloped over, zipping past him, close, and snapped at his arm. He turned to watch her skid to a stop, bark and run back at him, her joyous bounce achingly familiar before she stopped dead and nuzzled his hands.

"Hey, Baby," Jared said, petting her head. "I missed you."

She farted. Jared laughed and marvelled at her being there, with him.

You need to ask yourself how she's back from the dead, dumb-ass, his inner voice said.

He didn't care. If Baby was, like, a zombie dog and she was going to eat his face off to get to his brains, he didn't care. She was back. He could smell the cloud of fart wafting all around them. He could hug her, and he did, while she wagged her tail so hard her butt wiggled.

"Come on," he said. "I saved something for you."

He unlocked his door and took the steps two at a time, ripping open his sock drawer and taking out her squeaky squirrel. Baby barked from the doorway.

"Come in," Jared said, lifting the squirrel over his head to show her.

Baby barked again. She tilted her head like she was listening for something, and then took off, her bark fading as she left him behind.

Close the door, his inner voice said. *For God's sake, close the door.*

"Baby!" Jared shouted.

He scrambled through his room for something to use as a leash. He'd have to use a belt for her collar and catch her before some numb-nuts called the pound. The last thing he needed was to have to bum money off people to get her out of the SPCA after she'd gone through all the trouble to come back from the dead to be with him.

It's not Baby.

It is, it is, it is, he insisted. It's Baby.

He couldn't see her when he got back up the steps, and for a long moment he was alone again. Then he heard her bark again and he took off as fast as he could in that direction.

He stopped where the grass ended and the bushes in the ravine became a clump of woods, tall trees and darkness. He panted. Sweat dribbled down his skin. He could feel himself being watched, felt someone's eyes studying him. His skin prickled.

"Baby?" Jared said.

She barked in the darkness.

He whistled, and patted his thighs. Come. Come here. He whistled again and she barked, but didn't come. He looked around, and realized the lights in all the houses were off. No one was in their backyards. He was alone, and Baby wasn't acting like Baby anymore. Baby would never go into the woods at night. She was a big suck. She hated pissing in the backyard when it was dark. She held it in until first light and then whined and stuck her head in his armpit and snorted until he woke up and let her out.

That's. Not. Baby.

Baby yelped. He jerked forward, and then stopped. He wanted to help her, wanted to go to her because she was in pain, she sounded like she was in pain, but all the hairs on his neck and down his arms were standing up. Baby howled in agony.

Sarah walked out of the woods.

For fuck's sake, run. Run now.

She wore her Princess Leia dress and had her hair rolled into two buns. Baby cried for him. He heard her crying and he felt cold. Sarah smiled as she walked towards him. Her eyes were solidly black in the moonlight, two shiny points in her shadowed face. She stopped under the trees, out of reach.

"What are you doing out here?" she said.

"Me? What are you doing here?"

"It got intense. I needed space. You know how it goes."

"Yeah," Jared said.

She smiled. "Wanna have some make-up nookie?"

"I'm looking for my dog."

"There's a dog with its leg in a trap," she said. She held out her hand. "It was snapping at me, so I couldn't go near it. It's in a lot of pain."

She's lying.

I know, Jared thought. Sarah would never leave an animal in a trap. She'd call to him, but she wouldn't offer to make out while an animal was in agony in the background. And there weren't any fireflies spouting poetry over her head. This wasn't his Sarah. She was a decoy Sarah who was here to bring him into the woods. A part of his brain was trying to figure out how someone faked being someone else—prosthetics? lasers? Terminator technology?—while another part of his brain was pissed. They'd used Baby and Sarah as bait. They'd watched him long enough to know he missed his dog, and they'd used that to get him here, alone. He didn't know how they'd done it or why. He didn't know who they were, either.

Run.

"It's not funny," Jared said. "What you're doing isn't funny. It's mean. And it's hateful."

The Fake Sarah let her hand drop. The dog stopped squealing. In the sudden silence, the trees shushed in the breeze, a thousand small whispers. She stepped towards him, not smiling anymore. Jared dropped the squeaky squirrel, reached under his shirt and drew his revolver.

"That's close enough," he said.

"Your safety's on," Fake Sarah said.

"I know."

"What you're doing isn't funny," Fake Sarah said. "It's mean and it's hateful."

"I loved my dog," Jared said.

Little kids giggled in the darkness and the bushes snapped as things moved closer.

"You loved your dog because you were her master," Fake Sarah said.

"What?"

"You only love the ones that crawl to you and beg for food."

"Hey, I didn't do anything to you."

"Human," she said. "We're dying because you're killing us."

"I'm not killing anyone."

"You're killing the world and you have the nerve to wonder why we hate you."

Fake Sarah's face shifted, and then she shrank and her dress disappeared as her body was covered in sleek, dark brown fur. Her nose stretched her face and then turned black and her eyes glittered as she stared at him. Fake Sarah stood on her hind legs, her arms shrinking until they were legs with paws, her tail lengthening until it smacked the ground, whipping back and forth like a mad snake. Her ears shrank until they disappeared high on her head. She was about three feet tall and slender. Her paws were slightly webbed with long, sharp-looking claws. When she smiled, her teeth were pointed. His palms sweated as he carefully took the safety off his gun.

River otter, his inner voice told him.

A pack of river otters rippled through the bushes towards them, giggling as they swarmed the tallest one, who had been Fake Sarah.

"You need to be stopped," she said.

He could hear more of them in the woods, the brush crackling. He backed away, keeping the revolver pointed at them.

I'll be there as soon as I can, his inner voice said. *Just don't go running into the woods, okay? You might want to stay away from rivers, too. And the ocean. Just stay home and game. Don't even go to school.*

"Who are you?" Jared said.

No one answered. He made his way back to his room and locked the door. He held his gun and listened to the river otters banging on his windows as they ran past, giggling until first light. The ape men started coming through his walls and settled into their favourite corner, grumbling at each other as they got ready to go to sleep.

Nana, Jared texted her. *What do you know about river otters?*

His cellphone pinged almost instantly.

I'm coming, she wrote him.

34

SECRETS & LIES

Nana Sophia sent him a PDF of her itinerary. She was arriving on the afternoon Air Canada flight. She'd booked a car and a hotel room for the next three nights.

Don't come, Jared texted. *I was just asking. I'm okay. Please.*

I'll handle your mother, Nana texted him back.

God, Jared thought, his stomach clenching so tight he could taste bile.

Nana ignored the rest of his texts. Jared breathed deep. The possibility that Nana would not mention him staying with her this summer was nil. She would bring it up and his mom would react. The only way it wouldn't happen was if the sun suddenly exploded and wiped all life off the earth. Jared really, really wanted to drink. He wanted to get so hosed his eyes crossed. But Nana and his mom were still going to rumble whether or not he was smashed out of his gourd.

Jared thought, I'm so screwed.

There was no getting around it. No going over it, or under it, either. At 15:03 today, his nana was going to land at the airport, pick up her rental car and drive for forty-five minutes straight to their house. Sometime after that, his mother would shoot her, or Nana would slit his mother's throat, and they'd spend the night in Emergency either getting surgery or declaring an official time of death.

Hey, Mom, Jared texted her.

Whazzup?

U goin anywhere 2day?

Nope. House catting. Skip skool n watch junk wit me.

Oh, God, oh, God, oh, God. *Wanna go for a ride?*

2 tired. Got a plate of bacon here when u get hungry.

Sarah texted him. *U still mad? Can I come over?*

Family drama here—Nana coming, Jared texted back. *& yes. Still pissed.*

U no wut I think re monogamy.

Kinda busy.

Whatevs.

He wished he was still baking cookies. Getting his mom good and toasted before dropping the bombshell was the only way she wasn't going to react violently. He wasn't sure if telling her first was going to help. Maybe she'd just get more ammo. God, he'd been hoping he could finish grade ten before this shit blew up. He hadn't studied at all and finals were coming up. Which was the least of his worries.

Maybe he was exaggerating things. His mom was still kind of groggy and recovering. Her aim was off, anyway.

He scrubbed himself in the utility sink and put on clean underwear. He paused at the holster, not wanting to add more firepower to the fireworks, so to speak. But the morning felt off. He strapped it on. He finished dressing, leaving his shirt untucked.

The squeaky squirrel was outside his door. It was covered in something's blood. Flies swarmed the gory bits, flecks of a slick, livery-looking organ.

Jared scanned the yard, the trees down near the ravine, the street. He picked up the squeaky toy with a stick and tossed it in the garbage bin by the side of the house. The bloody outline of it remained on the concrete in front of his door. He'd have to hose it off, but bigger fish to fry. Fights to stop. Homicides to prevent.

He went up the stairs to the front door and considered turning around and hiding with Crashpad. Just for a moment. Then he opened the door and went inside. He could hear the T V tuned to *The Price Is Right*. His mom had a plate of bacon, and her hand poised over it as if deciding which chocolate in a box of assorted she was going to try next.

"Hey," she said.

"Hey," he said.

He sat close, but outside of striking distance.

"What's with the face? Who died?" his mom said.

"Nana's coming."

She sat up. Her expression went dark. "You're still talking to her."

Jared shrugged.

"Damn it, Jared. I told you to cool it with her. What the hell is wrong with you?"

"I'm tired of cutting people out of my life."

She swung her legs off the couch and flung the blanket away. She stood and started pacing. "What did you say to her? Why is she coming?"

"I didn't tell her about . . . you disappearing. Or why."

She stopped. She turned slowly. She knelt down so her face was close to his. "Then what?"

He had trouble saying the crazy. Admitting it. Because it was weird. And he didn't want her to see him as weaker than she already did.

"It's kinda nuts."

"Try me," she said.

"I don't even know why she's freaked. It's no big deal."

"Get to the good part. Now."

"I asked her about river otters. And she booked a plane."

His mom said, "Goddamn shit for brains, rotting cunt weasels. Jesus, that's just what I need."

As much as he was relieved she believed him, nothing added up. He opened his mouth and closed it, blinking fast.

"What happened?" she said. She snapped her fingers in front of his face. "Hey, stay with me. Don't zone, okay?"

Jared shook his head.

"Use your words, Jared. I'm not a mind reader."

"Am I asleep? I must be sleeping."

His mom slapped him upside the head.

"Ow."

"Did you see someone you loved? Someone you thought was dead, or far away?"

"Baby came back," he said, "but it wasn't Baby."

"No, it really wasn't," his mom said. "Does Nana know about this? Did you tell Nana?"

Jared shook his head. "And Sarah. But she wasn't Sarah. She looked like Sarah, but she didn't act like her."

"Fuck." She flopped on the couch and covered her eyes with her hands. "Fuck."

"Am I crazy?" Jared said.

"You're boning a witch," his mom said. "That's what this is about."

"This has nothing to do with Sarah. And can you stop calling her names?"

"Your freak's sparking all over the place. And she's not stable—magically, for fuck's sake. Good fucking Lord. Stop defending her."

"You think Sarah's a witch."

"The freak has juice. So does her gran—but the old broad's too much of a holy roller to use it." She sat up, rubbing her temples.

"Witches aren't real."

"Jared," his mom said. "You are knee-deep in witches. You are neighbours with one. You are boning her granddaughter. You are sitting beside one right fucking now."

The conversation had not gone in any direction he had expected. Witches? Juice? Either his mother was insane too, or he was dreaming this, or . . . or she was serious and the freaky shit he'd been dealing with had an explanation. Maybe not an explanation that he wanted to hear, but something that made sense, in a twisted, weird way. God, insanity was starting to look like the good option. His mom was a witch? He'd always known she wasn't a typical mother. And she'd dropped enough hints about having a spectacularly crappy childhood. But . . . but . . . but witches meant . . . meant . . . a world that he thought he knew turned into something he didn't know at all.

"Is Nana a witch?" Jared said.

"Halayt," his mom said.

"A hell what?"

"A high chief lady medicine woman."

"A what?"

"She's a look-down-your-nose-at-the-commoners, borrowing-her-power-from-the-cannibal-and-giving-herself-airs-about-it Halayt. She's nobility and secret society. She's bad fucking news."

"Cannibal? What cannibal? Nana doesn't know any cannibals."

"How far is your head up your ass?" his mom shouted at him. "You were invited to her last potlatch! She has a big name! She deals with the ogre!"

"Ogre? There's cannibals and ogres?"

"Holy crap, I need a drink. You are un-fucking-believable."

His mom stomped into the kitchen and came back with a bottle of vodka and two coffee cups. She poured herself a dollop, peeked into the cup and then poured in more. She poured Jared a couple of fingers.

"So you're a witch," Jared said.

She glared at him. "No shit, Sherlock."

Jared took a swig and felt the burn down his throat.

"You should have told me," Jared said.

She chugged her coffee mug, wincing. "You're a fucking bone-headed mule about magic. Always were when it came to the supernatural."

"'Hey, son. I'm a witch.' How hard is that?"

"When you were five, I was trying to teach you protection spells, and you wouldn't listen. You kept telling me why Percy was the best train."

"What?"

"You had a Thomas the Tank Engine obsession. Fucking drove me nuts. Fucking lame-ass Thomas. You just wouldn't listen. I couldn't make you listen."

"I'm listening now."

"Well, if you're listening now, we know the end is nigh." She clinked her coffee mug against his. "I gave up on ever seeing this day."

"Am I a witch?"

"Uh, no. You are special-needs magic."

"What?"

"You know how some parents are super musical and you expect their kids to be musical geniuses and—whoopsy doodle—they end up tone-deaf? You, sonny boy, aren't just tone-deaf. You don't even have the fucking holes where your ears should go."

Jared felt the vodka hitting his centres of reason, and knew that he felt outraged, but he wasn't even sure he fully believed his mom was a witch, so her telling him that he wasn't made his brain a wall of confusion. He took another swig.

"So Dad's a witch? Or a Halayt?"

She swished her vodka in the mug, staring into it like she was reading tea leaves. In the long, long silence, the ape guys starting crawling through the floors. The leader hooted loudly when he spotted Jared and the others echoed his hooting. No, Jared thought. Not now, guys.

"Get," his mom said, waving her hand.

The ape men puffed and spread wide, until they were a fog, and then spread wider, until they evaporated like steam.

"Holy crap," Jared said.

She turned to him. "I didn't think you could see them. You never have before."

"Are they gone?"

"Fuckers keep coming back. Some spirits are like cockroaches. It's like having a zoo downstairs."

"They're spirits? Really? Of who?"

"I don't even want to know where you and your freak picked them up. We should cleanse the house before your nana gets here or she'll be all up my ass about my housekeeping. When's Nana Scary due?"

"Can you not call her names?"

"Well?"

"Around four, maybe five. I don't think she'll visit Dad. She's still mad at him."

His mom stood. She sighed. She took another swig. "Come on."

"Do you see Sarah's fireflies? Do they ever talk to you?"

"What fireflies?"

"She's got a cloud of fireflies over . . ."

Jared stopped as his mom's non-existent eyebrows went up her forehead.

"We can save that for later. This is weird," Jared said.

She shrugged. "You get used to it."

He followed her upstairs to her bedroom and she pulled a chest out of her closet. Jared had always assumed it was her ammo locker because AMMO was stencilled on the side. It was half full of ziplock bags of stuff that looked herbal but smelled more like hippie tea. Also, weird hippie stuff that you would find in a New Age store.

"Crap," she said, pulling out an abalone shell and an eagle feather. "Go get the emergency candles in the kitchen pantry. All of them."

He took the steps two at a time and went through the kitchen to the pantry. The candles were in the back, behind the flour. He checked his cell to see if Nana had texted him. Or Sarah. He felt dizzy and closed his eyes tight, willing it to pass. The phone rang. He checked the call display before answering: P. Jaks.

"Hello?" he said.

"Gran's on the f-floor," Sarah said, crying. "She's not br-breathing."

"Call 911! Now!"

He was out the door and down the front steps. He tore across the yard and realized he still had the phone in his hands and his feet were wet because he was running across the lawn with no shoes. He ran around the corner. The Jakses' house was dark. He didn't notice the blue car parked in front of the house until a guy stood up from crouching behind it and clocked him.

35

THE CAVE

The muddy cave was full of bones. Jared raised himself up as best he could with his ankles bound and his hands stuck behind his back to try to figure out if there was a way out. The duct tape over his mouth was wound around and around his head. He could hear himself breathing, the catch in his breath. His head ached in a sharp, focused manner. The pain singled out his left eye. The top of the cave was covered in glowing slime that lit everything pale green. He was still wearing his jeans, but his T-shirt, gun and holster were gone. Duct tape held his ankles together. A cold breeze came from the darkest corner of the cave. In the distance, he could hear a river.

Sarah never used the land line. Sarah, the real Sarah, never would have phoned him from Mr. Jaks's phone. She was never sure if her gran was listening in on another phone in the house, so she always texted. He'd been tricked. And now he was screwed.

He shook from the cold. And the shock of being here. And the darkness. He pricked his hand against a sharp bone, recoiled and then felt around and picked it up, working it against the duct tape on his wrists. It took a long, long time of sawing to feel it give, which made him work harder. It snapped. His hands tingled. His fingers were swollen. He gripped the bone like a kid would grip his first pencil, awkwardly bending his knees to cut the duct tape around his ankles. He stuck the bone under the tape around his mouth and forced it up, then out, then over his nose, past his eyes. It slid off his head and he tossed it in the corner. He tucked the bone in the back of his jeans.

He felt his way towards the dark opening, recoiling when he touched tiny, slime-covered skulls and rib cages, the sharp, broken femurs and the cups of pelvises. Some were cats, some dogs. Others he didn't recognize. He paused at the sight of a human skull, man-sized and still covered with bits of scalp with strings of muddy hair, the eye holes festering with maggots.

"Mmm," he heard himself mumble, and he wanted to throw up.

The cave narrowed. And narrowed. He stopped, breathing hard, staring at the blackness in front of him, feeling the walls, clammy and close. He knelt and crawled, felt the mud squish through his fingers, soak his knees, his jeans. The rock sweated, slippery. The tunnel narrowed further in complete darkness and he stopped, hoping that he was going the right way. He got down on his belly and willed himself forward. His shoulders scraped the rock and sharp bits snagged his jeans. He imagined himself getting stuck, hollering in the darkness, listening to his heart fill his ears with panicked, jerky thumping.

Follow the sounds of the river, he told himself. They got you in here. There has to be a way out.

"Little worm, little worm," a woman said. "Tasty little bait."

He pushed with all his strength and then the pinch point opened and he could kneel again, crawling forward until he hit a rocky slope and slid into a small pool, splashing and shaking at the sudden dunking. He pulled himself out, but he couldn't see where he'd gone in or where he'd gotten out, and feeling around the floor, he couldn't find the wall, just rocks, jagged and slimy.

"Stick you on a hook. Set you out to sea. Wiggle you, jiggle you. Bring some fish to me."

All at once the darkness was filled with sounds of things moving towards him and he scrambled backwards and felt fur and yelped. A hand gripped his foot and he kicked. Teeth sank into his side and he screamed and grabbed the sharp bone from his jeans and stabbed, feeling the tip slide off a skull. Something shrieked. Teeth nipped his wrists, his arms, his sides, his legs and he fought until the bodies weighed him down and he heard himself weeping, felt himself bleeding.

"What kind of fish will we catch with you?"

A lighter flicked on, the yellow flame bright against the darkness. The cave was larger than the cave he'd crawled from and filled with otters that weren't otters, but had human arms on otter bodies, otter faces on human bodies, human faces on otter bodies. Jared bit his lips shut.

The world is hard.

He shook and the hands and claws tightened, and some of them giggled and some of them were silent. All of them watched him eagerly, eyes black and shining.

The Fake Sarah, the one without fireflies, held the lighter high. Another otter lowered a torch to the flame and it flared brightly, showing him a cave the size of a living room.

You have to be harder.

He felt hands lifting his left foot.

"This little worm went to market," Fake Sarah said.

The otters on his legs kept their grip, but pulled back so he could see his feet. He curled his toes and futilely yanked his leg. One of them licked his baby toe, and he wanted to beg, but he knew it wouldn't make a difference. The otter at his feet bared its teeth.

"Don't," Jared said. "Please. Don't."

The other otters held his foot still. The otter at his foot sniffed him and then struck, fast. He shrieked as the teeth ripped through the skin and ground against the bones in his foot. His head hit the cave floor as his back arched. The otter gnawed until his little toe came free.

Fake Sarah bent over and ran the lighter over the raw flesh. He smelled himself burning, sweet, like bacon. His screams echoed back to him and he wanted to pass out, he wanted to die, he wanted this to end and it didn't. He convulsed against them until Fake Sarah stopped roasting the flesh where his toe had been and then he collapsed, moaning.

They murmured as they wiped his wrists with their fur to clean away the mud. One of them brought a roll of duct tape out and they wound his wrists in front of him, sitting him up. They were warm and he was shaking, trying to be quiet, trying not to make them mad.

"How disappointing," Fake Sarah said. "We thought you had power."

"Power is tasty," said the otter with his blood on its mouth, smacking its lips. "You taste—what are we tasting?"

"Sp-special-needs magic," Jared stuttered.

Fake Sarah snorted. "Ha."

"C-couldn't magic my way . . . out of a p-paper bag."

Fake Sarah stroked his cheek, smiling. "Don't worry. You're still useful, Little Worm, even if you don't fill our bellies." She leaned in close, putting her lips so close to his ear the tiny hairs prickled at her breath. "Witches are so very tasty."

His toe screamed where the nerves had been cut and cauterized. The otter with the bloody mouth spat his toe out into a handkerchief and wrapped it like a present. They wanted his mom. They wanted to eat her. If he didn't start thinking, they would both die.

"M-Mom's scared of y-you. T-terrified."

"She should be. I'm going to let her watch while I eat you."

"Sh-she's g-g-going to run. Away. Fast. She won't come. For me." Giggling.

"So we should just eat you now?" Fake Sarah said. "Is that what you want, Little Worm?"

Jared shook his head. "I c-can't stop you."

"How many witches are in your coven?"

"C-c-coven?"

"No one's that dumb," Fake Sarah said. "How many toes do you want to lose?"

"M-M-Mom is always a-alone."

"You lie. Witches are never alone. We see the witches next door. Where are the others?"

Jared swallowed. He needed to get them off topic. What would get them off topic? "Anthropocene."

Fake Sarah nodded as the others murmured. "The world is burning."

"Humans take all the fish," another one said.

"Can't stay in the river," another spat. "The rivers burn and taste like shit."

"Soon the only thing left to eat," Fake Sarah said, "is you."

"I'm sorry," Jared said.

"We don't want you sorry," Fake Sarah said. "We want you dead."

"What kind of weaponry do you have?" Jared asked.

"Guns?" Fake Sarah said.

"Well, guns, yes. Bombs. Grenades. Intelligence."

"We're smart enough."

"No, like, intel. Like what you know. Who your allies are. Are you going to free the factory animals? They'd probably like to get in on this."

Fake Sarah frowned. "You . . . want us to free the chickens."

"Cows. Pigs. I'm sure the turkeys aren't that happy."

"Their minds are gone. They're mindless."

"Are you sure?"

Her lip curled in distaste. "We're not working with chickens."

"Isn't that, um, speciesism?" Jared said.

"Are you lecturing *us* about looking down on animals?"

"No, no. I'm just wondering if you have allies."

Fake Sarah sniffed him. "Is the coven listening to us? Are they behind your eyes too? Are you stalling until they get here?"

"No! No one's here but me. It's just me."

"Do you think we're idiots? Take all his toes. Take his fingers."

The otters chittered excitedly and Jared shouted, struggled, and then the otters stopped moving, froze as still as statues. The torch paused, mid-flicker. A drop of Jared's blood hung in the air like it was weightless.

A voice in his head said: *Hello, Son.*

Jared twisted and yanked himself out of the hands and claws holding him. He stumbled over the half-human, half-otter bodies and fell to the cave floor, vomiting. He heaved and heaved until he thought his stomach was going to come out his throat. His foot throbbed like a broken tooth. He didn't want to look at his missing toe, but he did. The stub was black. The surrounding flesh was red with blood, shiny in the dim torchlight. Some of the bites streamed blood and some of them were only pink where his flesh showed through. Bits of skin hung from the bite on his arm. The otter people stood like statues, like a paused movie.

He couldn't get himself off his knees, and his head swung, and he fought fainting. He crawled, without a destination, away from the otter people. A corner of the cave was lit with grey light, less dark than the walls. He crawled towards it and out the entrance and onto a riverbank.

The moon shone through a thin veil of clouds, and the moonlight would have sparkled off the river if the river hadn't been frozen. The bank fell away abruptly into the water. A muddy trail of small footprints led from the bank to the cave. An old, dark car was parked haphazardly off a nearby logging road, all the doors open. Jared used a tree to pull himself to standing.

"Hello?" Jared said.

This is a tricky spell, the voice said. *I've accelerated us in a temporal pocket, but I can't hold it. You need to come closer.*

"Where are you?"

Here.

Yeah, that's helpful, Jared thought. He limped towards the car. His wounds looked worse in the moonlight. The car keys weren't in the ignition. He was going to strip the wires to start the car when he felt someone watching him.

Up here.

A raven perched in a cottonwood tree. It cocked its head to get a better look at him.

You can heal yourself, you know.

Jared saw himself through the raven's eyes, and didn't want to anymore, and then was back in his own head.

"I don't like that," Jared said. "Please don't do that."

We all start as humans. The moment we realize we aren't is always awkward.

Jared put a hand over the bite on his arm that wouldn't stop bleeding. "I want to find Mom."

Your mom wrapped you in protection spells.

Jared burst out laughing, and his voice caught, and he jammed his fist in his mouth to stop himself from bawling like a baby. "I don't think they worked."

They were planning on eating you as soon as they got you alone.

"Which way do I go? Can you tell me that?"

You could come with me.

"I want Mom."

You need to shift out of this form and we need to fly away from here. Soon. This kind of spell is noisy and attracts all the wrong attention.

"I don't think I can do that."

You can.

The car seat was irresistible. He was pulled down, and felt himself going cold, colder. He lay down, his legs dangling out the door. Can't move. So tired.

Your adrenalin's wearing off. Jared, stay awake. Stay with me.

He pushed himself up and slid with a thump, landing on the dirt. His legs wobbled and wouldn't let him stand.

Any form you imagine, you can be.

Why are you here? Jared thought.

To save you.

Why? Why now?

You're this close to being otter chow, you stubborn, bone-headed mule.
Let go. Think of someone or something you'd like to be and let go.

You're the voice in my head.

Guilty as charged.

All this time.

Jared, not now.

Mom called me a bone-headed mule. Today.

She wasn't wrong.

Were you listening to us? Were you watching? Did you know the otter people were planning this?

Hey, I'm trying to help you here. Do you want my help or not?

You called me son. My dad is Phil. Nana did a paternity test.

You can't tell us apart from humans at the DNA level.

What?

We're different on the sub-quantum level. It's complicated. We don't have time. Jared, I will explain everything when we're away from here and you aren't about to get eaten.

How long have you been watching us?

Since time immemorial.

I meant me and Mom.

Since your first act of magic.

I don't do magic.

You tell yourself it was a dream. When you shifted your conscious-ness out of phase with your body and went wandering around, hello-ing through dimensions.

He saw himself holding Mrs. Jaks's hand as they walked back to the house, towards the ambulance. In the distance, faintly, he heard David's ragged voice calling his name. He wanted the raven out of his head, now.

He was alone then, and the vision disappeared.

"Did you pop some corn?" Jared said.

What?

"Did you enjoy the show? Give it two stars out of five? The worst moment of my life. And you watched. And didn't do fuck all."

You can't blame me for that.

"If I'm your son, where were you? All this time? Where the fuck have you been?"

Dead, if you must know. Your mother killed me. Blame her for the crappy childhood.

"You're pretty lively for a dead guy."

The raven puffed out its feathers and groomed itself. *I'm trying to help and this is the thanks I get.*

The fury roiling inside him was cold. He was confused about everything except David. David he couldn't forgive. So some random asshole listened in on the shittiest, crappiest moment of his life and, instead of helping, hung back, out of sight, making a smartass commentary track as Jared fell apart and slowly, painfully, glued his life back together. And only showed up now. Because? He thought Jared was a Trickster too? Because if he was just a human kid, he wasn't good enough to care about. Humans. Billions of them. La la la, hey, look, my son is getting tortured, but he's just human. Oh, wait. Nope, he's fucking magical. Let's help him now. Nice. Dad-of-the-Year trophies all around.

You're displacing your anger about David onto me, the raven said. *And I don't appreciate it. Especially when I'm here,* now, *trying to help you. God. Teenagers.*

"Go straight to hell," Jared said.

Jared, you are this close to answers. Everything you ever wanted to know. You don't have to suffer. You don't have to live in a shithole. You can go anywhere, any time you want. You can be anything, anything at all.

"I'm human. I don't know and I don't care what you think I am. I can't . . . morph into anything. I can't do any of the shit you do, and you know what? That's fine by me."

Wee'git croaked. He hopped around, flapping his feathers in a very annoyed way, and Jared could hear him, loud, in his head. The river suddenly started flowing again, and the trees rustled in a breeze. He heard the otter people shrieking outrage in the cave. The raven flew down to the ground as the otter people streamed out of the cave, barrelling towards Jared, then stopped still again. The sounds stopped.

I can't keep us out of sync much longer. Jared, think.

"I'd rather be otter chow than spend another second with you," Jared said.

Take a moment. You're angry. You don't know all the facts.

"I don't care."

The river rushed. The air was cold. The otter people surrounded them, hissing.

Last chance.

Jared wished he'd had the presence of mind to at least pick up a rock. His mom had always told him that most of a fight was mental, and when you were outnumbered, the only rule was fight dirty. Hit joints, knees, noses and eyes. Fight down to the ground.

"Collaborator," Fake Sarah said to Wee'git.

Wee'git hopped around the ground, dragging his wing. He cawed, and cawed, and hopped on the car.

The otters shoved Jared out of the way, intent on Wee'git, who screeched as otters swarmed the car. Jared fell and rolled, covering his head as he was trampled. When he looked up, the raven was gone and the otters were milling around the hood of the car, trying to figure out which one of them was now Wee'git. They bit each other, and clawed each other, and fought each other to the ground.

Run.

Jared limped away down the logging road as the otters circled each other, shrieking.

The ape men loped towards him, hooting when they saw him. The leader, in his necklace of finger bones and his loincloth, came up and sniffed Jared's foot, his bites. Jared heard his mother's truck before he saw it, the grinding shift and the sticky clutch. The headlights barrelled down the road, the tires spitting gravel. The otter people scattered, galloping towards the river in a sleek, dark brown mass.

Jared shielded his eyes as the truck ground to a halt in front of him. His mom hopped out the passenger side, and lobbed a couple of grenades at the river, but she was too far away for them to do any damage.

"You better run, fuckers!" she yelled after the explosions.

"Babe!" Richie yelled.

His mom swung Jared's arm over her shoulders and carried him to the truck. Richie helped her get him in. He casually evaluated the bites and said, "He'll live."

"But they won't," his mom said. "When I'm done with them, they're going to bleed out of every orifice."

"Heh, heh, heh," Richie said.

"Ew," Jared said weakly.

36

GOODBYE TO ALL THAT

"Bush party gone wrong," Jared told the admitting nurse as he bled on the plastic chair in Emerg. "Went to take a piss, got my foot stuck in an otter's den and then burnt it in the campfire trying to run away."

She shook her head. Then his mom pushed him in a wheelchair to the waiting room. Richie was already there, watching a show on the Discovery Channel called *Highway Thru Hell*. After a while one of the Emergency nurses came and got them and showed them to a room. He told her the bush party story and she glanced at his mom, looked her up and down, and didn't say anything. After she left, his mom got him some water and handed him a couple more pills from a bottle in her purse. They were big, white and hard to swallow.

His mom's cell buzzed. She read a text, then said, "Nana Scary wants to know if you're okay." She started typing a response.

"Is she really my nana?" Jared said.

"Jared," his mom said. "Focus."

Deflect, as Sarah would say. Which meant, possibly, that Nana was not his nana. Jared knew, when the pills wore off, that was going to hurt a lot more than it did right now. He was pleasantly numb. He could still feel all his aches, but they didn't bother him at all.

"Wee'git said you tried to kill him," he said.

"I thought we'd have a few more years without that son of a bitch poking his nose in our life. Someone must have owed him a big favour."

"Why did you try to kill him?"

His mom hissed, "Can we not talk about this with potential witnesses wandering up and down the hallway?"

"You must have missed."

"I didn't miss."

"He's alive, *ergo* you did."

"*Ergo?*"

"Eeergo."

"Okay, fly boy. Shut it before I shut it for you."

He studied his arm.

His mom touched his knee. "Did he say he was going to show you the world?"

Jared nodded.

"What did you tell him?"

"To go fuck himself."

She snorted. "Good."

He dozed in the wheelchair and the next thing he knew, he was getting stitched up. The doctor was wearing a tux.

"Fan-cy," Jared said.

"My daughter's wedding reception. Thanks for getting me out of the endless toasts."

"Hey, no problem."

"How much have you had to drink?"

"I dunno."

The doctor sighed. "You're too young to be losing toes."

"Is there a good time to lose your toes?"

"Jared," his mom said. "Have some water."

One hundred and twenty-nine stitches, some burn treatment and a prescription for antibiotics later, Jared was released. Richie popped a wheelie with his wheelchair in the parking lot and they all laughed. Richie lifted Jared into the truck. His mom slipped in the driver's side and took the middle seat. She put an arm around his shoulders. He dozed again, and then they were home.

Nana Sophia waited in the basement with the ape guys. She looked tired and her hair wasn't its usual perfection. She kissed his cheek, tearing up.

"Oh, Cutie," she said. "Oh. You look like hell. I wish I'd come sooner."

The ape men looked longingly at the ceiling. Nana held his arm over a bowl with a bunch of weeds in it and squeezed a little blood out of one of the bites. Nana lit the contents of the bowl. When she spoke words he couldn't understand, Jared saw something under her skin, something with a long, terrible beak. The smoke rose, and when it touched the ceiling, the drywall rippled like water. Jared watched the ape men crawl up the smoke and disappear.

"Bye," Jared said. "Thanks for the rescue."

"I'll let you get some rest," Nana Sophia said.

Not Nana. Sophia. A woman who was probably not his grand-mother.

"You can stay in my room," his mom said.

"I have a hotel room. Thank you."

"Are you okay?" Jared said.

Sophia cleared her throat and patted his shoulder. "I'll see you in the morning. No more wandering through the spirit world, okay? That could have been much, much worse."

After she left, Richie hit the hay and his mom brought him upstairs and they sprawled out on the couch, watching her *Sons of Anarchy* DVDs. Jared expected to crash, but his eyes wouldn't close.

Late, very late, when his mom was asleep, he heard the fireflies humming before he heard a knock on the door. Sarah waited on the porch in a nightgown and slippers. He stepped outside and carefully closed the door behind him.

"Hey," said Sarah.

"Hey," said Jared. "How's Mrs. Jaks?"

"Cranky. We drugged her so she'd stop being such a bear."

"But she's okay? No ambulances or anything?"

"Dude, she's fine. You still mad?"

"No. Not really."

"What's with the—" She pointed to the gauze and stitches.

He considered lying to her, just so she wouldn't think he was nuts, but he loved her and he didn't want any secrets. "Mom's a witch."

"She did that?"

"No, no. Otters. Mom thinks you're a witch too. She can see the ape guys and the fireflies. Nana did a spell and sent the ape guys home."

"Okay. What the hell have you been smoking?"

"Do you believe in magic?" Jared said.

"Hey, share-sies, dude."

Jared sat on the top step of the porch and Sarah sat beside him.

"The divine in all of us," the fireflies chimed in, "remembers being light."

No, Jared thought. No poetry. Please. Not now. Pleeeease.

"What are you looking at?" Sarah said.

"I'm going to tell you something," Jared said. "And it's going to sound nuts."

"You can tell me anything and I won't judge you."

"Oh. Okay. Here goes." Jared took a deep breath in and then let a shaky breath out. "I still see your fireflies."

"Really? Cool." Sarah looked up. "Are they here?"

Jared felt relieved she didn't think he was nuts, but then immediately wondered if she was nuts too for believing him so easily.

"Nana can send the fireflies home if you don't want them hanging around you."

"We're ultra-dimensional beings," the fireflies said. "Not fireflies."

"They say they're aliens," Jared said.

"You can hear them? They talk to you?"

"We're *ultra*-dimensional beings. *Not* extra-terrestrials."

"They say they're super aliens," Jared said. "And they're kind of douche-y about it. And shout-y."

Sarah touched his hand. "I used to hear them singing. When I was a little girl."

"Polymorphic creatures like yourself are a dime a dozen. But her mind shows signs of a unique quantum mechanical behaviour, a capacity for 'super entanglement,' if you will, far beyond normal carbon-based life forms. It's very exciting."

"Um, I think they just called me gay," Jared said. "And they think you're tangled, but they like it."

"Poly*morphic*. And that was *not* the point we were trying to make."

"Tangled?" Sarah said.

"What's polymorphic?" Jared said, ignoring her death stare.

"*Poly* is many. *Morphic* is shapes, I think. So they're polymorphic aliens? How are they talking to you?"

The fireflies hummed and shifted. "Each 'firefly' is a separate biological unit that can remain instantaneously connected via a quantum link. We touch and are one. When she touched us, we could understand your language, your culture, your world. And you."

"They mind-meld, like Vulcans. And they think that you can mind-meld."

Sarah's eyes narrowed suspiciously. "Either you're spending too much time bingeing crappy sci-fi with George or you're still mad about my not saying I love you back and you're passive-aggressively making fun of my belief system by taking my concepts of openness to the absurd."

"They're right there. Right above you."

"In the porch ceiling."

"Through it. But not touching it."

"I can't talk to you when you're being like this."

"I thought you said you were open to nutty shit."

"Screw you, Jared." Sarah hopped up and stomped down the walkway.

"I'm not making fun of you!" Jared shouted at her back.

"You're insufferable," the fireflies said before they took off after her. "Insufferable!"

"Assholes," Jared said.

Nana Sophia brought French toast and coffee in the morning. They sat at the kitchen table as his mom slept in the living room. Nana wore a dark suit, like she was going to a funeral. Jared had a few bites, but the antibiotics made him queasy, so he stuck to coffee.

"I thought I'd bring up our summer plans with your mother today," Nana Sophia said.

Jared felt the few bites of French toast promising to crawl back up his throat.

"I didn't realize things had gotten so bad here," she said, eyeballing the kitchen. "I assumed your mother was still relatively stable."

"I don't—I . . . I don't think—"

"Jared, I love your loyalty. But you were nearly eaten yesterday. And, forgive the judgment here, but your house looks like a crack den. I think it would be better if you stayed with me while you're healing."

Jared tried to casually sip his coffee, but his hands started shaking. He put the cup down.

"I know it's hard," she said.

It would be so easy to go with her. He would never have to worry about bills again. He'd live in a house where his bedroom opened onto a deck that looked out onto the ocean. Someone would clean up for him, and he'd get tutors if he wanted or Nana would pay someone to do his homework and take his tests. They'd travel. They'd have fun. If he kept his mouth shut. If he was willing to lie to her for the rest of their lives. If he was willing to use her love to live the good life.

Jared cleared his throat. "Wee'git came to the otters'. He said . . . he said you can't tell Tricksters apart at the DNA level."

"Wee'git was here."

"He was."

He watched her expression go cold. Her eyes lost their sparkle. Her wry smile disappeared. She let go of his hand and sat up straight. "What else did he say?"

"They lie," Jared said. "Tricksters lie, right?"

"What did he say?"

The thing under her skin raised its long sharp beak and cried, "Hok! Hok! Hok!"

In the distance, something answered in a voice as deep as a foghorn, "Wap."

Jared understood then why his mom called her Nana Scary. Now that it was too late to take anything back, he wished he'd kept his mouth shut. The thing under her skin had wild eyes and when they focused on him, he wanted to run.

Jared's mom came into the kitchen and put her hand on Jared's shoulder. "Sophia."

"Liar," Nana Sophia said.

"Phil knew," his mom said. "I told him everything. He didn't believe me."

"But you married him anyway."

"My sister wanted my baby. Said I was unfit. It was either marry Phil or lose Jared. It had nothing to do with you or your fucking blood money."

A red cloud came through the ceiling, thick and acrid. Jared hadn't thought anything could be worse than almost being eaten by otters, but he was wrong. Nana's eyes were wild and angry and the thing inside her was becoming clearer. He'd never seen a bird like that before, like a pterodactyl, with a long pointy beak and reptilian eyes. He'd been scared in the cave, but he didn't care about the otters the way he cared about Nana. It was so much worse when the person about to kill you was someone you loved.

"Then it's true," Jared said. "What he said. Wee'git."

Sophia and his mom stared each other down.

"Am I human?" Jared said. "Am I a fucking freak? What am I?"

"Not the time," his mom said.

"You're the son of Trickster," Nana Sophia said. "And a whore."

"That's rich coming from you, Sophia. What is your last name now? I lost track three dead husbands ago."

"So . . . we're not related. You're not . . . Nana."

"Apparently not," Sophia said.

All he seemed to be doing these days was crying. Why stop now, he thought, as he bent over and put his head on the table. He didn't care if Nana—if Sophia killed him. She'd been his lifeline when things got dark. She'd been the one person who could make the crap seem less crappy. And she hated him now. And he hated himself and his life, and he heard himself choking on his own snot and he was disgusted but he couldn't stop.

After a long moment, she pulled her chequebook out of her purse and wrote a cheque. "My son has been borrowing from you. He said he's keeping track so he can pay you back, but . . ."

She pushed the cheque across the table and he knew then that, in her head, their relationship was over.

"Please don't kill my mom," he said.

"Not one of my grandchildren has your wit," she said. "So dull and grasping. But blood is blood."

She stood and he walked her to the door. They always hugged, but this time they didn't. She stayed there for a long time, staring back at him, and then she left.

His mom sat beside him until he calmed down. She lit a cigarette and smoked while she waited, jiggling her left leg. "You almost got us killed. For the second time this week."

"Sorry," Jared said.

"I could have taken her," she said.

"So Granny Nita was right. I'm a monster."

"Uh, no. You're a dumb-ass. A human dumb-ass."

"How do you know?" Jared said. "How do you know I'm not a Trickster?"

She flicked her ashes in the French toast. "There'd be signs. You can't hide that shit. Not for long, anyways. Besides, if you were a Trickster, you'd be powerful, and that just ain't our luck, is it?"

"No," Jared said. "It really isn't."

Jared cashed Sophia's cheque and put the money in an envelope. The next day, he took the 6 a.m. Skeena Connector to Terrace, and walked the six blocks to Phil's apartment. He was hoping it wouldn't be Shirley, but she answered the door holding Ben. She glared at him, but let him in.

"We got child support," Destiny said. "And I have my own apartment. Want to see?"

"Maybe later," Jared said.

"I promise not to dump Ben on you. That was intense, huh? New-mom brain. Sorry."

"Yeah," Jared said. "I know."

Phil finally came out of the bedroom and glared at Jared. They went out to the front step and Phil crossed his arms over his chest. "Did your mom finally get sick of you?" he said.

"What?"

"Who did the number on you?"

"Oh. That. Drunken bush party gone wrong."

His dad sighed and shook his head.

"You were a good dad," Jared said.

"Is that sarcasm?"

"No. I think we owe you. For taking us in."

"Until I ditched you?"

Jared handed him the envelope and Phil opened it suspiciously.

"What's this?"

Jared shrugged. "Nana gave it to me, but I don't need it."

Phil considered the money and tried to hand it back, but Jared wouldn't take it.

"I'm still going to pay you back," Phil said. "Every penny. I'm keeping track."

"You don't have to," Jared said.

"Listen," Phil said. "Your mom's half cracked. Whatever she told you, she's delusional. Okay? Take everything she says with a bucket of salt."

"I know."

"I don't think you do. She's got this whole imaginary world going where she's a big powerful witch and she's being chased by mythical creatures and it's, you know, insane."

They stood on the front steps and watched the world go by. Phil seemed to want him to say something, to agree with him, and Jared wanted to but couldn't.

"Are you happy?" Jared said.

"Mostly," Phil said.

"Better than nothing," Jared said.

"Yeah," Phil said. "Well, what I'm saying is, if it gets too crazy, come park with us."

Jared missed being that clueless. He envied it. "I appreciate that."

"Least I can do. See you later, son."

"Later," Jared said.

As he limped back to the bus stop, a part of his brain was working on a clever text to Nana Sophia and another part of his brain was achingly aware that the last thing she wanted was to hear from him. No one liked being reminded that they'd been someone's sucker.

37

TWO TICKETS TO PARADISE

His mom kept him home from school for a few days. She asked the tenants if one of them wanted to trade rooms and then Richie helped move him back upstairs into his old room. Richie didn't grumble about it, and then left on his rounds. Jared climbed into his mom's bed. After she changed his dressings, they snuggled like he was five. It was weird. But comfortable. Except for the weirdness.

"This is weird," Jared said.

She lit a cigarette and blew the smoke up to the ceiling. "Stay close until the weasels are dead."

Jared shifted, trying to find a position that wouldn't hurt. "Are we hunting them down?"

"I cursed them."

"I don't think swearing can actually kill anyone."

"My magic moron," she said. She hugged him, holding her lit cigarette away from his face. "The evil eye. Hexing. It's a talent. Actually, it's my only real magical talent."

"That sucks."

She puffed out some smoke rings. "You can make a lot of money with curses. But you have to listen to a bunch of whiny, spineless douches too gutless to do the deed themselves. You get so sick of it you want to scream *Fucking buy a gun like normal people!* Plus the pitchfork crowd blames you for every little thing: *My lawn mower won't start. My cat has hairballs. I didn't win at bingo.*"

Jared shifted again. "Maybe the weasels will go away on their own."

"They're kind of 'roidy. It's kill or be killed, bucko. Get with the programme."

They paused to listen to two of the tenants arguing downstairs. It sounded more sports-related than anything they'd have to deal with. Lots of stats being thrown around and *yo mama*s.

Jared cleared his throat. "So you tried to kill Wee'git."

"Oh, I did more than try. I blew his head off with a thirty odd. Stuffed him in the trunk of his car. Pushed it into the ocean."

"Holy."

"He messed with Mom and then with me. Fucker. You can't really kill Tricksters," she said, "but you can put them out of commission while they pull themselves back together. I'll just have to bury him deeper next time."

"I don't think he's coming back."

"He'll be back."

Jared had a few things he'd like to say to the guy too. He couldn't imagine blowing anyone's head off even if he knew they wouldn't really die, but he was perfectly willing to watch his mom give it the old college try.

A large moving truck hissed as it slowed down and stopped in front of the Jakses' house. After a few minutes, Jared could hear Mr. Jaks's

voice stridently arguing in Czech. Jared got up from the top step of
the porch and went inside to put on his runners, then checked the
street carefully before he made his way to their place.

The uniformed movers stood silently while Mr. Jaks blocked
them from entering the house. Sarah stood at the side of the walk,
while Mrs. Jaks tried to pull her husband inside. Dawn went down
and talked to the movers. They shrugged and went back to their
moving truck. Once they'd left, Mr. Jaks allowed himself to be per-
suaded inside.

Sarah gave him a hug.

"You okay?" Jared said.

"No. I'm really not."

"Sorry."

"Yeah."

The fireflies were silent. Jared didn't want to see them anymore.
He wanted his normal, ordinary human sight back.

His cell buzzed.

Where u @? his mom texted him.

Saying goodbye.

No magic wit da baby witch. Shez not ready.

Ya, ya. TTYL

TTFN

They went inside and had soup, everyone quietly sitting around
the table. Mr. Jaks started tossing his cutlery and then his bowl and
then Mrs. Jaks started crying. Jared took Mr. Jaks to the bathroom
and cleaned him up while Dawn and Sarah calmed Mrs. Jaks down.
Mr. Jaks's eyes showed white all around, the fear radiating off him,
making him shake.

"You're okay," Jared said. "You're going to be okay."

Mr. Jaks didn't look like he believed him. Or maybe he didn't understand. They stood in the bathroom, looking at each other's reflection. Then Mr. Jaks opened all the drawers, all the cupboards, and they were empty. He sat on the toilet, looking lost and alone. Jared didn't know what to say to make it better. He didn't know what to do except sit on the side of the tub beside him and wait until Mr. Jaks was ready to go back to the living room.

A round of tranquilizers later, Mr. Jaks passed out in the recliner and Mrs. Jaks went to lie down in her bedroom. Dawn told him the drama was coming home to roost.

"What?" Jared said.

"My mom's coming tomorrow," Sarah said. "She wants me home."

"Does she?" Jared said.

"I think she doesn't want me going rez."

"We'll slather you in bear grease," Dawn said. "And she won't be able to grab you."

Sarah giggled.

"I don't feel like cooking tonight. A&W or Dairy Queen," Dawn said. "Your choice."

"A&W," Sarah said. "Just the garden salad."

"She'll eat most of my fries," Jared said.

Sarah bumped him.

"Ah, to be young and in love," Dawn said. "I'm going to chill out at keno before I get supper. Don't do anything I wouldn't do."

After the rumble of Dawn's diesel truck faded completely, Sarah said, "Wanna screw? This could be our last kick at the can."

"It's sad that I'm the romantic one in this relationship," Jared said.

Sarah wanted to put a sleeping bag down in the basement, but Jared was weirded out by screwing with the Jakses passed out in the house. It felt wrong, and not in the good way. Sarah ran her hand along his scalp. She cocked an eyebrow.

"Go for it," Jared said.

She sat him down on a kitchen chair and pulled off his T-shirt. She lightly touched the dressing and he flinched.

"Holy chew toy, Batman," she said.

"They were pretty mad," Jared said.

"Otters."

"Otters."

"Huh."

He could tell she thought he wasn't entirely on the level, but she wrapped a towel over his shoulders and used Mr. Jaks's clippers to buzz his head. When she was finished, she ran her tongue from his neck to the top of his head. Jared squinted, imagining the fine cuttings of his hair in her mouth.

"Can I buzz your pits?"

"No."

"Come on."

"No."

"Square."

She kissed him anyway. They went into her bedroom, which was packed up, the bed bare. She unwrapped the gauze around his foot and studied his missing toe.

"Looks painful."

Jared said, "Sometimes it's itchy, and I want to scratch it even though I know it's not there."

She wrapped it up in the gauze again and kissed his ankle, his shins, his knees, avoiding the bites and stitches until she reached the tender part of his thighs. He flinched when she pressed against one of the cuts.

"Sorry," she said.

"Everything's kind of sore. Circle jerk?"

"Let's get drunk before we descend to mutual masturbation," she said.

The only alcohol in the house was Mrs. Jaks's raspberry cordial. It was syrupy and sickeningly sweet. He put a bit on her nipple and then smeared more over her chest and they laughed.

"I'm going to miss you," Jared said.

"No end credits," she said. "You'll visit. We'll butcher moose and make sausages."

"'Kay."

She grabbed the bottle and took a swig, smacking her lips. "Wow. I think it's like a hundred proof."

"I think we're supposed to cut it. Or pour it on ice cream."

They kissed, and kissed, and came up for air and kissed until his lips felt bruised. Sarah slid her hand beneath the band of his underwear and squeezed his ass. He stroked her leg, the soft skin beneath her dress, third base. He felt dizzy, and gripped her shoulder until he steadied.

"Whee," he said.

She giggled.

They both stopped to listen, and then Sarah got up and put on her bathrobe. She came back a few minutes later and said the oldies were still out cold.

Jared took out the condom from his wallet and they tried to position themselves sitting on the bed, facing each other, not hitting any of his stitches. Sarah moaned against his neck, and he felt a line of tension, of pleasure, from his cock up his spine, down his arms and his legs as they moved together. Their breathing quickened. Jared closed his eyes and heard music, and hoped that Dawn wasn't coming home when they were so close, so close.

"That's the song I've heard in my dreams," Sarah breathed.

Jared's eyes snapped open and, above them, the fireflies had formed a figure eight. The edges of Sarah were shredding and lifting, floating up as the fireflies came down.

"No!" Jared said.

He pulled away from her and she reached up, her fingertips sparkling with tendrils of light. Her delight, her wonder, her glowing face.

"I thought you were delusional," Sarah said. "Or lying. Look. Look at us."

He was shredding too, bits of himself spiralling away from his skin, twining with bits of Sarah. "Damn it."

He willed the fireflies gone. He willed himself into one solid, normal human being, but he kept shredding and shredding, and the fireflies sparkled.

Jared stumbled off the bed and pulled on his underwear. He pulled on his shirt, staggering, while Sarah ignored him, her face uplifted and serene.

"I'm going," Jared said. "Sarah. Sarah!"

She refused to move, so he went into the kitchen and filled a glass from the tap. The shredded tendrils sank back into his body. The glow of his skin faded. He went into the living room and sat on the couch.

He heard the fireflies coming with her down the hallway, and he didn't want to see them. He willed them away, but they wouldn't go.

"Come back," Sarah said. "I can't hear them if you aren't there."

"No," Jared said.

"I've never felt anything like that."

"You're coming apart," Jared said. "It's taking you apart."

"We're joining."

"No, you're shredding."

"I'm not scared."

"I am."

"Jared, come back to bed."

"No."

A string of fireflies came at him, like a strand of DNA. It wound around his head and Jared ducked. They coiled tight and then sprang straight for his eye.

"I'm here," Sarah said. "I'm right—"

Think of magic as a tree. Orange sparks floated through the darkness, wafting upwards from the bonfire on the beach. *Asteroids were due to boom through the atmosphere like falling angels, wings afire.* A chief tree spirit peeked out from behind a cedar, its eyes too large for its head like a bat's, watching a canoe carver tap the trunk in the solemn gloom of a forest dripping moss. *Come closer and let me speak to the creatures that swim in your ancient oceans, the old ones that sing to you in your dreams.* A longhouse high in the mountains with a smoke hole spewing terrible red smoke, acrid and sweet, like burning flesh. *Unless you are a Trickster.*

———

"—here!" Sarah shouted.

"Are those all your memories?" the fireflies said to him. "So strange. You aren't quite human, are you?"

Mr. Jaks grumbled as Sarah put her palm on Jared's forehead.

"I want to see what you see," she said.

Another Sarah came through the wall. The bone showed through half her face while the rest of her skin was pocked with boils and pustules. She smiled.

"I want to see too," the other Sarah said, lifting her hand and putting it on top of Sarah's.

Her fingers were cold as they sank through Jared and past him. She flickered. The ghosts of the otter people crawled through the walls, crawled along the floor, following Jared as he pushed past Sarah, towards the door.

"Jared!" The real Sarah grabbed his arm and Jared pulled away, yanked firmly, stepping over the dead to get outside.

He limped home with Sarah following him and the ghosts following her and the cloud of fireflies swirling happily above all the craziness. He led his entourage up the stairs to the front door. His mom met him there, saw the ghosts and smirked.

"I told you curses work," she said.

"Do you see them? Do you see all of them?" Jared whispered.

"Hey, Sarah," his mom said. "We're going to have a little family moment. Do you mind?"

"Jared?" Sarah said.

Jared shook his head, wordless.

She waited at the bottom of his steps, looking forlorn, then walked away backwards, holding her hand to her heart as the fireflies followed her.

"Beat it," his mom said to the otter people's ghosts when Sarah was out of sight. "Before I exorcise the crap out of your ever-living souls."

"We owe you pain," Fake Sarah said. "Witch."

"See you in hell," his mom said. "Bitch."

When Richie came home, a grizzly as large as a VW Bug followed him, coming through the bedroom wall. Richie tried hard not to look annoyed, and failed. The grizzly stopped and pawed the ground when it saw Jared, swaying its great shaggy head back and forth, lowing.

"Holy crap," Jared said.

"Settle," his mom said to the bear.

It growled, but sat with a resounding thump.

"He can see it?" Richie said. "Is he a witch now too?"

"No, but he's boning one."

"Man," Richie said. "I wish I could see it. That's not fair."

"Someone's having a bad night," his mom said. "Would you mind sleeping in Jared's room?"

The bear roared, a piercing sound that rattled the windows and boomed through the house.

"Yeah, whatevs," Richie said. "I'm tired anyway."

"I owe you," his mom said.

"Need anything?"

"We're good."

The bear got up and came over to sniff Jared. His breath was hot and smelled like a full Dumpster on a hot summer's day. Jared pulled back and his mom got off the desk chair beside the bed and smacked the bear's nose.

"Beat it," she said.

It lumbered through the walls and disappeared. His mom lifted the comforter and crawled in beside him.

"Get some sleep," she said.

He couldn't. His brain hummed, and he couldn't stop shaking. He couldn't close his eyes. He saw the longhouse, smelled the smoke and felt dread, deep, deep in his bones.

Jared stayed home from school again and didn't look at his texts, but he could hear the alert pinging on his cellphone every time Sarah messaged him. His mom wouldn't let her in the house. He wanted to talk to her before she left town, but he wanted to do it when his brains weren't spilling out of his head.

That night his mom offered him a large white pill and he shook his head. Jared didn't remember falling asleep, but he must have, because he woke and the bedroom was dark and he could hear two different kinds of sirens wailing down the street, a police car and an ambulance. In the distance, he could hear a fire truck. His mom lifted the bedroom curtain, lit by flickering red lights.

"I think it's your freak," his mom said.

He struggled to get out of bed and stood beside her at the window, in time to see the ambulance take off down the street. He moved to go downstairs, but his mom wrapped her arms around him, holding him still.

"I think you've done enough," she said. "Let her be."

38

WE'LL ALWAYS
HAVE ALDERAAN

Jared went over in the morning and knocked on the door. No one answered and when he tried the handle, the door was locked. He sat on the porch, waiting. He heard the rumble of Dawn's diesel truck before he saw it round the corner. He walked down to help the Jakses out.

"Sarah's okay," Dawn said. "She said she did some 'shrooms and she doesn't remember . . . anything."

"She cut herself," Mrs. Jaks said.

"Come on," Dawn said. "Let's get inside."

The house looked normal until you got to the kitchen. Mrs. Jaks put the back of her hand to her mouth as they stared at the damage. Dawn sighed.

"We're on it," she said.

They were lucky Sarah had cut herself in the kitchen; blood was impossible to get out of carpet. Dawn brought Jared the bucket and mop, and told Mrs. Jaks to go watch TV. He could tell she was still shaken because she didn't argue. Mr. Jaks's heavy-duty tranquilizers kept him zoned on the recliner. Jared rolled up his sleeves.

They moved the kitchen table to the side, sponging the blood off the legs. He put the chairs on top. He poured half the bleach into the mop bucket, filled it with water. Carefully, he soaked the worst spots.

This time, the uncles were driving down with the moving truck and Sarah's mom was coming in order to sign the paperwork to get Sarah out of psych. Mrs. Jaks didn't want any of them to see the kitchen looking like a murder scene.

Jared used a scrub brush to get the hard spots off the floor. Dawn burned through the paper towels. They filled a garbage bag with used towels and cleaners. After another mopping with water and then Mr. Clean and then water again, the kitchen smelled less like a slaughterhouse. Jared moved an old area rug up from the basement and laid it down. He put the table over it. If you didn't know what had happened, it was a perfectly clean, normal kitchen.

Jared opened a can of chicken noodle soup, heated it up and brought it to Mrs. Jaks in a mug. Mr. Jaks woke up and Jared went to get him a cup too. He stood at the stove and stared at a spot he'd missed, a handprint on the oven-door handle where Sarah had probably pulled herself up.

They huddled together in the living room. Mr. Jaks fell asleep again on the recliner. Mrs. Jaks sipped her soup. Jared drank coffee. They stared at the TV and, eventually, morning came.

Jared's mom got him out of final exams by faking a family death. He asked Dylan to drive him to school and back home. As he walked in, kids went quiet and he knew they'd found out about Sarah. At some point since he'd last been to school, she had hot-glued some flies in the shape of a heart to his locker door. She'd possibly been trying to remind him of the fireflies, but there weren't any fireflies around, so she'd made do with houseflies, carefully painting their butts yellow.

Which, if you didn't know her, looked nuts. He considered scraping them off, but he was getting enough unwanted attention just showing up for school. He dumped everything from his locker into his backpack.

Dylan blasted the tunes in the truck, turning them down when Jared opened the door and piled in.

"Man, you're lucky you're skipping finals," Dylan said.

Jared put his seat belt on. "Yeah, I feel lucky."

Dylan lurched out of the parking lot. "Hey, I've had plenty of chicks try to off themselves to get my attention. You get used to it."

"They did?"

"Sure. Well, okay, they were mostly all talk and threats, except for Amanda, who said she was going to throw herself off the overpass and stayed there all night with her friends and shit."

"Yeah?" Jared said.

"We'd gone on a couple of dates. You know, beers with friends, movie nights, nothing serious. But she was telling everyone we were going to prom and shit. It got intense. Then her parents got a restraining order on me and my dad blocked their number and she was going to all these houses so she could phone us . . ."

As Dylan talked, Jared zoned, glad to be on the sidelines of someone else's drama. His eyes burned from staying awake. He wished he could sleep. He wished he could shut his brain off.

"Okay?" Dylan said.

Jared nodded automatically.

Dylan slugged his shoulder. "You can feel as guilty as all hell, but it won't do you or her any good. Okay? Got it?"

"I'm not used to you being thoughtful," Jared said. "It's weird."

"Fuck you."

"There's the Dylan I know."

"Serves me right for trying to help you, you mouthy douche."

"Sorry. Duck's gotta quack."

Dylan pulled up in front of the house. Cars plugged the driveway. "You can stay at my place."

Jared sighed. "Your mom and dad'll freak."

"They don't hate you," Dylan said.

"Well, they aren't throwing confetti, either."

"It would help if you didn't fucking irritate the crap out of them."

"Thanks for the lift."

"Later."

"Later."

The lights were all on at the Jaks house. Jared stood and watched for shadows, for movement, for signs that people were alive and well.

His mom brought a Hungry-Man TV dinner to his bedroom. Hot turkey, his favourite. She smoked while he ate.

"So how's the nut job?" she said.

"You missed your calling as a sensitivity trainer."

"I call 'em like I see 'em."

"She's not a nut job."

"If someone dumps you, you key their car. You don't try to off yourself in front of your grandparents, for fuck's sake."

"I didn't dump her. And she wasn't trying to kill herself. She has these weird aliens following her, saying crazy-ass shit, and she was on 'shrooms."

"Oh, that makes it better."

"Can we save this touching heart-to-heart for later?"

"I warned you she wasn't ready. Didn't I warn you?"

"Mom."

"What?"

She was trying to help. In her own way, this was warm and fuzzy. "Thanks for supper."

"It wasn't even on sale," she said. "I paid full price for that crap."

"When someone pays retail, that's love," Jared said.

She tucked her cigarette in the corner of her mouth and got him in a headlock.

"All right, all right, get off me," he said.

"I fucking love you, you sarcastic little shit."

"Hallmark! Hallmark!"

A black Ford Explorer with a rental sticker on the bumper sat in the Jakses' driveway. Jared hesitated, but went up the front steps and knocked. After a few minutes, a woman with straight black hair parted to the side cracked the door open.

"Hello," she said.

"Hi, I'm Jared."

"Oh," she said.

"Is Sarah in?"

"She's resting."

"Can I see her?"

"I don't think that's a good idea."

"Can you tell her I dropped by?"

"Jared," she said, slipping outside and quietly closing the door behind her. She was trim and wearing black yoga pants and a matching hoodie zipped down just enough to reveal a hot pink yoga top.

She would have been tall but for an apologetic hunch to her shoulders. "This is a delicate time. I think Sarah needs some space, okay?"

Jared studied her. "Okay."

"I'm not blaming you, but did you give her the drugs?"

"No," Jared said. "I don't like 'shrooms."

"But you didn't stop her."

"You know, it kind of does sound like you're blaming me."

"I'm not. I'm trying to understand how this happened." She stood, rigid, with her arms crossed, a good arm's length away, not meeting his eye for very long, like she smelled something rotten and wanted to keep out of the stink zone.

"It happened because you sent your daughter to take care of your dying parents," Jared said. "And she cracked under the pressure. That's what happened."

"*You* broke her heart."

"No, you dumped her like a sack of kittens on the side of the highway and now you're looking for someone to blame."

"I think you should leave."

"You're covering your ass."

"I'm calling the police." She backed away from him and went inside. "I want you off our property."

The deadbolt clicked and he heard her slide the chain in place. He swallowed all the things he wanted to say and glared at the door.

"Don't come back!" she shouted through the door. "You're not welcome here!"

He'd never understood his mom's urge to kick, smash or shoot things to smithereens. But he got it now. If he had a gun, he would have shot the door open just to see her skitter.

His mom was cackling on the phone when he came through the front door.

"Yeah?" She waved at him. "Honey, you send the cops over if that'll make you feel better."

"Oh, God," Jared said, reaching for the phone.

She smacked his hand away. "If you were my mom, I'd off myself too so I wouldn't have to hear your whiny, stuck-up, ball-curling voice. Fuck off, cunt, and stay—" She looked at the phone and then at Jared. "She hung up. Right in the middle of our conversation. How rude."

"Some people," Jared said.

"Come here," she said, holding her arms open.

"I didn't mean to get you involved."

"No, no, that's not it." Her eyes watered. She blinked back her tears.

"I'm sorry," Jared said. He hugged her hard. "I'm sorry, Mom."

"Look at you, scaring respectable folk," she said.

"Mom."

"My baby has a backbone. Thank you, sweet Jesus! I was starting to think you were as spineless as your good-for-nothing daddy."

"Nice. Way to get in all your digs."

She laughed and pecked his cheek and then hugged him closer. "I'm so proud of you."

"We should hold up a liquor store. You know, for the family bonding."

"We'll save that for Christmas," she said. "And we'll wear cute little matching ski masks."

"I'm joking," Jared said. "I hope you are."

"We can use our mug shots for the Christmas cards."

"Yeah, haha, Mom. Funny."

Dylan had promised him a quiet night at Gruchy's Beach, and it was low-key if you didn't count the other fifty or so drunken teenagers shouting and flirting, frisking in and out of Lakelse Lake, throwing random shit on the bonfire. Dylan brought him a beer, patted him on the shoulder and then got distracted by girls taking their T-shirts off to have a splash fight.

Jared sat on a log watching the sparks float up. The beer was one of those weird craft things that had an orange aftertaste he didn't particularly like. But it was hard to argue with free. And he was out of the house for the first time in days.

Hey, Crashpad, he texted.

Hey.

Wutz up?

Ketchup.

@the lake.

Pre-final blowout?

Ya.

Howz it goin?

No fights yet.

U bord?

Achy. Lonely. Wishing it wasn't such a shitty year. *Ya.*

Me 2. Mom sad about her cuz dying. In her room cryin tryna be quiet. Dad doin nother double shift. Pizza pops 4 supper.

Sorry.

Sorry bout S.

Shitty year.

Ya.

Watcha watchin?

Series 3, Primeval.

Thatz the dino 1, rite?

Um, no, loser. It's the epic dino 1. Walking Dead marathon 2morrow?

"Hey," Ebs said. She wore a party dress with someone's ratty sweater over it. Her flip-flops had lost a flower.

Jared paused, mid-text, stunned. "Hey."

"Can I sit?" she said, sitting.

"It's a free beach."

Ebs here. Gotta go, Jared texted.

Repeat: da power of Xrist compels u.

"What's so funny?" Ebs said.

"Crashpad."

"He's weird."

"But funny."

"You haven't changed," Ebs said, taking a drink.

"Neither have you," Jared said.

"I'm sensing judgment."

"Caution," Jared said. "Are you taping this?"

She side-eyed him. "You pushed me."

"I told Dylan to stop shoving Crashpad into a snowbank. Why was it a deal?"

"Why didn't you talk to me?"

"I had family shit."

"We all have family shit."

"You don't have my rez-ass family shit."

"You'd be wrong if you believed that for a second," she said.

Dylan wrestled some guy in the shallows, laughing. The girls splashed them. Ebs dropped her gaze to her bottle.

"Sorry," Ebs said. "About the video. It was a pretty low thing to do."

"I should thank you," Jared said. "Actually made me more popular."

"That would never happen to a girl," Ebs said. "Guys have it easy."

"Your mom's not expecting you to rob banks for a living."

She laughed. "Mine expects me to land a rich husband so she can lounge around my swimming pool. Are we good?"

"We're good," Jared said.

"Are you still baking cookies?" Ebony said.

"I don't think we should be in business together. I don't think that works."

"Your cookies are good," Ebony said. "I'm good at sales. Think about it."

They watched the other kids goofing around the beach. After a while, Ebs asked him if he wanted to leave.

"I'll talk to Dylan," Jared said.

"You need his permission?"

"I don't play games."

"Everyone plays games."

"I don't wanna play those games."

"Suit yourself."

Dylan shrugged, grimly cool. "Whatevs."

"'Kay. Later."

"Later."

The trail to the parking lot was dark. Ebs spritzed herself with Deep Woods OFF! She offered him the bottle. He shook his head. She pulled out a stainless steel flashlight that lit the trail with a beam so bright you could probably see it from space.

"What else have you got in your purse?" Jared said.

"Water, gum, makeup, hair product, bear spray, night-vision drone—"

"Bullshit."

She held up a little white box. "Dad special-ordered it. I couldn't leave it in the Jeep 'cause I took the top off and if I lose it, he'll mope forever."

"Who's he spying on?"

"He thinks the neighbours are whizzing in his flower garden. I told him it's cats, but he's sure it's human whizz. He's between jobs. And bored. And driving us all crazy."

"Wow."

"Yeah."

Frogs chirped. Things skittered in the underbrush. Salmon splashed in the nearby creek, smacking the water. Mosquitoes whined in a thick halo above his head. He slapped his neck and then his legs.

"Don't be such a fucking guy," Ebs said. "Use the OFF!"

"I'm fine."

"I hear the West Nile virus is all the rage," Ebs said. "I'm sure the hospital is lovely this time of year."

"Holy. Way to worst-case-scenario things." But he let her spritz him and it was nice not to be feeding the entire winged-insect population of northern BC.

In the Jeep, Ebs tied her hair in a ponytail then wound it into a low bun. She threw her purse in the back seat and jumped over the door with a confident plop. The Jeep was standard. She shifted without grinding the gears or rolling back down the hill at the stop sign. The dashboard lit her face green. The horizon glowed with the promise of long summer nights. The highway was empty and they sped down the road with the wind making small talk impossible.

Ebs cranked the tunes and bounced along to the beat when M.I.A.'s "Bad Girls" came on.

"'I'm coming in the Cherokee,'" she sang. "'Gasoline. There's steam on the window screen.'"

Ebs parked at his house. He got out and stood beside the driver's window and they shot the shit, comparing their year. Her dad had been laid off twice, but there was a lot of work, so he rolled with it. Ebs was planning on doing her summer job cleaning rooms out at the Kemano work camp with her mom. Plan B was waitressing at either Mr. Mikes or Rosarios. Jared suspected that she was being super nice to him to get back on Cookie Dude's good side. He did need the money. Maybe it wasn't such a bad idea. He was about to tell her he'd think about a cookie sell when his eye was caught by a glowing cloud of fireflies.

Sarah wore her white robe with her hair up in buns on the sides of her head. Above her, fireflies moved in a lethargic haze.

"Is that a Leia outfit?" Ebs said.

"You should go," Jared said.

"Um, no," Ebs said. "She should be arrested for being such a freak show. Who wears that shit when it isn't Halloween?"

"Chill, okay? She's had a rough week."

As she crossed the street towards them, he could hear the fire-flies hum. He dragged his eyes away from them as they spun and flickered and glowed.

"Hey, Jared," Sarah said. "Ebs."

"Love the outfit," Ebs said.

"Jared's not going to screw you, Ebony," Sarah said. "So go find another one of Dylan's dumb-ass friends to revenge-fuck."

"I'm off," Ebs said. "Try not to kill yourself with your grand-parents watching."

"Whoa, ladies. Time out, okay? Okay? We're all—"

Sarah pulled out her cellphone. "I wonder who Dylan's screwing tonight? Let's check his Instagram and see which lucky lady is next."

Jared threw himself on the Jeep door to stop Ebony from launch-ing herself through it. "I don't think this is hel—"

"Shut up, Jared," they both said.

"Real sensitive, Sarah," Ebs said. "But what can you expect from a snotty head case who thinks she's so hip when she's trailer trash in dorky outfits."

"You're the one ashamed of your class," Sarah said. "I'm blue-collar to the bone."

"What the hell does that mean? Do you even know what you're saying or are you ripping off lines you found on Wackadoodle.com?"

"It means my mother wishes I had your shallow-ass, grasping, self-aggrandizing, fashion-whore herd mentality."

"You're the fucking cow, bitch!"

"Moo! Moo! Everyone's wearing short sleeves today! Moooo!"

"Okay, okay, okay," Jared said. "Ebs, thanks for the ride. Sarah, um, I think your mom's coming to get you."

They all paused to watch Sarah's mom creep down the street in her black Ford Explorer, gripping the steering wheel like she was about to be attacked by a zombie horde.

"Enjoy the funny farm," Ebs said, revving her engine. "I hear the long-sleeved jackets are especially becoming on sallow, pasty losers."

"I hope your spray tan gives you cancer!" Sarah shouted at the rear bumper of Ebs's Jeep as it sped away.

"Classy," Jared said.

"She started it."

"She did dis the Leia. But you called her a whore."

"A fashion whore. God, learn to speak girl."

Sarah's mom braked suddenly and lifted her cellphone to her ear, staring past them at the house. Jared turned and saw his mother striding onto the porch with a paintball gun.

"Damn it," he called. "Mom! Chill!"

"Shut it," his mom said, aiming and firing off a round. It splattered green a few feet short of the Explorer's hood. "Move a little closer, Hon! You're out of range."

"I love you," Sarah said.

Jared studied her. "I can't. Go there. With you."

"We were so close."

"Sarah, you almost died . . . I . . . I had to clean up your blood."

"I never felt anything like that. It was . . . it was . . . like coming home. Like being alive for the first time ever."

"I can't do this anymore."

His mom stomped down the steps as Sarah's mom hastily backed up. The neighbours' lights clicked on up and down the street. The fireflies sparked and spun faster.

"Do you see them? Right now?" Sarah said.

"God. Let it go," Jared said.

She looked up. "I want to see them again."

"It's like when Vader used the Death Star to blow up Alderaan," Jared said. "Once you blast a place to smithereens, you can never go back."

Her eyes narrowed to a dangerous squint. "It's a movie, dumbass. Not a religion."

"She grabbed the shotgun first," Richie said, bouncing Jared's mom in his lap. "Everyone's damn lucky I made her take the paintball gun."

"Fucker," his mom said, playfully slapping him.

"Don't mind if I do," Richie said.

They slobbered over each other.

Jared said, "Get a room, Bonnie and Clyde."

"You know, the little nut job grows on you," his mom said. "She's got spunk."

"Seeing as how her mom's dragging her off to rehab in the morning, yeah, that means squat, Mom."

"Rehab's not forever," his mom said.

"Hear, hear," Richie said.

They clinked beer bottles.

"I was wrong," Jared said. "You should write for Disney."

"*Rehab Princess: The Bride Wore Blood*," his mom said.

"She ate his heart with fava beans and a nice Chianti," Richie said.

His mom kissed Richie and Richie slapped her ass as he stood and asked if she needed anything from the corner store.

"Smokes. Thanks, Babe."

"You owe me lots," Richie said cheerfully.

After he was gone, his mom tapped Jared's arm. "We should run through some protection spells."

"No. No, I'm done. So seriously done. No more magic."

"You stubborn dumb-ass," his mom said, slapping him lightly upside the head. "You may be done with magic, but that doesn't mean magic is done with you."

Early in the morning, Jared woke and knew she'd be there when he got to the window. He could hear the fireflies, and saw them like a halo over her head as Sarah stood on the lawn, looking up at his window, the sun sending golden fingers through the trees on the top of the mountains. He put his hand up and waved. She waved back and then put her hand on her heart. She didn't come any closer to the house and he didn't go downstairs. They watched each other until Sarah's mother drove up and honked. Then Sarah turned and walked slowly to the black SUV and they drove away.

The sequence of events that led him to the Jakses' house that night would always remain fuzzy. Drinking had been involved. A lot of drinking. Jared found himself crying in Mr. Jaks's lap as the old dude sat at the kitchen table. Jared knelt on the floor. Mr. Jaks stroked his head, saying soothing things in Czech. Jared slowly became aware of Mrs. Jaks and Dawn standing close but saying nothing. And then, beyond them, in the living room, the uncles busily carted boxes on dollies out the front door.

Jared wiped his nose. His throat was raw. He hoped it was from drinking and not from howling or bawling. Mr. Jaks patted Jared's head and Jared stumbled to his feet.

"Sorry," he mumbled. "Sorry."

Mrs. Jaks put a cup of coffee in his hands and led him to a kitchen chair. She kissed his forehead. "You can stay here until we leave."

"Don't go," Jared said.

"We're going to miss you too," Mrs. Jaks said.

"Please. Don't leave me."

"Shh," she said. "Drink your coffee, Jared. Dawn, can you take Petr to the garden?"

Jared heard Dawn and Mr. Jaks walking to the back door.

Mrs. Jaks reached over and held his hand. "It's been a hard go, hasn't it?"

Jared laughed, wiping his eyes.

"I'm not afraid of dying," Mrs. Jaks said. "But knowing that Petr will be alone frightens me. The family tries, they do. But they have children. And jobs. And my sweet Petr will be alone."

"I'm sorry," Jared said.

"I wish life was more fair. For you and for him. You deserve better."

"So do you."

"I'm sorry I was angry with you. I'm sorry I wasted that time when we could have been together. I wish I could take that back. I was wrong and I'm sorry."

"S'okay."

"It isn't. You were good to Sarah. She was good for you."

The uncles banged around upstairs and Mrs. Jaks flinched.

"I'm going to miss you," Jared said.

"I know everything hurts right now," Mrs. Jaks said. "But don't drink your life away. Find love. Have babies. You're a good boy, Jared. I wish only good things for you. I wish this with all my heart."

39

SUMMERTIME SADNESS

Jared watched the grizzly the size of a VW Bug ramble through the kitchen. No one else besides his mom could see the bear raise its head and sniff the air. The low-key party went on. People chatted, holding bottles of overpriced beer or cider as the bear walked through them, swinging its head threateningly. Music thumped in the background, too quiet to be made out against the murmuring conversation and the laughter and the roar of the Ultimate Fighting Championship mixed martial arts pay-per-view pre-match show on the living room TV. His mom's new money-maker was to charge for booze but not for pay-per-view. It seemed to be working. The grizzly moaned, a deep rumble like a jet breaking the sound barrier. A white woman with dirty-blond hair teased into a lion's mane backed away from the bear. She wore an overly zippered denim dress and pink stilettos. Her matching pink purse with a gold chain strap banged against her hip.

"Stop it," she said, shoving the bear's head away from her purse.

The bear bumped her with its snout. She danced around the bear and came straight at Jared. People walked through her as she stood in front of him.

"I know you can see me," she said.

Jared sipped his beer. The bear lumbered after her, snorting and pawing the ground.

"I need your help!" she shouted as the bear backed her through the party guests. "I need you to tell my daughter I was killed! I didn't leave her! I was murdered!"

His mom stomped into the kitchen from the living room. She wore her black Georges St-Pierre tank top over tight leather pants and her shitkickers, custom-made black cowboy boots with embedded steel toes for an extra "something-something" in unexpected brawls. She flipped her braid over her shoulder as she reached through the chest of the denim-clad ghost, who promptly puffed out of existence.

"Needy fuckers," she said, wiping her hands against her pants as she came and plopped herself in the kitchen chair beside him. "How you doing, Ghost Whisperer?"

"Peachy," Jared said.

"God, stop being a lump."

"Mom."

"Come on. Shogun versus Sonnen."

Jared constantly felt shaky, like his brains were hanging out. Which was not a good place to be to watch two guys try to kick, punch and slam each other into tomorrow. "I'm good."

The TV crowd roared, and the people in the living room hooted excitedly.

"Okay, it's starting," she said. "And I paid a buttload of money for this. Don't fucking do anything stupid, okay? Stay close."

"I'm going to bed. Can you call off the bear?"

She sighed, an aggravated, annoyed sigh. "Are you going to learn some protection spells?"

"Night," Jared said.

The bear curled up near the fridge. Jared scanned the kitchen. No further ghost incursions. He supposed learning a couple of zap-it spells wouldn't kill him. But he had a lot of trouble caring. He barely had enough care left in him to get up to piss in the toilet instead of in a can by the bed, much less about protection from the dead.

Summer was winding down and his mom said he could drop out of school if he didn't feel like going back. She'd gotten by on her grade eight education. Jared could bake cookies for her and Richie without a high school diploma. Cookies. Dylan wanted cookies too. He was going to swing by later and they'd get drunk and game. Or just get drunk. Dylan had started seeing Martina and she wasn't a gamer girl. If there wasn't booze or drugs involved, she wasn't interested.

He made his way up to his room and the bear followed him. He lay in his bed. Dylan and Martina came in an hour or so later and made out on the desk. Jared smoked a j. The bear moaned, irritated that Dylan and Martina were dry-humping near its feet. They fell off the desk and their make-out session dissolved into giggles.

Dylan went downstairs to watch pay-per-view. Martina smoked and swayed to music playing on her phone's speaker. She caught her reflection in the dresser mirror and dug around her purse for liquid eyeliner. She leaned in close, touching up her makeup. A woman who sounded like she'd done too much lithium sang a slow song about someone leaving her.

"Who's the mopey chick?" Jared said.

"You're the mopey chick," Martina said. "Lana Del Rey's an underappreciated lyrical genius."

"I like Nickelback."

She met his eye in the mirror. "Goody for you. Can you give us some privacy when Dylan gets back?"

"It's my room," Jared said. "I'll hang if I want to."

"Perv."

Jared never thought he'd miss arguing with Sarah. It wasn't that she made him think, or that he agreed with any of her points, but she always had something to say like: *Aren't you bothered by the inherent misogyny of glamourizing rape culture in pop music?* Martina left his room in an annoyed huff, and a few minutes later Dylan dropped by to say they were heading out to the lake.

"Later," Jared said.

"You might want to take a bath," Dylan said. "You're smelling pretty hobo."

Alex Gunborg and his Goth friends came up to his room and gave him some beer so he'd let them drink in his room. Jared cracked open a can and toasted them, then they ignored each other. Some kids brought pot. Some brought ciders. His mom wouldn't kick them out as long as they were in Jared's room and so they got to party indoors. He'd been picky about who he partied with before, but he found lately he didn't give a rat's ass. Besides, they weren't really hanging out with him. The kids partied together in the room while he drank or smoked himself unconscious. The bear didn't like it and tended to sleep with his head through the wall, grumbling when things got too rowdy.

"Man, you've got the life," Alex said enviously, watching him drink. "Fuck."

"Living the dream," Jared said.

———

Dylan threw him off the dock. Jared sank under the water, watching the dock fall away and the swimmers' legs cutting the water. He sank, and sank, and touched the bottom because it was low tide. Skeletons of salmon were piled in a mound where someone had tossed them, bits of flesh and guts gone pale and waving in the tide. Jared felt his heart trip-hammer, and for a second he was back in the cave, and he fought his way back to the surface to take a great gasp of air. Dylan was trying to pick up Martina to throw her in, but she was whacking him in a way that meant business. The bear glanced up, then put his head back between his paws.

The bites had healed. He didn't feel his missing toe anymore. He should be over it by now, he thought, but as he treaded water, he wanted to get drunk, immediately. He wanted to not feel terrified or dumped or used anymore. He wanted to get out of his head and never, ever crawl back in.

Martina wanted to have couples time, so Dylan dropped Jared off in front of his house and honked as he sped away. Jared wobbled down the street to Mr. and Mrs. Jaks's old house. He swayed on the sidewalk, remembering all the times he'd been there. The new owners twitched the living room curtains closed. Jared was about to go home when he saw the burgundy Caddy cruise down the street and come slowly to a stop beside him. The bear roared, and roared, and took a great breath then roared again, pawing the ground, huffing.

"Hello, Jared," Monster Gran said.

"Hey," Jared said.

"Would you like to get a bite to eat?"

"Sure."

"Oh, my," Monster Gran said as he plopped into the passenger seat. She waved her hand in front of his face. "Having ourselves a little party, are we?"

"Yup."

"Shh," Monster Gran said as the bear roared into her window.

The grizzly dropped and curled up on the sidewalk like a puppy, sound asleep.

"Off we go," she singsonged.

Jared watched the monster shimmering under her skin. She didn't have air conditioning, so she had the windows down. Jared put his hand out the window and closed his eyes, enjoying the breeze.

He had assumed he was the bite to eat and was surprised when Monster Gran lined up at the Dairy Queen takeout window. The sudden stop of the breeze made the car uncomfortably hot.

"Wee'git's my brother," Monster Gran said. "Which makes you my nephew."

Jared turned to study her, trying to focus. His mouth was suddenly dry and he felt a prickle of alarm. "Yeah?"

"Before you get all excited, he has 532 children. You're baby boy 361. There's a website if you want to meet any of them."

"Meh," Jared said.

"He's not actually the giant whore other people would have you believe. We've been alive since these mountains were lumps of gravel, bare and treeless. When you've lived that long, you tend to accumulate exes and children."

"Huh."

"He got all the power, but I don't really care about that," she said. "I just want as normal a life as I can manage."

The cars moved forward. The heat made the air wavy. Jared sweated and felt the first knock of a headache, dull and insistent like a rotten tooth.

"What do you want?" Monster Gran said.

Or Monster Aunt. Being drunk helped with the shock.

"A chocolate dip," Jared said. "I haven't had one of those in ages."

"Me neither," she said.

Jared dug around his pants for change, but she laughed and said she could afford a couple of ice creams.

She kept both hands on the steering wheel even though they were idling in the lineup. "Are you curious about anything? Any questions?"

"Nope."

"None at all."

"Nada."

"Well, you've certainly changed," she said. "The boy I met was chock full of questions."

"I had a shitty year."

"So I heard. You hurt his feelings, you know."

"Boo hoo."

"He deserved to have his feelings hurt. But to be fair, he has a lot of children to watch."

"Yeah, he's a prince."

"I'm not trying to make you like him. I'm trying to give you information. Hopefully, you'll be less hard on yourself. I like you, Jared."

Jared mulled that statement. They finally pulled up to the drive-through microphone and Monster Aunt carefully enunciated her order. They pulled forward into the line for the takeout window.

As they waited, Jared painfully sobered up, sweating and aching. She paid for the ice creams with exact change, counting out dimes and quarters and bemoaning the disappearance of pennies. The girl at the takeout window sighed angrily and constantly while holding out her hand, waiting for the final bits of coin. She handed over the ice cream cones and threw some napkins at them when Monster Aunt asked for more.

"Thank you, dear," Monster Aunt said.

Jared held the ice cream cones while Monster Aunt drove them to the viewpoint in the park. They sat on a bench in the sunshine as a wedding party posed in front of the vista of the Douglas Channel and the surrounding mountains, fading into lighter shades of blue and the sparkling ocean in the distance. Flowers swayed in the breeze. Leaves rustled. Jared ate all the chocolate coating before realizing the ice cream was making him nauseous. He ate a bit more and then hurled the rest over the drop-off. The nearby flower girl started crying because she didn't want to pose for pictures anymore.

"You seem like you're in a lot of pain. I'd like to show you a place where you can find peace," Monster Aunt said. "Would you like that, Jared?"

Jared tasted his mouth and tried to remember the last time he'd brushed his teeth. "Whatevs."

They ended up at a church and walked down the steps to the basement. Jared felt mildly pissed off that she was religious and wanted to convert him. He didn't want to spend time with Bible-thumpers. Some people were setting up chairs and he could smell coffee. Jared poured himself a cup and saw Alcoholics Anonymous pamphlets on the table.

"Crap," Jared said.

"We can leave if you want to," Monster Aunt said. "But give it a chance, please?"

Jared did want to leave, but he didn't have any pressing engagements, as Nana Sophia would have said if she was still talking to him. He had nowhere to go but home, so he drank his coffee and followed his aunt to some folding chairs at the back of the meeting. The room was warm and he kept his head down as people filed in. He was worried that someone he knew would see him here.

It started off boring, and the stories were sad, and sometimes they tried to be funny and mostly weren't. They were broken, like he was, and they weren't trying to front anyone. They weren't pretending they were all right. They weren't faking a good time.

He had a fuzzy moment, and he realized everyone had turned to look at him. Something about first-timers. And his aunt made him stand up and he almost swallowed his tongue.

"Hey, I'm Jared," he said.

"Hi, Jared."

"I'm half-cut, so I don't know if I'm supposed to be here."

"You're welcome here, Jared," the guy at the podium said.

"Okay, that's all I want to say."

"He'd like to listen," his aunt said.

The meeting wound down. He turned, anxious to get the hell out of here and get royally hosed, when he bumped into Mr. Wilkinson, Dylan's dad.

"I want to shake your hand," Mr. Wilkinson said. And he held out his hand, and he was attracting attention, so Jared reluctantly shook. "It took a lot of guts to come here. I wish I'd been as together as you are when I was your age. I'm proud of you, Jared."

Jared started crying. Leaking tears. And then bawling and shaking. And feeling like a phony and a loser. Mr. Wilkinson wrapped his arms around him and let him cry.

"I'll take him home," Mr. Wilkinson said.

The party at his mom's house was in full swing when Mr. Wilkinson drove him home.

"I grew up in a party palace too," he said. "Any time you need a ride to a meeting, you call me, okay?"

"'Kay," Jared said.

"Look, I know you aren't sober yet, so this is a bit of cheat, but I've got seven of them, so I'm not going to miss one." He handed Jared a white chip. "Be safe."

"Later."

Jared went to his room and Alex and his Goths raised their beers to him. Jared lay down in his bed, and listened to the party going on around him, turning the plastic chip over and over.

One day at a time, the chip read. On the other side: *Recovery . . . begins with one sober hour.*

40

SUCKS TO BE YOU

Dear Granny Anita,

Hello. This is Jared. I'm okay and so is Mom. She told me about your time in residential school and the TB sanatorium and I wanted to tell you I think you're tough. What you went through sounds like hell. I hold you in the deepest respect.

I met Wee'git and his sister, Jwa'sins. I don't really want anything to do with Wee'git, but Jwa'sins seems okay. She says she's sorry her brother is such an ass.

I hope to visit you someday, but I won't if you aren't ready. Thank you for praying for us. I hope you are okay,

Love,

Jared.

He found a couple making out on his bed. He slung his backpack on the desk and took off his shoes.

"Hey, we're trying to have a party here, you fucking pervert," the guy said. "Get the fuck out before I kick your ass out!"

"It's my bedroom," Jared said. "That's my bed. My mom's Maggie."

"Give us two minutes," the guy said.

"Oh, fuck that," the woman said, shoving him off and reaching for her shirt.

"I didn't mean— What the— Hey, thanks for ruining my night, you fucking douche."

They left and Jared could hear them arguing in the bathroom next door. The arguing turned into wet smacking sounds. Jared put his noise-cancelling headphones on and cracked his textbooks open. He hadn't realized how much time he'd spent getting hosed and recovering from hangovers until he went dry. He finished his homework and still had hours and hours of free time left. He considered doing another meeting. He'd done one before school, but an evening one couldn't hurt. He had enough time to make the fire hall meeting.

"You're home," his mom said, pulling off his headphones.

"Hey," he said.

She slammed the textbook shut. "You're like a Stepford kid now."

"A what?"

"A brainwashed robot. Fuck. I want my son back."

"I'm still me, Mom."

"You aren't. I never thought I'd miss your smart mouth or your smug fucking attitude."

"I'm right here."

"Judge-y and self-righteous, just like my mom."

"I'm not judging you. I love you."

"You want me to quit drinking now, right? Stop partying. Be a good fucking girl and keep your legs fucking shut and obey everybody. Right?"

"This doesn't have anything to do with you. This is my sobriety."

"Can you stop quoting your cult?"

"You don't have to change," Jared said. "You don't—"

She whacked him upside the head.

"Later," Jared said.

He got up and she shoved him back down.

She leaned over and grabbed his chin. "Sitting there thinking you're better than me. You aren't better than me, you self-righteous prick."

"Got it," Jared said. "Not better than Mom."

She shoved him and his chair tipped over. He caught himself on the desk. He reached for his textbook to put it in his backpack. She grabbed it and hurled it at the wall. She started throwing all the stuff on the desk and screaming. Richie popped his head in. The grizzly moaned in the hallway, but wouldn't come near Jared since Monster Aunt had put him to sleep.

"Hey, Babe," Richie said. "Got a sitch downstairs. I could really use your help."

"Good," she said. "I'm in the mood for a massacre."

Richie waited until she was clear of the room to shake his head at Jared.

"Thanks," Jared said.

"It's like you're spitting on her traditions," Richie said.

"I don't think partying's a sacred part of our culture."

"Yeah," Richie said. "I can see why she wants to murder you."

Jared would see people from the meetings in the outside world and it was weird knowing everything they'd shared. One of the managers at the Dairy Queen was in his morning meetings. She was sitting on the interview board when Jared applied for work. After Jared got offered a fry-cook job, she took him aside and congratulated him and then warned him if she caught him drinking on the job, she'd have to fire his ass, but she'd help him get back on the wagon.

Home was uncomfortable, so all he really wanted was some spending money and a place to hang after school. He trained and filled his orders. One day Dylan showed up and shouted his name until Jared turned around.

"You used to be cool!" Dylan accused him from the front counter.

The supervisor went over to Dylan, but he shook her hand off.

"Look at you now, Mr. Hairnet. How fucking lame is that! It's fucking lame, Jared. You're fucking lame."

Dylan stomped off. The rest of the employees whispered and Jared went back to flipping burgers. Dylan wasn't okay with Jared's new-found sobriety. Dylan ignored him at school, his eyes grimly skipping past Jared like he was something disgusting to behold. But at night, Dylan drunk-dialed him and told him what he really thought about Jared stealing his dad. All the kids who used to party with him avoided him like he had scabies, lice and bedbugs, and turned their faces away from him in the school hallway if he came near. The good kids seemed super nervous around someone who'd been hard-core enough to need Alcoholics Anonymous.

"It's like I've got the plague," Jared said to George, the only person in the school willing to hang with him.

"Welcome to my world," George said, as they sat down for lunch. "Sucks to be us."

"It really, really does," Jared said.

"Wagon Wheel?"

"Thanks. I appreciate your friendship and your food."

"Oh, ugh, dude, can we not get all emo and shit?"

"Got it. Canning the emo," Jared said.

Dear Jared,

I was very happy to get your letter. I'm glad you and your mother are doing well. Any time you want to visit me, you can come down.

I don't know Jwa'sins. You be careful around her, though. Supernatural creatures don't think like us. If she is paying attention to you, she has a plan. They are very patient when they want something from you.

Tell your mother I love her and I miss her. I'm sorry. I'm sorry a thousand times. I hope to see you soon, Jared.

All my love, thought and prayers,

Anita Moody

ACKNOWLEDGEMENTS

Thank you to the Canada Council for the Arts and the British Columbia Arts Council for taking a chance on the early drafts of this novel in its bleak infancy.

Thank you to my very first readers, Erika T. Wurth and Robert W. Gray, whose comments led me to expand and explain the short story into a novella and then a novel.

Thank you to my writerly, technical and cultural consultants for helping me create a make-believe world founded in our world (in alphabetical order): James Ferron Anderson, Rob Budde, Laura Cranmer, Blair Grant, Raija Reid, Carla Robinson, Karen Smith-Paul and Richard Van Camp.

Thank you to my undauntable agent, Denise Bukowski, for the cheerleading, the mildly exasperated explanations of the really dull parts of the contracts and generally being a typical Capricorn.

Thank you to my fabulous editor, Anne Collins, for knowing the right questions to ask, pushing things deeper and reminding me that internal logic applies even when the world you're creating is insane.

Thank you to the good people of Ci'mot'sa and Waglisla for being you.

Haisla/Heiltsuk novelist EDEN ROBINSON is the author of a collection of short stories written when she was a Goth, called *Traplines*. Her two previous novels, *Monkey Beach* and *Blood Sports*, were written before she discovered she was gluten-intolerant and tend to be quite grim, the latter being especially gruesome because, halfway through writing the manuscript, Robinson gave up a two-pack-a-day cigarette habit and the more she suffered, the more her characters suffered. *Son of a Trickster* was written under the influence of pan-fried tofu and nutritional yeast, which may explain things but probably doesn't.